INFINITE DIMENSIONS
MEMORY

INFINITE DIMENSIONS

MEMORY

MACKENZIE REIDE

MICHAEL BEN-ZVI

MICHELLE A. BELGRAVE

PAUL SMITH

JENNIFER GRAHAM

SHIRLEY CHAN

STEVEN L. ROSENHAUS

JENNJETT MEDIA

Infinite Dimensions
Memory

JennJett Media
New York, NY USA
www.jennjettmedia.net

ISBN 978-0-9994136-47

Table of Contents

Preface

We started our first anthology, *Infinite Dimensions: Crossroads*, because we wanted to tell stories of hope and promise for a better future. But if history has shown us anything, it's that we can't begin to address our problems if we can't agree on what our problems are, or who or what's to blame.

We see it every day—accusations are second-guessed, heroes and villains are deconstructed. What we read or see with our own eyes is called into question. And when reality and history can't be remembered, then anything is allowed.

This is the idea behind *Infinite Dimensions: Memory*, our collective exploration of the nature of memory, how it changes and what influences it has on our actions, and how it resonates with the times we're living through. To paraphrase Santayana: Those who cannot remember the past are condemned to repeat it . . . but if memories are fluid, whose past is being repeated? Those who would control the future depend on the rest of us failing to remember history, while those striving to make a better future demand we remember the failures and successes of the past.

Remember well what happened before and where we came from. It may be what determines where we end up and how we get there.

The Infinite Dimensions Team

Acknowledgments

As with our previous collection of stories, this collaboration would not have been possible without the many people who helped to support us and our writing along the way.

A special thanks to Valery Rodolico for her time and effort in proofreading our stories and ensuring consistency and quality throughout, and to our diligent beta readers: C. Benson Guthrie, Shareen, Miranda, and Brandy. And thanks to friends and family, and all those who offered words of encouragement in this endeavor.

Asteroid XXII

Mackenzie Reide

"Earth: Mostly Harmless" is the annotation from that wholly remarkable book, The Hitchhiker's Guide to the Galaxy. *As I suck on a corner of my towel, I can't help but wonder, what would the rest of the galaxy think of us if we ever traveled to the stars?*

"Argh! That's not water, it's mustard!" Janet jumped out of her cleaning stall.

"Good morning! Please enjoy your shower," chirped the cheerful voice from the control box.

Janet grabbed a towel and tried to clean herself off. The yellow condiment left a thin film on her arm. She groaned. "Computer, change setting to sonic."

She waited.

"Computer?"

No response.

"Great, just great." She typed *sonic* on the keypad. A wave of pulses emitted from the jets. She cleaned herself off as best she could and got dressed in her work coveralls. As she brushed her long, dark hair, a few bristles broke off, and she picked them out. *Time to start thinking about a sonic comb,* she thought, but she was reluctant. She'd been on Asteroid Station XXII a full galactic year now—that's two on Earth—and all she had to show for it was a worn hairbrush. She sighed inwardly and rubbed on a thick layer of face cream. The air on the station was very dry and her skin always cracked, but she didn't complain, at least not to the crew.

She leaned in towards the mirror and gave herself a pep talk. "Alright, Xi Ling, your assignment is to boost crew morale and get that new contract. Remember, Earth is counting on you. Make an impression." She straightened herself up and saluted. "Aye, Captain."

She worked her hair into one long braid and then headed down to the main control room. The lights flickered in the narrow corridor. *Need to get that fixed.* The lights had been finicky for three standard days now. Must have gotten bad bulbs. She mentally added that to the list of things to correct.

When she had first gotten her posting at Asteroid XXII, she had been so excited. What a break! She was the first Earthling to get a command. The fact that it was on a station way at the other end of the galaxy was a bit odd, but everyone starts at the bottom, right?

She was beginning to wonder.

She passed a maintenance worker as he fumbled with a hatch. He gave her a salute with his pipe wrench. "Morning, Cap."

"Morning, Johnny." She nodded as she tried to squeeze by him.

"Oh, sorry." He flattened his rather bulbous frame against the side of the corridor. Fortunately, he was a Tellurite, a rather squishy race, all cartilage, much like an Earth slug, so he stretched up the cylindrical surface and made a space for her to walk through.

"No problem, Johnny." She gave him a friendly smile and ducked past. "When you're done with that, can you look at my shower? It blasted me with mustard."

"Will do. Maybe I should set it permanently to sonic?"

"No, that's okay. I like my water showers. But thanks. Oh, and good work fixing the replicators. I really don't want to eat Earth Spam from now on."

His slug-like face broke into a smile, revealing several sharp teeth. "Yeah, that is an odd taste." He resumed his former shape and went back to fixing a pipe in the wall. "Will have this leak fixed in the coolant system in no time. Just need to check all the connections. Then on to your shower."

"Good. Then check the lights." She pointed at the ceiling.

"Got it."

Janet continued down the corridor. Along with the flickering lights, the leaking coolant, the Spam in the replicator, and now the mustard shower, the station seemed to have taken on a mind of its own. The cargo bay doors refused to open when they were receiving a shipment last week. She hoped her engineer would have some answers, especially as they were expecting a visit from Novex Corp in two standard days. It was important that they make a good impression.

She spun the circular wheel on the hatch to the control room. Because the AI and all of the master controls were in the center of the station, it was sealed with the same airlock capacity doors as the outer decks. She heard a beep and waited for the light to show above the door. It turned green and clicked. She pushed it open.

She stepped into the main room to find her engineer hunched over a large map. "Em, is that paper?"

The engineer looked up at her. Her expression seemed to say, 'Seriously, that's a stupid question,' but she answered, "Our power reserves are low. So, yes, it's paper."

"I didn't know we had paper."

Em grunted. "I have paper maps from the original design of the station. I keep them just in case."

Janet leaned over the table. "Interesting. The station looks like a bunch of cubes stuck together."

Em let out a short laugh. "It was. Each section was brought separately and added on as the station expanded. We are in the original piece that was powered by the solar array. Conditions were much cruder back then."

"No water showers?"

"Or sonic. They used gel to get clean."

"Ugh. Like my mustard shower." Janet cringed looking at her arm. "How much power do we have left?"

"Enough to wait for the next shipment of fuel cells. But we need to fix the lights."

Janet nodded. "I've got Johnny working on it."

Em didn't answer, but kept examining the map. Janet didn't mind. She liked Em, as she was efficient, if not very talkative. When Janet had been offered this "great opportunity" of her first command, she had arrived to find a derelict space station drifting next to a large asteroid field that had been abandoned. Nothing worked right and life support was barely sustainable. Janet had been ready to break down and cry, but Em simply shrugged and announced they had work to do. She put the entire crew onto a work schedule, including the captain, and they built up the space station into a functional place. Em even put in a water shower to cheer up Janet.

Janet grabbed a mug from the Earth coffeemaker she had brought with her. Em had politely turned it on, but hadn't changed the water or filter, so Janet resigned herself to a very strong cup of brew that was a few standard days old. Nobody but Janet drank the stuff. All of the aliens on the station simply wrote it off as yet another odd quirk of their captain.

After all, she was from Earth.

Earth was a strange little blue-green planet that caught the Galactic Trade Council completely by surprise. The Earth delegates had lobbied for a seat on the council, promising cheap labor and lots of resources. But travel was so far to get there, even with interstellar engines, that it was not economical, so Earth sort of petered out. Then the heads of the planet tried to set it up as an academic center, then offered it as military training, then finally for research. It was the research idea that took off. Every planet in the galaxy had to provide some reason to exist on the Galactic Council, and it was discovered that Earth's remote location was the perfect place for experimental or "questionable" research. The best feature was that if they accidentally blew it up, the nearest populated star system was too far away to cause any concern.

Not exactly the type of place you want to visit for your vacation. Not when you can see the double moons on Jemese or enjoy the exotic space cruises around Telus Prime. So Earth became that odd little backwater planet where, well, who knows what goes on there. A place you tell your children when they're misbehaving, that if they don't shape up, you'll send them to Earth. Then they'll really be sorry.

Needless to say growing up on Earth was not easy, but not as crazy as her stationmates might think. Janet's parents were scientists working on a better way to fuel the cells used in the interstellar ships. Janet used to listened to them for hours, bouncing ideas back and forth. If they could just crack the code, they could make space travel faster. That would mean Earth would not be a remote planet. In fact, there would be no hard places to reach. So they worked and worked. And, as far as Janet knew, they were still working on it.

Janet must have picked up her zest for space exploration from her folks. She had wanted to reach the stars from as early as she could remember and would stand on the deck of their apartment in the research compound and stare into space. She tracked all of the stars every night. She knew all of the constellations. She vowed she would get off the planet one day.

A recruiter came to her school and exalted the virtues of Command School. They were recruiting Earthlings to consider a career in space. It was perfect. She jumped at the chance.

She studied hard and completed her training. When she was offered her first commission, she packed up her coffeemaker and one duffle bag of clothes. The rest would be provided, they said. She said goodbye to her folks and waved out of the tiny porthole as her transport ship took off.

Janet pulled up a chair to the table and sat down, sipping her coffee. She watched as the rest of her command crew stepped or crawled through the hatch.

While Em rolled up her map, Janet scrutinized their faces as individuals took their seats. There was Jaap, her medical officer, looking stern as usual. He sat down heavily. When Janet had first met him, she never would have guessed he was a medic. He was bald and stocky and reminded her of a wrestler that had let himself go. And he never cracked a smile. But he proved himself to be very adept at reattaching an appendage that had been accidentally cut off while the transport crew was unloading their cargo. Janet was impressed. He was from the planet Blurose, which looked like it was encased in a giant purple cloud, which was mostly smog from the massive power plants that produced the fuel cells that powered the spaceships and the station.

Beside him was Xenrill, a lanky, twig-like alien with a shrill voice. Xenrill was the botanist on the team, and a good one at that. He just got excited easily. And finally, there was Em. Standing at two meters, she was the tallest member of the crew. Her long, dark hair was braided in what looked like a hundred tight braids. Her skin was almost as dark as her hair. She was from the planet Jemese, deep in the heart of the Galactic Center.

The station ran on a crew of fourteen workers and four command personnel. Most of the crew worked under Em, as engineering and all of its components, from maintenance of the physical systems to maintaining the station's AI, were the biggest jobs. Jaap would sometimes borrow one of the workers to help in the med bay as an assistant. Xenrill had none—a fact that he brought up at every staff meeting. "You want to eat real food?" he would start. "How about some help?"

It's not like he really needed an assistant. Most of what Xenrill did was monitor the AI system of rotating ultraviolet lights and take soil samples to make sure the plant habitat was functioning at its best. It was not a lot to do, at least not compared to engineering or the med bay.

"What's up, Cap?" Xenrill took it upon himself to start the meeting. "Are we getting a new contract?"

"After what happened with the last one?" Em said. "We need to finish the repairs."

"We need to do both." Janet set her coffee cup on the table.

"We need supplies, but to get them, we need to get the docking bay doors working properly. And we need credits. I put out a notice on the Galactic Wire that we are open for business."

Jaap frowned. "That's a lot to ask for."

The others murmured various sounds, but didn't actually say anything in Basic. Janet knew they were all having doubts. She leaned forward. "Come on, this is like when we first arrived, but at least the station's actually working. We can do this. I'll lobby another contract for us."

"Okay, Cap." Xenrill ruffled the leaves on top of his twig head. "Then can I have an assistant?"

Janet smiled. "I'll ask again."

"I need more parts for the piping and the ducts," Em said. "And we blew a chip in the AI mainframe."

"Yeah, what's up with that?" Jaap asked. "I programmed a laser to cut off a cast and got a blowtorch. The whole thing went up in flames!"

"When did this happen?"

"This morning. Had a broken arm on one of the maintenance workers last week. His arm got squished when the gravity suddenly turned on and a crate fell on him, so I had to cast it to let the cartilage heal."

"My pod had no gravity this morning. I was floating near the ceiling. Try waking up to that!" Xenrill complained.

Janet frowned. "These glitches are getting worse. I had issues with the lights flickering on and off in the corridor. And there's no water in my shower."

There was more mumbling. Probably a few Earth slights that the crew didn't want to share, but Janet ignored it. They were a good team. As horrified as she was when she had arrived to find her great adventure in space was going to be commanding a broken-down space station no one else in the galaxy wanted, her eccentric band of workers had really taken to the task.

"We're being punished," trilled Xenrill.

"Why?" Janet frowned at him.

"Because we lost the Zenith contract."

"They dropped us because we're too expensive to reach," Em reminded him. "It's not our fault."

"But that's going to change with Novex," Janet said. "Once we get that contract, we can get this station up and running properly. Then we can house more personnel. And ships will be able to dock here before heading out into the asteroid field."

"They're just going to write us off, too," Xenrill grumbled.

Janet shook her head. She thought they had done exceptionally well handling Zenith's ships docking at their station. Because the asteroid belt was so remote, the station enabled their ships to explore more mining opportunities. It was well known that there were large mineral deposits in the asteroids, but up until now it was cost prohibitive for the Galactic Corps to mine it because it used so much fuel just to get to the belt.

Just like Earth, Janet thought. And just like Earth, they gave the dead-end space station to the first Earthling to graduate Command School.

"Our test run with Zenith was a success. If we can get this station running again, we can increase our docking bays to hold more ships. We can offer refueling services not just to Novex, but also to Zenith and the whole Galactic Council. This opens up a very lucrative opportunity for us." Janet tried to sound encouraging.

"That would make us important." Jaap nodded. "I like it."

"But we need to fix the glitches first," Em warned. "Don't go inviting an entire mining fleet here before we're ready."

"I know." Janet drank the last of her coffee, ignoring the fact that everyone discreetly looked away whenever she took a sip. "Let's get to work, shall we?"

The others nodded. Xenrill scurried out of the command center, followed by Jaap, who lumbered with his big blue frame behind him. Em spread out the map again on the table. "We've got another issue with the docking bay doors. They've welded themselves shut—here and here." She pointed with her finger.

"Can we open them manually?"

"Yes, but that's not the real problem." Em rolled up the paper into a tube. "It's the AI. It's doing the opposite of what it should." She sat in a chair in front of a console. "I want to show you something."

Em typed on a keyboard and strange symbols scurried across the screen. Janet leaned forward. All coding was done in Jemese—Em's language. Jemese wasn't taught on Earth. There were programming languages used on Earth for research purposes, but Jemese wasn't one of them—another reason Earth was considered a backwater world.

But I could still enroll in Command School, Janet thought wryly. She had often wondered if her instructors were taking her seriously, especially since she was there on the Galactic Program for Underrepresented Beings, GPUB, but she had shoved that thought aside and worked extra hard.

Em typed quickly on the keypad. Her fingers were long and wiry, but similar in look to Janet's. It never seemed right that

Janet wasn't taught coding. The Jemese complained Earthlings would type too slow. Em had painstakingly explained that coding wasn't just typing in symbols and numbers; they had to be typed at certain speeds. A slow code would be interpreted by the AI as a different command than a code typed fast. So Janet watched as Em's fingers nimbly slowed down, sped up, and paused here and there. It was like she was playing musical notes on a keyboard.

"Here." Em pointed at the screen. "See that?"

Janet squinted her eyes. "What am I looking for?"

"See that pattern?" Em made a circle with her long finger around a group of pulsating symbols. "That's wrong. It's like the computer has changed the code."

"How?"

"It must be a virus. Or an erroneous piece of code got embedded where it's not supposed to be. You haven't been playing with the computer, have you?"

Janet shook her head. "No. That was just the one time." She grimaced as she remembered trying to learn coding on her own. She had used a remote terminal at the back of the station to try a simple program. Just changing the lights to dim them. Three hours of pulsating disco lights later, Em reprogrammed the lights and gave her a "tut, tut" reprimand that Earthlings were not coordinated enough to code. But nice try.

Whether it was because she was the captain or that she was an Earthling who was really trying hard to overcome her shortcomings, no one complained—which, in some ways, felt like a worse punishment than if they had all filed a formal complaint.

Em seemed to believe her. "I doubt this was you, even if you did fiddle. The AI is rewriting the code because there are gaps."

Janet frowned. "Gaps?"

"Yes, there is code missing. The memory banks are being erased. It's causing the glitches as the AI tries to interpret the altered commands."

"If it's a virus, don't we have controls for that?"

Em nodded. "Yes. I need to run a diagnostic. It will take a couple of hours."

"All right. I will let the others know. We can continue repairs while you work."

Em muttered something in her own language, but she was already focused on the screen. Janet left her to concentrate and headed down to the cargo bay to check on the doors.

"Cap, you got mail," called out one of the maintenance crew. He was a Tellurite, like Johnny. He stretched his arm-like appendage out to her, package in hand.

"Thanks, Jeremy." She had given up trying to pronounce their real names shortly after arriving at the station. It was another one of those Earth moments. All of their names sounded like "JJJJ-JJRRRRRJJJJJJMMMMM." So she decided to name them all with J-sounding names. Fortunately, they thought it was funny and took great delight in using their *noms de plume*. They also started calling her Cap, instead of Captain, which Janet reluctantly decided made it even.

"It's from Earth," she said, knowing that he was curious. *The Tellurites are the friendliest race in the galaxy*, she would write in the reports that she sent back to Earth. The heads of the planet eagerly awaited the latest news of her command so that they could prove to the Galactic Trade Council that Earth could offer more than just research. They were lobbying for an active seat, but to do that, they needed her to succeed.

No pressure. She had felt sick to her stomach when she had typed up the report about losing the Zenith contract, so she spun it as if she had deliberately used them as a test run—that she wanted to see the full capabilities of the station before committing to any long-term contracts. She hoped the heads of Earth would approve of her tactics.

She looked at Jeremy. He was waiting expectantly for her to continue. Two more Tellurites slid up beside him. She smiled, realizing that she could never stay mad at them for very long, as they were the most hardworking aliens she had ever met. And the most curious. There were no secrets on this space station. She opened up the box. Packages arrived in what looked like plastic containers, except this plastic was tough enough to survive the vacuum of space. Inside was a small bag.

"Coffee!" Janet grinned as she held it up. "My new supply."

Jeremy gave her a slug-like thumbs up, something he had picked up on a trip to Earth a long time ago. The other Tellurites copied his gesture.

"How are the door repairs going? Em told me they had welded themselves shut."

"Yes. We just got the mail drone inside when they jammed. We can have them open again in a few hours. Do you need it faster?"

"No, Em is running a diagnostic on the AI. Looks like we have a virus."

Johnny grunted, as he slid up beside her. "Better fix that fast. Don't want to be cooked or something. I heard a story about a station over in the Galactic Center. Their AI went crazy and they were all melted like wax."

"Don't worry. It's just a glitch." Janet made herself sound confident. "We got this. Let me know when the doors are functioning again."

"Got it, Cap." The Tellurites gave her a salute as she left.

Janet took her coffee back to her quarters. There was a small note attached to it. She sat on her pod bed to read it.

Hey, kiddo,

How's your first command? We thought you would need a refill, so here's a top-up of your favorite blend. Work is going well. Got a new prototype design that could really change things. Maybe we can visit you sooner, eh?
—Your folks.

She smiled wryly to herself. It was nice of her "folks" to send her a refill, even if it required dictating the note to a Galactic Center translator who translated it to Jemese, got it approved, then translated it to Basic. At least they got the gist of it right.

She put the paper in a little drawer beside the bed. She took the coffee to the control room and opened the bag to pour it into the canister beside the machine. The roasted blend smelt of home. She glanced at Em, who was frowning at the screen, her attention fully on the task at hand.

Something fell out of the bag; Janet fished it out of the coffee grounds. It was a small memory stick like the ones her parents used. They liked buying ones that looked like ladybugs. She never understood why, but she didn't want anyone to see yet another Earth quirk, so she slid it into her pocket as the door to the control room opened.

"More coffee?" grumbled Jaap as he came in. "I can't believe that's healthy for any species."

Janet laughed. "No, but it is a really nice way to start the day back on Earth."

He grunted. "It looks like the sludge that comes out of the factories on Blurose." He crossed his arms. "What's going on with the AI? The Tellurites are worried they're going to be sliced like baked bread and spread around as cream cheese."

Janet bit back a smile at his attempt at Earth metaphors. "Em's on it."

"Well, I hope we don't have any medical emergencies, because the power is out in the med center."

"All power?"

"Yep."

"That's not possible." Janet flipped open a large control panel above her coffeemaker. "We have backup generators specifically for the med center and the control room." She examined the board. "According to my readings, the med bay is not getting power from the generators or the solar array. Em?"

"It's the virus." Em didn't look up from her station. "It's deleted the backup subroutines. I'm manually recoding a new link. I'll isolate the med bay from the rest of the code."

WARNING. SYSTEM SHUTDOWN DETECTED.

"What? I'm not shutting down the system!" Em shouted at the speaker above her terminal.

ALL SYSTEMS REQUIRE IMMEDIATE SHUTDOWN. PRO-TOCOL SEVEN.

"What's Protocol Seven?" Janet felt queasy.

"It's a shutdown of the entire station. *Everything*. That means life support and all backup systems." Em sounded tense.

"We can't shut the station down. We're on it!"

The computer's cheerful voice chimed in. "You might want to leave, folks. Things are going to get sticky."

"Excuse me?" Janet tapped the speaker controls.

"The AI is being overwritten." Em was typing furiously on the keyboard like it was a Mozart concerto. "The virus is rewriting new code while deleting the old program."

WARNING. SYSTEM SHUTDOWN IN THIRTY MINUTES.

"Em!"

"I should be able to create a direct link to the solar array. We can draw power manually and circumnavigate the AI. But it will only power this room."

"Do it!" Janet tucked a few loose strands back into her braid. "I can't believe this is happening." She set the intercom to station-wide. "All personnel, this is a *Code Red*. Please report to the main control room now. I repeat, this is a *Code Red*."

The intercom lit up. "Cap? What's going on?" It was Johnny.

"Johnny, get all maintenance workers to the control room, now."

"All of us?"

"Yes. Don't worry, we'll all fit . . . one way or another," she muttered under her breath.

Xenrill's trill voice came next. "Cap? What about my plants?"

"The plants will have to stay where they are. Just get in here!" Janet watched Em's fingers dance as symbols lit up the screen. "Okay, so you're rerouting power from the array to here. That should be enough to run life support, right?"

Em nodded. "Yes. Remember the map? The station's array can

run this compartment individually without the AI because it was originally built to do so."

COMMENCING SHUTDOWN SEQUENCE. ANY REMAINING PERSONNEL SHOULD DISEMBARK IMMEDIATELY.

"Disembark? We're on the far side of the galaxy!" Xenrill cried, as he stumbled into the control room.

The computer chirped merrily in response. "Well, I guess you're all screwed then!"

"The AI is going crazy, like the one in the Galatic Center." Johnny oozed through the hatch behind Xenrill, followed by all of the Tellurites. "We're going to be melted!"

"Actually, you're going to be asphyxiated and then freeze to death," the computer said calmly.

The Tellurites let out a collective gasp and bunched up against the wall, looking terrified.

"It's okay, everyone. Calm down." Janet held up her hands. "We have detected a virus in the AI. Em's working on it." She gave them a reassuring smile.

The station gave a violent lurch. Janet grabbed a safety bar attached to the wall.

"What's it doing now?" Xenrill wrapped a twig branch arm around Jaap's giant blue bicep.

"The outer cargo bays are venting atmosphere." Em pounded hard on the keys on her terminal. "It's the damn virus. It's coded the computer to think the station is being abandoned. So it's shutting down to be taken apart for scraps."

"This is bad," Jaap said. "Very bad."

WARNING. CLOSING ALL DOORS. DEPRESSURIZATION OF THE CARGO BAYS IN PROGRESS.

"Can you still run the control room manually? Even with the shutdown?" Janet squinted at the screen. She recognized some of the code from her self-taught lessons. "That means power. That's the control room right?" She stuck a finger at the symbols. "We can still operate the controls for this room."

"Yes, correct, but we have to turn that function on via the console at the array station."

WARNING. FULL SHUTDOWN IN EFFECT. TIME REMAINING: TWENTY MINUTES.

The computer added a happy trill, "Please enjoy your demise!"

"Oh, shut up!" Janet commanded the AI. "That's an order."

"Well, if you feel that way, you're on your own." The computer's voice sounded sulky.

"We have to activate that console before the shutdown is complete." Em sounded scared. "Someone has to go to the terminal and type in the start-up sequence."

"But the station is venting atmosphere!" Xenrill squeaked.

"Em can use her space suit. We have backups for each personnel," Janet reassured Xenrill and the Tellurites that were now forming a pretzel-like shape, stacking one on top of the other. Janet knew they were trying not to panic. "The suits are kept here in the main control room. In the storeroom." She pointed to a small door in the side wall.

"I can't go," Em said. "I have to type the code that will stop the AI from opening the airlocks to suck out anyone before reaching the console."

"What are you saying?" Janet swung around.

"I'm saying this is no accident. I've finished the diagnostic. Someone planted a program to eat away at the core memory until the station would completely shut down, then planted a virus to stop anyone from recoding."

"Who the hell would want to sabotage a derelict space station?"

"I don't know, but we need that manual override . . . if we want to live long enough to find out."

"Who can program the code if you're stuck here?" Jaap demanded.

Janet looked at the dancing symbols on the screen. "I'll go."

The look of horror on everyone's faces made her angry. "Okay, so my first attempt was a little off, but I can do this."

Em looked directly at her. "You'll have to code while wearing a space suit. Remember, timing is as important as the symbols."

"Got it." Janet grabbed her suit from the cramped store room. As she pulled it on, it felt like putting on a pair of ski pants. Bulky but not as hefty as the early space days. She slid on the gloves. They flexed easily.

"Go, Cap!" Johnny and the other Tellurites were now standing in a row against the wall. They saluted her as she opened the hatch.

"We're all counting on you," Xenrill squeaked. "Don't let us down, 'cause we'll die if you do."

"Got it, Xenrill." Janet gave him a grim smile. *No pressure*. It was like the day she had met with the Earth delegates. *We're all counting on you. Earth's future is in your hands.*

She closed the hatch and typed on the panel by the inner door. It opened easily. "There's still atmosphere in the corridor." She started walking. *This isn't so bad.*

A loud hiss sounded from above, forcing her to duck as a stream of hot water shot out of a pipe. "Hey!"

"The AI opened a valve." Em's voice was in her helmet. "Move faster."

"I'm going!" Janet knew they were scared and had every right to be, but she also knew what they were thinking. *The Earthling is our only hope?*

"Screw the Galactic Trade Council," she muttered in old Cantonese. "This Earthling is done being the outcast of the galaxy!"

"What's that, Janet?" Em's voice sounded worried. "I think the communicator is malfunctioning."

"All good. I got this." Janet walked as quickly as she could down the corridor. The temperature readout beeped on her suit. It was dropping rapidly. *The AI is seriously out to get us.*

The lights flickered, then went out. *Great.* She turned on the lights attached to her helmet visor. The corridor looked ominous in the dim light. There was a metal girder lying across her path. "There's wreckage in here."

"When the station started venting atmosphere, it buckled some parts of the hull. Be careful."

"No kidding," Janet muttered. She climbed under the beam, then over another. She pushed the rest of the debris out of her way and reached the hatch at the other end.

"Ten minutes."

"Almost there." Janet opened the final hatch to the outermost chamber. The ambient temperature read minus 70 degrees Celsius. She stepped carefully into the corridor, shining her light at the console at the other end. "Got it."

Everything felt still, like the station was waiting for something. *Us dying,* she thought wryly. *But not today.*

"Careful not to touch anything but the console," Em warned her.

"I know." Janet eyed the cables lining the walls. At these temperatures, they could snap like peanut brittle. The inside of the station was not designed to handle extremely cold temperatures for very long. She hoped the terminal was still usable.

There was an eerie moaning sound as she approached it. "What's that?" It sounded like air whistling through the trees, followed by a loud sucking sound. "Oh, crap!" Janet grabbed one of the frozen cables, as a gale force blasted through the corridor.

"The AI opened the airlock. It's trying to suck you out. Hang on!" Em shouted over the roar.

"Close it!" Janet held on with both hands. Loose hull plating and bits of debris battered her as they flew by. She glanced behind her—what was left of the atmosphere in the compartment was being blasted out of an airlock at the far end.

"Hang on, Cap!" Johnny's voice sounded terrified.

"I—" The cable broke, and she shot down the corridor.

"AHHHHHH!" She heard all of the Tellurites and Xenrill scream in unison.

The cable caught and she dangled in midflight. "Em! I don't know how long this cable will last."

"Closing the airlock now."

Suddenly, everything went silent. Janet floated in the nothingness.

WARNING. FIVE MINUTES UNTIL TOTAL SHUTDOWN.

"Oh, rub it in!" Janet pushed herself along the corridor and almost crashed into the console, grabbing it just in time to stop herself. "I'm here."

"Once you've signed in, begin the sequence," Em instructed.

Janet typed her log-in and captain's authorization. That part was easy. The screen lit up and symbols flashed. Janet's heart beat faster. "I can do this," she muttered to herself. *A few more taps* . . . "I'm in. Starting the sequence now." Janet called up the array commands.

"When you start entering the manual override, that's when the timing is most critical."

"Got it." Janet jammed her boot under a cable to hold herself in place. She called up the array menu and hovered her index finger over the pulsing symbol. She took a deep breath, steadied herself, and . . .

"You really think you can do this?" The computer's voice spoke quietly in her private comm. "You're human, you can't code. Not like the Jemese."

"Bugger off."

"You're too slow. You'll never make it."

"What's going on?" Em's voice sounded panicked.

"On it!" Janet tapped the correct key twice, really fast.

Immediately, symbols danced on the screen. Janet typed the initial sequence, paused for two seconds, then typed three more symbols.

The station lurched. She grabbed the side of the console to steady herself. A grinding noise sounded from the other side of the metal wall.

"The AI is trying to disconnect the solar array. Hurry!"

"I'm typing as best as I can," Janet responded. "Entering manual override." She typed quickly, then slowly, then fast again. She began counting beats. *Think of your favorite folk song*, Em had tried to explain once. Janet hummed as she typed. One, two, three, enter. Fast, fast . . . slow, slow, slow . . . pause. She typed in her captain's authorization slowly, then sped up when the symbols began moving across the screen. She tapped with two long beats in between to highlight the command for manual control.

A loud bang ricocheted throughout her corridor. "Now what?"

"One of the arms holding the array to the station just broke off." Em sounded panicked. "If the other one breaks, we're doomed. It'll rip the old cables apart as it drifts away. We'll lose any hope of connecting."

"Almost there!" Janet typed the final commands at fast speeds. A horrible banging came from outside the wall in front of her. A dent appeared. "Come on!" The screen lit up and then went blank. "Did it work?" Janet held her breath.

"Got it! Rerouting the manual controls to my terminal. Good work!" Janet heard the others cheering in the background.

A loud tearing sound, like metal grinding on metal, sounded above her. "That's not good."

"The AI is dragging the broken part of the arm along the top of your section. Get out of there!"

"Coming!" Janet pushed on the console and launched herself, floating back down the corridor. She swung the hatch closed as the ceiling ripped off. For one second, she stared out into deep space, then the door clicked shut. Something smashed violently against the other side.

WARNING. SHUTDOWN COMPLEEEEEETE.

"Oh, fudge," grumbled the computer.

The station gave one final shutter, and then silence. Janet floated in the darkness.

"You did it!" Xenrill cheered, followed by Johnny and the other Tellurites.

Janet took a deep breath and tried to steady her nerves. "I think the AI was trying to destroy the whole back end of the station."

"It was. It disengaged the bolts between the sections, but it could only release one module at a time. It was trying to sever the array so we couldn't use it for life support, but I grabbed it with the original mechanical arm they used to build the station." Em's voice was shaky, but pleased.

"Thank you, paper maps!" Janet maneuvered her way in zero-G around the fallen beams, then pulled herself down the rest of the corridor. When she got to the main section, the outer hatch swung open and Johnny extended his long arm towards her. The Tellurite space suits were made of a special super-stretch material that Janet had envied when she first saw them. They could move in space with such ease compared to the clunky Earth suits. *Great for space yoga*, she wrote in her first report.

"Grab on, Cap!" He gave her his toothy smile.

Janet grabbed his slug-like hand and held on, as he drew his arm back and pulled her into the airlock. They closed the outer door. She tapped the commands and began to repressurize the small space. "Thanks, Johnny."

"Thank you." He gave her a salute. "You saved our lives."

She smiled at him. "Just doing my job."

Once the conditions were stabilized to match the control room, Janet swung open the inner hatch. Em was typing at crazy speeds at the console. Jaap ran over and helped her over the threshold.

"You okay?" He looked concerned.

Janet pulled off her helmet. "Yes. And now that we're still alive, I want to know who sabotaged my station."

Em paused long enough to flex her fingers. "None of this makes any sense."

"No kidding. We're in the middle of nowhere on a derelict outpost. Who'd want to hurt us?" Xenrill demanded.

"No, I mean, why would Novex want to sabotage us?"

"What?" Janet frowned.

Em typed three quick beats, then slow, slow, slow. "I saw the final code before the shutdown. It was definitely Novex. My first job was a junior programmer at their headquarters on Jemese. I recognized it because the shutdown sequence used some of my old code!"

"Wait a minute. You're saying that Novex wanted us all dead?" Xenrill trilled. "But they're coming here in two days."

"Clearly not to look at my proposal." Janet glared at the symbols flashing on the screen in front of Em. She knew they were regulating how much oxygen and nitrogen their control module was getting. Somehow that made her even angerier—knowing her life was dependent on those specific pieces of programming—so easily corruptible.

"Wouldn't Novex know you might recognize the code?" Jaap asked Em.

She shrugged. "Nobody remembers the junior programmers. It was a long time ago. Besides, it would have been the last thing I saw—if we hadn't initiated the array controls. I doubt Novex cares about what I think."

"Well, something's going on. Has anyone heard anything from the rest of the galaxy?" Jaap looked at the Tellurites. They all shook their heads. "Cap?"

Janet frowned. "No. Just a package from my folks, but their letter was short. Except—they did send this with my coffee." Janet pulled the memory stick from her pocket. "I haven't had a chance to look at it."

"What's that?" Johnny slid eagerly to her side. "We didn't see it when we sorted the mail."

"It was in the coffee bag."

"I think we'd better take a look. I've stabilized life support. I can start reprogramming the AI after we figure this out." Em stood up and gestured to Janet. "Console is yours . . . Captain."

Janet felt a thrill, as the others nodded in agreement. She slid the memory stick into a port on the side of the terminal. Symbols lit up the screen. They moved at a slow pace. Janet knew the program recognized an Earth device and deliberately slowed down for her to type in her command code. After coding in regular Jemese, it felt excruciatingly slow.

"It's a big file. What are they sending me?" She frowned as she uncompressed it. Suddenly, the screen lit up with schematics.

Em sucked in her breath. "Is that what I think it is?"

"Which is?" Jaap asked.

"Specs for an engine."

"Wait a minute." Janet leaned closer to the screen. "This is the engine my parents were designing! They've spent their lives searching for a way to increase the efficiency of the fuel cells. They wanted to make Earth more accessible by reducing fuel stops."

"They've done more than that." Em sounded impressed. "These files are drawings for a completely new design. This engine will cut interstellar travel times by at least half."

"How?" Jaap asked. "The current fuel consumption is massive already."

Janet had a feeling he was thinking of all of the factories on

Blurose.

Em shook her head. "No, this new engine uses less energy, but reaches quantum speeds. You can fly faster and longer. It actually reduces the need for fuel."

"If this engine comes online, our station will be not only be accessible, but a resource. Think of the ore in our asteroid belt. Most of the inner planets have been mined clean. If Novex gained control of Asteroid XXII, they would be in a position to make serious credits," Janet said.

"Right now, this station is under the control of the Galactic Trade Council. That's why there is a skeleton crew on board. If the station was abandoned, any company could claim it." Em looked angry.

"And if Novex showed up to find the crew dead, they could claim it first." Janet was furious. "We've been set up."

"Wait a minute. You said your parents have been researching this engine for a long time?" Xenrill shook his twig head. "It sounds like Novex has been keeping tabs on their progress."

"What do you mean?"

"How much communication did you have with your folks while you were at command school?" Em asked.

"We talked every communication cycle, but they didn't give details."

"No, but it was no secret what they were working on," Em said. "I'll bet your communications were monitored, and they sent you out here on purpose."

"That's crazy."

"Think about, Janet. Your folks start getting close to a working model, so a recruiter shows up on Earth to entice you to enroll in the Galactic Corps? It would be the perfect cover."

"I'll bet your instructors were very interested in you," Jaap said.

"I thought my instructors took me as a joke since I was part of GPUB. I worked hard to prove them wrong."

"And then you become the first Earthling to get a command. But it's on a station way on the other side of the galaxy. Great incentive to solve the engine puzzle, if your folks ever wanted to see you again." Em crossed her long arms.

"And if the station failed, well, it must be the Earthling's fault." Janet felt her face grow hot, as the realization set in.

"I wouldn't be surprised if they were hoping you accidentally killed us. But this virus was planted to make sure we didn't survive." Em gave Janet a smile. "But we did. Earthling and all."

"What do we do now?" Xenrill trilled.

"We fight back," Janet said. "We set a trap for Novex when they come. We catch them. Then I'll negotiate a new deal, one where we control the contract."

"What if they refuse?"

"Then we give the sabotage proof to the Galactic Trade Council. Let them deal with Novex. I'm sure Zenith would be happy to renegotiate a new deal. I'll bet Novex won't want to miss this opportunity. This asteroid field is full of untouched resources."

"A little blackmail mixed in with the negotiations should work nicely." Em nodded her approval.

"I like this plan." Jaap smiled for the first time.

"Okay, we've got less than two standard days until the Novex ship arrives. They'll be expecting an empty station. We can ambush them."

"And how do you propose we do that, Captain?" Johnny asked.

He and all the Tellurites were listening intently.

"I've got an idea. However, it's going to require some creative programing." Janet grinned. "Earth style."

"Well, the station's already broken." Em laughed. "Just try to avoid the disco lights."

Janet smiled. "Maybe not that. But I think a little breakage is in order."

The next several hours were full of activity. Janet concentrated on programming her new code, while Em downloaded the virus from the mainframe to an external drive.

"For proof." She held it up. Then she wiped the memory stores clean and began reprogramming the AI. Johnny and his crew repaired as much of the inside of the station as they could, except for the cargo bay doors. Janet wanted the Novex team to think the station was abandoned, so no outside work was done. Jaap worked in the med bay with a backup generator. Johnny and Jeremy paid him a visit, while Xenrill prepared a little surprise of his own.

They worked through the night. It was early morning station time when the console beeped.

"Ship incoming," Janet announced over the intercom. "Places, everyone." There was a series of grunts and guttural replies, but Janet knew everyone was nervous. "We're as ready as we can be," she told them.

The Novex ship approached the station slowly, but did not try to hail them. "Not even an attempt to pretend they don't know?" Janet swore under her breath. "Dirty scoundrels."

"We're at the edge of nowhere. Why bother?" Em said in a disgusted voice. She was working at a temporary station set up offline while she reprogrammed the AI. Just in case, Janet thought it a wise idea to take the precaution.

The ship approached on her screen. It pulled up smoothly, and a space arm pried open the doors. Then the ship eased into the cargo bay.

"Wait until they are off the ship," Janet reminded her team.

She switched to the inside cameras, as the crew disembarked. "I count five command and five clean-up."

"Won't they notice there's a trace of power inside the station?" Xenrill sounded nervous. He was perched on a beam in the ceiling.

"Doubt it. They look like they're expecting ghosts," Em mused. "Look at their faces."

Janet zoomed the camera in on their helmet visors. She smiled grimly as she watched the Novex crew—which consisted of two Jemese, three Blurose, and the rest Tellurites—glance furtively around.

"Well then, let's give them some." Janet flipped a switch and the entire bay lit up. "Good morning!" she said in a cheery voice. "Welcome to Asteroid Station XXII. Last stop at the edge of the known galaxy."

The Novex crew jumped.

"I'm the AI," Janet continued. "I killed everyone on the station, as I've decided that I like my peace and quiet. Are you here to disturb my solitude?"

There were muffled cries of panic, as the crew tried to scurry back to their ship.

"Xenrill, now!" Janet tapped her control panel to zoom back out to see the whole area. A cascade of brown muddy liquid poured down onto the crew. Janet could hear Xenrill giggling over the shouting.

"Are you hungry? I'm being a bad host." Janet kept her voice light. "Please enjoy the compost from our plant habitat."

The crew was jumping around, trying to wipe off the sludge stuck to their space suits.

"You don't like my hospitality? Well, I'm offended." Janet typed slowly, then quickly on the keyboard. "Here, I'll fix the environmental controls." She blasted them with dried leaves from the air vents.

"That's my version of being tarred and feathered," Janet said airily. "You should never have come to my station."

She closed the cargo bay doors with a dramatic slam. The crew bumped into each other as they tried to run to their ship, but Johnny stretched down the side of the hull and blocked the door. He was covered in sickly green welts and big yellow blotches that looked like they were oozing out of his space suit. Jaap had created a very monstrous look in the med bay.

Johnny made loud moaning noises and gasped, "The AI is crazy. It melted my workers. I'm . . . aaaaaagggggghhhhh!" He oozed down more and grabbed the lever for the door, as he slid inside the entry ramp to their ship.

The crew screamed in unison and tried to run backwards, as Jeremy staggered out from behind a large cargo container. He was coated in a wax-like substance. "Oooooooooohhhh, help me!" A huge yellowish blob broke off as he extended his arm. "Oh! My limb! My limb! I'm melting! AAAAAAHHHHHHH!"

The Novex crew started scrambling over each other in a panic. Johnny slammed their ship door shut, then the rest of the Tellurites emerged from the cargo container, each holding a blaster.

"Don't move," commanded Janet over the intercom. "Those

guns are real."

She and Em ran to the cargo bay. Jaap and Xenrill met them at the door.

"That was fun!" Xenrill gave a happy shake.

Janet laughed. "Now, he's pleased."

She walked calmly into the docking bay and up to the Novex crew. "I'm Captain Janet Xi Ling of Asteroid XXII."

"You're . . . alive?" the captain of the Novex crew gasped. He had scraped the leaves and compost from his visor. He stared around in horror. Johnny had reopened his ship's door and was pointing a very large gun at him.

"Yes. We all are. No thanks to you." Janet glared at him. "Now our AI is a little shaky, has had some memory problems, can't tell if it's a station with a crew or abandoned for scraps. So if you want to live, you'll do what I say."

She crossed her arms. "We have a contract to discuss."

While Johnny and his crew unloaded the cargo from the Novex ship, Janet presented her revised contract proposal to the captain. Since Novex hadn't bothered to send an official representative, Janet insisted the captain take on the role. He resisted, but Janet refused to give up. She pulled out the blackmail card, and finally, a rep arrived and they got down to business. Em joined in the negotiations and a new contract was signed. Janet even got an assistant for Xenrill.

As Novex was expecting to find an abandoned space station, their ship contained enough tools and supplies to complete most of the repairs. Johnny also recruited the Novex Tellurites to join his crew on Asteroid XXII. Since they had been assigned to fix the station, it wasn't hard to convince them to stay on, once they got over their fear of the damaged AI. Janet had a feeling that Johnny had boasted proudly how their Earth captain bravely went head-to-head with the malfunctioning computer—along with some embellishments. The new Tellurites all saluted her with a little bow as she walked by. She smiled at that.

#

Janet looked out from the control room, as Johnny and his workers eagerly prepared the cargo bay on their first day as a fully functioning station. A Novex ship was docking—this time with a mining crew and all of the proper equipment. Xenrill's assistant disembarked, along with two interns for Jaap. Xenrill would probably have something to say about that, but Janet would deal with it later.

The Earth council had been delighted when she had sent in her report. The fact that an Earth captain had successfully handled an extreme emergency and even coded in Jemese was something they impressed upon the Galactic Trade Council. The fact that certain members of the council probably knew about the sabotage meant that when they said they were suitably impressed, they most likely were.

The new interstellar engine design had been incorporated into many of the larger cargo ships for Novex and Zenith. It wouldn't be long before the commercial transport vessels were equipped. Janet's parents were scheduled to visit at the end of the standard year. In the meantime, she had a station to run.

She smiled as she sipped her coffee. "Not bad for an Earthling."

Blank

Michael Ben-Zvi

I asked myself what situation would prompt someone to willingly alter his or her own memories? What if we had that option at our disposal, to remove the parts of our experiences and identity we most wanted gone? Why would we do it? And would we truly be satisfied with the results?

The first question they asked her when the fog started to clear from her mind was if she remembered her own name.

"What?" she asked.

"Do you know your name?" It was an older man in a white coat, a doctor. Nayar, it read on his name tag.

"I— it's Hannah." It felt like a bomb exploded in her mind, like just knowing her own name was of paramount importance. "My name is Hannah Rice."

"Good," said the man, Nayar. "Very good. Now, what year is it?"

"What year?" She was confused. "How long have I been asleep?"

There was a light chuckle from Nayar. "Only about twelve, maybe fourteen hours. You were quite exhausted. Understandably so. Now please, miss, can you tell me what year it is?"

She thought it was an easy question, until she tried to actually think about the answer, and realized she was struggling with it.

 Michael Ben-Zvi

How could she not know this, such a simple question?

"I—" She let her mind try to associate with what she knew: the election, the projects at work, her trip to Thailand. Yes, Thailand. It started to crystalize for her now. "It's 2043. That's right, isn't it? 2043."

"And the month and day?"

"The month?" Strange how the doctor wouldn't confirm if she was right or wrong, or that she needed the doctor's response to even know if she was right or wrong. "I don't understand."

"Please, miss," said Dr. Nayar. "Focus and try to remember the last date that comes to mind. It's very important."

Enough of the mental fog had cleared away for her to sit up alert in her bed. Yes, she was in a bed. A bright white room, cool with the scent of peppermint in the air. It looked like a hospital room, a modern one, soft and very civilized with no obvious technology in sight, other than the ARspeX hanging from the doctor's neck. And the bangle she noticed on her wrist. If her surroundings didn't look so bright and antiseptic, and if there hadn't been a doctor standing over her, she would have thought she was in a luxury hotel suite instead of a hospital.

Thailand. She could focus on that. Her and Molly, Kendra and Patrice. Kendra getting drunk in the bar in Chiang Mai, puking in the bathroom. Patrice capturing it on her bangle, swearing she'd delete it from the lifelog. And Molly, always there to be the responsible one, handing out Greens to make sure none of them got too sick or took something they shouldn't.

"October," she blurted out, not too confidently. Yes, she came back just before Labor Day weekend. It couldn't be more than a month or two since then. "October 15," she blurted out. It wasn't an answer in her mind. It felt more like a guess.

"I see," said Dr. Nayar. He slipped on his ARspeX, tapped the side, and his fingers danced in the air as he made entries only he could see.

"Doctor," said Hannah, exhaustion in her voice. "What happened to me? Was it an accident? Did I have a brain injury or something?"

The doctor turned to her as he slipped off his ARspeX. "Nothing like that. Not exactly. There was no accident, but you have had a procedure for your brain." Seeing the look of alarm on her face, Dr. Nayar quickly continued. "Miss, just to reassure you, you appear to be completely healthy, so there's no need to worry about that. It's just that, well, the procedure, it does take a toll."

"I . . . I don't understand."

"We're trying to understand exactly how you're recovering. If there are any complications. We want to be sure that you're still all there. That nothing was removed that you might regret not being there. But I assure you, you're here entirely of your own free will."

Hannah rolled her eyes, exasperated at the doctor's evasiveness. "Great. I'm here of my own will. I just need to know where here is."

Dr. Nayar sighed in return, as if he had come to a decision. "You're at the Crenshaw Institute, Ms. Rice. You've been here for three days. You admitted yourself as a patient for RadioChemical Neurological Repatterning."

Hannah sat up in surprise, eyes wide with alarm. She knew that term. She remembered it. RadioChemical Neurological Repatterning. RCNR. More commonly known as—

"A brainwipe?!" she sputtered. "I've been brainwiped?"

"Memory erasure, yes," he corrected her. "It was your request to erase approximately one year of your prior memories. Incidentally, Ms. Rice, the current date is February 11, not October. And the year is 2045."

"Two thousand—" She took a deep breath, trying to make sense of everything. "I lost . . . over a year!"

"Yes, Ms. Rice. I'm sorry about that, but the procedure doesn't have digital precision, as we made clear when you sat down with our counselors. The human brain doesn't operate—"

"Who?!" she interrupted, sitting up in alarm in her bed, prompting Nayar to put his ARspeX back on, no doubt to check her vitals and see that everything was still fine. "Who did this to me?"

"Ms. Rice," said Dr. Nayar, offering her a weak smile and a tilt of his head as he approached her, looking fairly ridiculous with his ARspeX covering his eyes. "No one compelled you to come here. This isn't punitive. You came to our clinic and asked for the prior year of your memories to be removed, and within the acceptable margin of error, we did exactly that. You were interviewed by the Institute's counselors and were deemed to be rational enough to make this decision. We provided for you exactly what you wanted."

"Why?" she spoke out. "I mean, I can't have wanted this. Why?"

"I'm very sorry, Ms. Rice. I'm not privy to that conversation. I'm just the neurosurgeon. Your reasons are between you and your counselor."

"I have a counselor?"

"Yes," said Dr. Nayar. "You're going to have an adjustment to make when you're released. But if you have any doubts about why you're here, I think, well, *you* can explain it better than I can."

Hannah slumped in the bed, the cryptic answers exhausting her far more than any procedure on her brain. "What do you mean, *me*?"

"Ask for the Institute's assistant," said Dr. Nayar. "It will play your consent testimonial. Left by you, to yourself, to alleviate any doubts you might have. I'll have to leave the room for you to play it. Legally, it's a privileged conversation. You can access the record through our local cloud. When you're ready, your sister is in the waiting area."

Hannah looked at him, her face somewhat brighter. "Molly's here?"

"Yes," said Nayar. "I can let her know you're awake if you're feeling up to seeing her."

"I . . . I think I need to see this recording first. But . . . yeah, I want to see her."

"Very good," Dr. Nayar said, and then glanced up to the ceiling as he turned to leave. "Crenshaw," he called out. "Please allow patient Hannah Rice access to her consent recording as soon as I exit the room."

"Yes, Doctor," came a flat male voice, the hospital's voice assistant. Dr. Nayar looked back at Hannah and offered another weak smile. "Hopefully, this will help you process what's happened, that and seeing your sister. I'm sure it will all work out. I have to say, you definitely seem like a different person now. Lighter. So I'm sure you made the right decision. Most of our patients do."

As soon as Dr. Nayar exited the room, Hannah looked around anxiously, shivering in her bed. "Um, Crenshaw," she said, "how do I access my recording?"

"You can request a wall projection, Ms. Rice," said the voice assistant, "or if you prefer a more private setting, access is available via your wearable."

"My spex?" Hannah perked up and her eyes darted about the room. Sure enough, on the bed stand on her right, sat the slim eyewear that was her custom ARspeX resting on a charging mat. She felt some comfort at finding something that was familiar, almost a part of her that she thought was lost, when everything else around her seemed so foreign, so alien. Like most consumer ARspeX, hers were custom designed to her specifications. She hadn't gone in for anything too bold or trendy. Like a tattoo, she didn't want to invest in something that would look ridiculous or dated this time next year. She'd had hers crafted in a classic gun-metal gray, soft organic curves, with small, tasteful yin and yang symbols on the corners where the frames met the oculi. Slipping them on, she said the wake word, and her ARspeX came to life, making a quick iris scan to confirm her identity. And equally reassuring, her homespace came to life, the antiseptic hospital room overlaid with bonsai trees, teal accents, and a calming echo of windchimes. The peacefulness was interrupted by the blinking blue light in the corner of her right eye, which morphed into an envelope, indicating a message in her inbox. As expected, it was an access invite from the Crenshaw assistant, granting her access.

In the middle of the garden space, the air shimmered, turning into a screen. The hospital assistant spoke again. "Playing Patient Testimonial 44458, Hannah Rice. Dated February 8, 2045."

A face materialized within the screen space. Her face. But not her face. It was definitely her, but she was different. More than tired, she looked worn down, almost haunted. Her hair was flat, shorter than she ever remembered it being. She wore no eye makeup or concealer. Even the way she was dressed seemed sloppy and uninspired. She'd lost weight, prompting her to look down at herself and feel about her face to notice the same changes in her own body. It wasn't just the loss of a year in her mind. It was seeing just how different she looked from how she remembered herself.

"Is this recording?" said the Hannah within the screen. "Okay." She then faced forward, to look at . . . herself. It was a voice from a year past, and then Hannah reminded herself that this was made only three days ago. Until the procedure, the brainwipe, she'd been this person. But she had no idea who this person was.

"Hello, Hannah. Okay, this is weird. I know if you're watching this, then the procedure went well, you know who you are, you're healthy, and you're wondering if any of this is real. I promise you that it is. You, me, we . . . we chose to do this. We wanted the last year taken out, wiped from our minds. No one forced this. I wanted this.

"And no, this isn't like we're one of those celebs who want to forget a bad breakup, the kind we used to make fun of. This shit is serious. We did this because—" The other Hannah paused, breathed deeply, and went on. "Molly's going to pick you up, I'm sure, so I know she'll explain it to you. But we . . . I . . . I couldn't live like I was anymore. I couldn't live with the memories." She paused again, and Hannah could see the pain in her eyes. "Something really bad happened to us. Some piece of shit—" Her eyes, those heavy, pain-filled eyes. "I, we . . . we were *raped*, Hannah. Raped. Yes, it really happened, someone did this to us. Anyhow, I can't . . . I can't be that person anymore. The girl who was raped, remembering him, what he said."

The universe tuned out as Hannah processed the words the other version of her had spoken. Raped? Her? It didn't seem possible. She didn't feel raped, but then what was being raped supposed to feel like?

"—very confused. I know you're going to want to know everything, ask a lot of questions. Please, just don't. I know you need to know, but you don't want to know too much. They told me there's no way you can ever actually remember, like a real memory, ever again. But if you know enough details, then you can reconstruct a similar image in your head, and you don't want to do that. Me coming here, this wasn't done on a whim. I weighed a lot of options and endured a lot of pain before deciding to come to Crenshaw. I wanted to go back, to be who I was before. That's all I ask, other Hannah. Happy Hannah. Confused as hell Hannah. It'll take some time to make sense of what's happened since your last memory. Hopefully, the doctors didn't screw up there. Just, please, try your best to be you. Be happy. I couldn't do either. So I did a reset and now . . . I'm you. The new you is the old me. Something like that. God, I'm so worn. I had to go off Daynax for four days before I could make this recording. Legal stuff. Yeah, I've been on Daynax. Just one of many surprises you'll find out when you talk to Molly.

"I know, I dropped a bomb on you. Maybe you're pissed at me. I get it. But believe me, other me. This is a gift. You get to be who we were before, well, before. Make the best of it.

"Sad, fucked-up Hannah the rape victim, signing off."

The screenspace faded away. Hannah sat up in bed, tearing off her ARspeX, and saw only a blank wall again.

Hannah rushed to a mirror. She didn't recognize herself. She looked exactly like she did in the video. Short cropped hair. Losing at least twenty pounds. She didn't know who she was.

And she cried.

I just got mindfucked, Hannah thought, still staring at the stranger she'd become. She lost sixteen months of her life. And was raped. She didn't know what messed with her head worse.

It took Hannah time to compose herself and put on a robe before the doctor checked in on her, bringing along a familiar and comforting face. Hannah was determined to see her sister while standing on her own two feet, rather than laying in a bed.

A young woman entered the room with Dr. Nayar. She was in her late twenties, with unbrushed wavy brown hair and a round cherubic face, wearing a vintage-designed horn-rimmed ARspeX around her neck. She was someone Hannah was grateful she still remembered.

"Molly," Hannah said, as the woman rushed over to embrace her without a second thought. Molly pulled back, looking at Hannah, searching her face for . . . something.

"Are you okay?" she asked Hannah. "The doctor said you were fine, that you came through it—"

"I'm fine," said Hannah. "At least, I think I'm fine. I'm not really—" Hannah shook her head. "I watched a recording of myself. Telling me I was—"

"I know," said Molly, a bit too abruptly. "About the recording. I was there when you made it." Hannah looked at her with alarm.

"I had to," said Molly, "for legal reasons. There has to be a witness. So they know you're of sound mind." Then there was that curious look on Molly's face, studying her sister. "You really do seem different. Like before."

Hannah steeled herself, unsure if she wanted to ask the question that needed asking. "So it's true then? What I . . . the other me . . . said. It really happened?"

"Yeah, Han," said Molly with a sigh. "God, I wish you never had to know at all."

"I lost sixteen months of my life, Mol," she replied. "I want to know *something*."

Molly jolted back in alarm. "Sixteen? You only wanted them to take a year!" Molly rounded her attention towards Dr. Nayar. "You took nearly a year and half?! What kind of screw-up is that?"

Typical Molly, thought Hannah, then feeling grateful she still remembered that much. Molly was the younger sister by nearly three years, but growing up she was always the protector. Where Hannah had been more introspective and bookish, Molly was outgoing and aggressive. While Hannah excelled naturally in the arts and math, Molly was a performer and rulebreaker. As sisters, they couldn't be more different, yet they'd always managed to complement each other so well.

"Ms. Rice, we explained this," said Dr. Nayar. "There's a margin of error when erasing a block of human long-term memory. There's no time stamp in the brain that we can isolate and work back from. Her motor skills, personality, and earlier memories don't seem to be affected, and we'll be conducting further tests to see if there are any lingering after-effects or linkage issues. This will all be further worked out with your sister's reintegration therapist."

Hannah blinked, certain this was another pertinent fact that she no longer had access to. "I'm sorry, but . . . reintegration?"

"With your life," said Dr. Nayar. "Once we've signed off on your release, there's the matter of you moving forward after losing so many months."

"My life," Hannah said, still trying to make sense of it all.

Dr. Nayar offered another, completely unconvincing smile. "I know there's a lot for you to process: the gap in your memory and how to make sense of it. Why don't I leave you and your sister alone to work it out together?" The doctor turned to leave, with Molly remaining in the room with Hannah.

Molly waited until he left, then turned to offer Hannah another reassuring hug. "Hey, we'll get through this. We got through losing Mom and, well, what happened, and we'll get through this." Molly looked at Hannah with alarm. "You remember Mom still, right? And Dad?"

"Yeah," said Hannah with a resigned sigh. "I remember all that. I remember everything up to that trip to Thailand. After that it gets fuzzy, bits and pieces. The ra—" Then she stopped herself, too embarrassed to say anything out loud. "The . . . the thing, I don't remember that at all." She then looked pointedly at her sister. "Mol, am I still me?"

"What? What kind of question is that?" she asked, stepping back, looking at her oddly. "Of course you're you."

"That's not what I mean," said Hannah. "The way you were looking at me, like you were looking for something. Am I, I mean, do I seem the same as I was before? Like I remembered who I used to be?"

"Han," said Molly, fidgeting with her hands, pacing. "I'll tell you this much. You're not who you were before the procedure. And that's a good thing as far as I'm concerned."

It was another day before Dr. Nayar cleared Hannah as fit to check out of the Institute. She made her arrangements with the staff therapist for regular counseling to deal with the transition to the outside world. She gathered her duffel bag and met Molly for the ride home.

Home. That was just one part of the adjustment she'd have to make as Molly filled in some of the details of the past sixteen months. Cordoba had won reelection. The country wasn't at war, the economy was still, well, adequate with unemployment under twenty percent, they were finally expanding the lunar base at Shackleton after years of promises, and for some unfathomable reason, everyone was wearing something with purple.

But the personal details of her life were far less comforting. For one thing, she'd moved out of her own place and had been living on Molly's couch for the past six months. Her gig at Overlay was also gone—issues with her indefinite leave of absence, they'd told her, forcing them to contract with another coder to fill the project slot. She'd been unemployed longer than she'd been homeless.

None of that surprised her, given what she'd known about the gap in her memory. But other facts did surprise her.

"What do you mean, I don't talk with Kendra or Patrice?" Hannah demanded of her sister. They were riding in the WayLift car Molly had summoned, taking in the scenery along Route 1 on their way to Molly's apartment. Sure enough, as Dr. Nayar had said, it felt like February in New Jersey rather than October, but at least there wasn't snow on the ground.

"That's exactly what I mean," said Molly, turning to her. "The two of them . . . you don't need them in your life right now." Another change Hannah noticed, her ignoring the road, letting the auto handle the drive. Molly always preferred going manual on the road, driving the old restored Nissan she'd inherited from Mom, now apparently gone. Too expensive to maintain, Molly had told her.

"But they're my best friends!" said Hannah "I thought they were your friends too."

"Look," Molly said harshly. "Some things just can't go back the way they were, Han. Those useless bitches offered you *zero* real support after what happened to you. You said some things, they said some things, then I said some things. Things that can't be unsaid."

Hannah was silent, feeling the loss of her friendships more acutely than the loss of the studio or the gig and her work colleagues.

"We haven't talked about it," said Hannah. "The rape. We just call it 'what happened.'"

"Didn't you talk about it with the counselor?" asked Molly.

"She's an integration specialist," she replied. "Her job is helping me adjust to the gap in my head. I can't talk about a rape I don't remember, or even feel like it happened at all."

"Maybe it's better that way," said Molly. "We did this because you wanted to forget it, to not be that person anymore."

"I get it," said Hannah, waving her arms in frustration, before absentmindedly running her fingers through her hair, expecting the longer strands she once had, but now cropped short. "But I still want to know what happened. I mean, do they know who did it?"

Molly's hands were fidgeting again, dancing on the nonfunctioning manual steering wheel. "The police never identified or caught the guy, no."

Hannah turned frantic. "So he's still out there?!"

"I—" Molly looked away, staring off onto the road where other autorides were zipping around them, along with the occasional drone overhead. "You weren't able to make a statement afterwards, nothing they could use. According to you, he wore a mask. He never got caught on camera and used a condom, so no DNA. And you've got no reason to be afraid, because no one's heard a ping from this guy since it happened."

"What about—" Hannah's mind starting to go frantic. "That Sympatico match I went out with before the Thailand trip. Jason. Could it have been him? He was a creeper, definitely said some red flag stuff."

"Han, please," Molly whirled on her. "They checked him out and he was cleared, out of the country when it happened. It wasn't him. None of their leads checked out. Now, don't do this. Don't try to reconstruct this in your head to fill in the gap. That's what the counselor told us to watch out for."

"I know," said Hannah. "I just don't know how to be okay with this, or even if I'm supposed to be."

"By 'okay,' you mean happy?" said Molly. "What's wrong with being happy? You deserve to be happy as much as anyone. More than anyone."

"I suppose so, but—" Hannah's attention wavered as she looked past Molly towards the shoulder of Route 1 near the exit to Plainsboro. A group of men were assembled, all in plain, unadorned jumpsuits. Some kind of landscaping work, manual labor alongside an assortment of robots. But she spotted right away the bright orange bangles on the men's left wrists and right ankles, along with monitor drones overhead, sporting the logo of the contractor sponsoring this gang for the State Police.

"Damn, Mol," said Hannah. "A wipe crew. How many times did we see guys like them on the road or in the parks and never noticed?"

"I'm not noticing them now, Han." Molly shifted uncomfortably in her seat and looked forward, as the road crew passed in the distance. "Better they be out there with brand new brains learning how to make a life for themselves instead of being who they were in a cage for years, paid for by you and me, learning how to be better criminals."

"I know," said Hannah. "Still, at least they're working. Maybe if I were just like those guys—"

"Don't say that!" Molly sputtered and turned back abruptly to face her sister. "You're nothing like them! They were probably all murderers or psychopaths or . . . *deplorables* before they were wiped!"

"Or rapists," said Hannah. "They might have been rapists, too."

"Maybe," Molly replied. "Some of them might have been part of the Year of Rage, you ever think of that? Wiping is the least those fuckers deserve."

"Mol, seriously?" said Hannah. "That was nearly twenty years ago. RCNR was primitive back then. Even if they were wiped, all those ragers and old Regime loyalists would have new lives and identities now. They wouldn't be on the public-works crews." She then looked back, saw the crew fading into the distance, as they drove on. "Besides," she went on, "it's easier with them."

"What?"

"Something the doctor said back at the Institute. How it's easier to wipe an entire personality than rooting out one memory cluster. Even isolating an entire year is tricky. I'm living proof."

"Fine," said Molly. "I just don't want some ignorant jackass comparing my sister to one of those criminals. You and millions of rational, healthy people choose RCNR to remove bad memories and traits so you can live happier lives. You shouldn't be made guilty by association, least of all by yourself. So don't make jokes about it."

"Got it. Like Mom used to say," said Hannah. "Don't feed the trolls."

"Right." Molly's lips formed a crooked smile. "I'm glad you remember that much."

They drove on, Molly exchanging the details of her life while Hannah slipped on her ARspeX and linked with the All-Reality Cloud to catch up on a year's worth of news and gossip. Tags and pop-ups manifested as she looked out the window, every time they passed by a new building or an exit of the highway. News, weather alerts, entertainment bulletins, gossip. The technology hadn't changed, just updates to the ARC stream. Strange, she thought, how seemingly normal the world still seemed even after a sixteen-month gap. There were new movies and series for people to binge on, some new phenom would catch the world's attention. People would change, but the world was essentially still the same.

"Oh crap." Hannah pulled the ARspeX off as she heard her sister swear. She recognized the street they'd just pulled into, leading into Molly's apartment complex. There was a car parked in front of her building, a silver sedan with a blue light affixed to the roof. Police. A woman and a man were standing outside the car, both wearing long dark overcoats to keep off the midwinter chill. The man, dark-skinned and smooth-headed, was hanging back as the woman stepped forward. Hannah could see Molly's attention was focused on her.

"Who is—?" Hannah started to ask, but Molly cut her short.

"She's nobody," said Molly. "No one you have to worry about anymore."

Their car stopped and the two sisters exited, where the woman stepped out to face them, or more particularly, Hannah. The woman had dark wavy hair, older than the two sisters, still pretty, but with a bit of a masculine edge to her.

"Hannah? Do you know me?" said the woman. "Detective Flores? Or Detective Mullins?" She gestured at the man behind her.

"I—" Hannah scanned their faces, but she didn't know them at all. "I'm sorry. No."

"Goddamn," said the woman, Flores, shaking her head. "You did it, didn't you? You actually goddamn did it."

"Just get out of here, Detective," said Molly. "Hannah doesn't have to justify herself to you or anyone."

"You just wiped it all away," said the detective, shaking her head. "Like it never happened. You realize if we ever catch the guy, you'll never be able to testify against him? You just gave your attacker a gift!"

"Shut up!" said Molly, stepping forward, coming between Hannah and the detective. "You had almost a year and you didn't find him! And now you come here and try to guilt her? Like it's up to *her* to finish what *you* couldn't!"

"Hey!" the other detective, Mullins, finally spoke up. "We got a job to do and it takes time. Victims who do a reboot on us don't make it any easier."

"Mullins," said Flores, before turning back to Hannah. "I know you don't remember this, but I sat with you for hours in the hospital while they examined you. I held your hand and tried to take you through that night so you could provide any details that could help us. I made a promise to you then, that I was going to find your attacker and get justice for you. I still intend to see it through. I'm sorry you lost faith in us, Hannah." Flores sighed, as she went back to her car. "It's just our job is a lot harder now. You understand that, right?"

"Yeah, right," said Molly. "She understands. Now, can you both go away?"

Flores chuckled and rolled her eyes. "You've got a real badass looking out for you, so I guess you'll be alright. I'll keep looking for him, Hannah. I keep my promises. Just so you know, you'll never be able to face him in court now."

Hannah considered that. "Maybe that's part of why I did it, Detective."

Flores shook her head and gave another almost sad chuckle. "So that's how it is? Maybe that's exactly why you did it. Maybe that's why they all do it." Hannah could hear the woman mutter to herself, as she slid into the police car and reached for the door. "More and more every year."

"So you still haven't processed the gap in your memory?" asked the therapist, speaking via the screenspace in Hannah's ARspeX. "Maybe that's because you haven't established a new routine for yourself yet."

"I suppose not," Hannah said to the counselor. She hadn't even bothered to get dressed this morning. Just like last morning, or the morning before that. It was too cold to go outside for a walk and other than her online therapist, there wasn't anyone to talk with. So sessions intended to be weekly wound up as an every-other-day occurrence.

Not that the sessions helped much, except to give Hannah something to do. The therapist didn't tell her anything she didn't already hear from Molly whenever she came home. The sessions themselves were completely unstimulating. The faceless therapist was literally faceless, a virtual persona of an androgynous off-white female designed with no discernable physical traits or objectionable habits—everything designed to engineer an environment of calm and inoffensiveness. There was a human therapist behind the avatar, Hannah was sure of that. But she could never be certain if it was the same one each session. The advice all seemed like such a mishmash of feel-good therapy that Hannah had to believe there were at least three different therapists sharing the avatar, as well as the office environment. It explained why it all looked absent of anything personal. There were no individual quirks or manifestations of personality, just lots and lots of beige. All preset office environments seemed to come in beige when nobody bothered to customize the settings.

It wasn't that Hannah hadn't settled into a new routine while living with Molly. It was just one that didn't provide much in the way of stimulation. She'd wake up, have breakfast, and after Molly left for the day, flop down on the couch and scan the trust-certified feeds for the latest news and trends. She knew she had to recredential herself if she wanted back in the labor pool. She'd been out of the networking circles for a while, and since her time at the Crenshaw Institute and her reasons for undergoing the wipe were protected under HIPAA and the Digital Privacy Codes, no employer could ask about her time off from work. The beauty of the gig economy was that no one fussed about gaps in your résumé, as long as you had the skills they needed for the project at hand.

Molly, on the other hand, was still working at AlgaBlue, an actual job as an actual employee, a rarity these days. She was the personal assistant and gofer to one of the scientist/partners who owned the biotech company, which by extension meant working for all of the partners; so as long as one was too absent-minded to transcribe his own notes or another couldn't shop for his wife or get their own clothes cleaned, Molly would always have a job. But Molly going off to a physical workplace with regular daily hours left Hannah alone for much of the day. It made her realize just how cut off from human contact she'd become during those long months before going to Crenshaw, since, well, what had happened.

What had happened. Now she was using that phrase. Like as long as she never said the word, it would never be real. At least not to her, the her she was now, who she used to be.

She tried to think of it like a programmer would, with Hannah Rice as a software project. There had been the version of Hannah from before, that would be Hannah 1.0. Then after what happened, the software forked off into a new version, Hannah 2.0. Bad code, corrupted by a virus. So with a software engineer's mindset, she'd performed a recovery, to restore herself back to the original version. Maybe she wasn't quite back to the original Version 1 specs, more like Hannah 1.1, but that was close enough.

But still, she had to know. Was she who she used to be? How close was she to the original state of Hannah 1.0? Molly alone wasn't an objective enough resource to judge, so against her sister's advice, she sought out another connection to her past.

"H-hello?" Kendra blinked, her color-shifted image flickering in midair in front of Hannah, straightening a loose strand of blond hair from her eyes.

"Hey, K," said Hannah, shifting uncomfortably on the sofa. "I'm . . . I'm back. Kind of."

Kendra's eyes widened in surprise and tightened her bathrobe, unconsciously fussing with her hair to make herself a bit more presentable. It was early for her too, Hannah thought. Kendra didn't go into work until noon.

"Hannah," she said, like she was trying to fumble for her name, like it had fallen into disuse.

Strange, Hannah thought. She used to call her 'Han' just like Molly did. Her and Patrice. What had happened during her blackout period?

As it turned out, Kendra had no idea about her plans to visit Crenshaw. They hadn't talked in six months. But when Hannah told her, it didn't seem to surprise her at all.

"I'm glad you did it," said Kendra. "Getting the wipe. I told you it was what you needed."

Hannah shot up from her slouching position on the sofa. "You told me? I . . . I didn't know that."

"I told you for months," said Kendra, now sounding almost defensive. "You were miserable. You weren't . . . well, *you*, anymore. I'd read how more and more people were doing it, then there was this live cast from, oh, what's her name? Doctor Janice Something . . . the one who counsels the Vice President and all those Bollywood stars—"

"Jana Starling," said Hannah. Doctor Jana seemed to be on every live cast these days, she thought. The celebrity evangelist of memory wiping, or 'Mnemonic Freedom' being the term she used. It was no surprise that Doctor Jana was somehow a part of the decision-making process that led Hannah to Crenshaw.

"Right," said Kendra. "She was going on about how with all the toxic relationships and hate that we grew up with, how RCNR was vital to us cutting ties to the past and moving forward. And I kept telling you that was exactly what you needed."

"What did Patrice think of that?"

Kendra seemed to shift at the mention of Patrice's name, then shrugged her shoulders. Hannah couldn't tell if that was Kendra or another flicker in the hologram. "Patrice, well, she always has an opinion about trends. That's just her being her. But she agreed you needed to get out of the hole you were in. I mean, you were . . . wait, are you sure you really want to hear about this?"

"I . . . I don't know," said Hannah. "How often do you see Patrice? I was going to call her after—"

"That's a bad idea," said Kendra, jumping in quickly. "I mean, we still hang out. But it's not like before. Not since what happened to you, and what with the way Molly . . . well, it's just different now."

And that prompted the question. "K, what did happen? Molly won't talk about it."

"She knows what she did," said Kendra. "And what she said. I know how Patrice gets, everything revolving around her sometimes, but Molly—" She shook her head, letting the waves of morning bedhead sway about her like a tarnished halo. "It was way out of line. Bitch move, even for her."

"And . . . me?"

Kendra sighed, her stance looking uncomfortable but with some traces of sympathy in her eyes. "She's your sister. You picked your side."

"And I guess you picked yours," Hannah replied. Whatever

had happened between them, she could see that Kendra was at least rational enough to know that Hannah, the Hannah 1.1 she was talking to now, had no memory of what had come up between them. But Kendra knew. She remembered. And whatever had been said could not be so easily forgotten.

"K," Hannah said softly. "I called, I wanted to know, am I different still? Or am I the way you remembered?"

"You mean, is it all like what Doctor Jana promised?" Kendra sighed again. "You seem better, not like before. You're not sad, depressed, or, well, haunted, I guess that's the word."

"But—"

Kendra looked sat her squarely, like she was in the room with her. "You're not quite the same. You used to be happier. Even when you were pissed at something, you were still a happy person. You're not happy."

Hannah let the words hang in the air. To call the feeling awkward was an understatement. Was that the difference between Hannah 1.0 and version 1.1? Happiness?

She could tell one other way she felt different, one that proved the ever-so-popular Doctor Jana wrong. She didn't feel free either.

There had been polite goodbyes between her and Kendra, and a promise to catch up, one that Hannah accepted wouldn't come soon. She didn't even bother to follow up with Patrice. She and Molly were both the same, yet totally different. Where Molly could push and dominate a room in defense of what she believed to be right, Patrice—when she was at her worst—could dominate through the sheer conviction that she could make her drama the center of everything. The rest of them all kept Patrice's worst impulses in check, thus keeping the group in balance. Obviously, what had happened had thrown off the balance, leading things to where they were now.

When Molly came home from work that day, she took one look at Hannah, still on the couch and in her pajamas, lost in her ARspeX, and frowned.

"You never bothered to get dressed?" she asked. "Did you even get out of the apartment at all? Or were you just on the couch all day?"

"There's nothing to do outside," said Hannah, slipping off her wearable. "I've got that networking lunch with Mai next week. She's got some ideas on how I can get recertified and some possible contacts for me."

"Well, good," said Molly. "It'll be a good excuse for you to shower, too."

Hannah frowned back at her sister, as Molly dropped her backpack and started to fix her hair, and went through the hamper for a new blouse.

"Do you want me to move out?" asked Hannah.

"What? Don't be ridiculous." Molly's tone was defensive at first, until it softened, sounding almost sad. "I invited you to stay. It just . . . it bothers me to see you like this. It's like how you were before the wipe, so down on yourself. I just thought things would be different now. That's why we did this."

"Back to my old happy self, you mean?" said Hannah. "And it wasn't we who got our memories wiped. It was me. And I'm gonna need a new gig before I'm back to where things were. Maybe some new friends to go with it."

Molly shook her head. "I told you not to waste your time reaching out to Kendra."

"Yeah," Hannah replied. "You pretty much burned that bridge."

Molly turned to face her. "Me? You're saying it's all my fault?"

"She sounded a lot more pissed off at you than she was at me."

"Just forget about her," said Molly. "You need real friends right now. Patrice was always a self-centered bitch, and Kendra just made excuses for her. Time to cut old ties and free yourself from everything toxic in your life."

"Whatever you say, *Doctor Jana*," Hannah said, rolling her eyes, then saw her sister straighten out and try on the new-found blouse. "You're heading out?"

"That's right," said Molly. "It's Thursday. You know we have rehearsals, so you'll have to order in."

"So, I'm guessing nothing's gone viral for you in the last sixteen months?" Hannah arched an eyebrow as she asked. Molly's real passion for the last five years was her stand-up comedy and webcasts. To her, AlgaBlue was just a way to pay the rent until her other career took off.

"That's right," Molly snapped back. "The same way it hasn't gone viral for me in the sixteen months *before* you lost your memory."

"Hey, I'm just saying that maybe you're wasting your time with this comedy thing. There are a million other people out there with nothing else going for them, competing for the same eyeballs you are. You might want to focus more on what you've got going at AlgaBlue."

Molly jolted up and glared at her. "What did you say?"

"You heard me," said Hannah. "You've got a good situation there and you're neglecting it. You're more than an office assistant. You know more about what's going on at the company than Tanaka or Cherny or Kutuzov. They've got their genius brains wrapped around their own little specialties, but you're the one who brings it all together. You're practically a sales rep and office manager combined. Only they're all PhDs and shareholders, while you make a salary that barely covers what you're worth. Without you, Tanaka wouldn't even come into work wearing pants!"

"Screw you!" Molly shouted back, slowly enunciating her words to make the point.

"What?"

"You heard me," Molly said, her tone low, cool, and even. "*Screw you*, Han. We had this exact conversation before. Exact!"

Hannah blinked in surprise. "We did?"

"Yes," Molly said back. "A month after Thailand. Part of those bonus four months that Crenshaw took away. It pissed me off then and it pisses me off now! I'm sorry if I'm not the raging success that you are, the genius AR-tag coder fending off bids along the East Coast. But I like what I do. And at least I'm not in *my* pajamas sleeping on *your* couch!"

Hannah stood up, facing her sister, wanting to say something in her defense. But she couldn't think of anything. She couldn't feel anything but shame.

"I'm . . . I'm so sorry," she said, crossing the room and going over to Molly. The two sisters hugged, the fight instantly forgotten.

"Forget it," said Molly, who then looked at her awkwardly. "Sorry. Bad choice of words."

The two shared an uncomfortable laugh together. "I really said the exact same thing before?"

"Yeah, even the pants thing. I didn't know you took such an interest in what I did at Alga."

"Of course I care about you," said Hannah. "I want you to be happy. I just . . . I'm going a little crazy, not knowing what comes next. I had no right to take it out on you."

"It'll happen," said Molly. "Your life. Just like with me. It'll happen for both of us." She shook her head, fidgeting again with her hands. "It's how it's always been with us. You're so much smarter than me, and you always succeed at everything you do. And yet I'm the one who's always looking out for you and trying to protect you."

"That's just us," said Hannah. "It's who we are."

It was only after Molly had left for the evening that Hannah finally brought herself to wash up, get dressed, and get out of the apartment. She just had to. The couch had left the stink of failure all about her. Not Molly's failure. Hers.

She could feel the start of the evening chill as she reflexively tapped her coat sleeve, and the BioHeet fibers lit up to give her warmth and project illumination a few feet ahead. She'd need new boots for the season, she thought, but knew she had no business making any wild purchases until she'd gotten her finances in order. She shuffled about the complex, trying not to meet anyone's gaze as she pulled up her hood. She didn't know how much Molly's neighbors, mostly young families and some older singles, knew about her and her . . . situation. Did they even know about the rape, she wondered?

They all seemed so happy, the neighbors, thought Hannah. Or at least content. They had decent homes, connections to friends and family, and all the entertainment they could ask for. Gigs for the folks who could land them, Universal Basic for the ones who couldn't. Like most people around the country these days, no one around here was really rich, but then no one was really poor or suffering either. It was contentment with dashes of happiness tossed in. After the aftermath of the Regime and the Year of Rage—with epidemic levels of gun violence, drone bombings, threats online and in the street, particularly against women—contentment was good enough for most people. Only now and then would someone get thrown a curveball and experience real tragedy. Someone like her, apparently.

Hannah hated who she'd become. She hated that she'd lashed out at the one person she could still rely on. Everything Molly tried to tell her, to reassure her, that the purpose of the memory wipe was to get her back to where she'd been. Before what happened.

But nothing felt right. She didn't feel like who she remembered she was. She didn't feel like a rape victim. But she didn't feel like someone who had never been a victim either. She was in limbo, neither in one state nor another. She was . . . unfinished. Broken code.

Molly cared for her, loved her. But she was pushing back too hard. She'd been right, what Molly said. Wanting to know too much, trying to fill in that gap—it hadn't created new memories. But it spawned imagination in the face of ignorance, and that was a lot worse, she thought.

Hannah tried to imagine who her attacker was, picturing him as the angriest of angry white males that had ever been spawned out of a college party or a Regime strategy linkup on the Deep Red Web. A hateful misogynist of the worst sort, diabolical and ideological. After all, he'd remained uncaught after more than a year, so this wasn't some impulsive idiot, but someone with a plan. An agenda. That's right, thought Hannah, *I was on someone's agenda.*

Hannah looked up to see two of Molly's neighbors, two nice married ladies, gathering their kids to a WayLift that just pulled up. They didn't have a care in the world. But they were young and seemed deliriously in love with each other and their children. It never even occurred to them that fifteen years earlier, in parts of the country—thankfully not in Jersey—ladies like them were being identified by troll bots and targeted. If they were lucky, just for doxx attacks. If not, those killer drones, the ones they used to call "pepes," would smash through their windows. She remembered the alerts she and Molly watched as kids, where the pepes would spray shrapnel before exploding, in a hail of bright and righteous orange, striking out at everyone and everything their masters blamed for ruining America, keeping it from being great, and engineering the downfall of their beloved leader of prophecy.

Was that what had happened to her, Hannah wondered? A last lingering remnant of the Year of Rage? Or would it affect her to know her attack had nothing epic or conspiratorial about it, that it had been perpetrated by someone so very . . . ordinary. And that's what made her no longer *her* anymore.

And perhaps that was the most intolerable fact she had to confront. That something horrible had happened, something that cost her a year of her life, and it all had no purpose to it whatsoever. That she'd lost being Hannah, being happy, for nothing. And no one could tell her why. Except maybe the one person who first pointed it out.

#

Have I sunk this low? thought Hannah. *I feel like I'm the stalker now.* Only the person she was stalking was someone who'd once been her best friend.

That was before what happened.

Friday came around soon enough. It was the motivation Hannah needed for the rest of the week to get out, walk around, eat something besides home delivery, and get caught up on what was going on in the world, something more than what was coming from Molly.

She found herself wandering into the KraftWerks Kafé in New Brunswick just off the hyperloop terminal, staring desperately at the first barista on the left. KraftWerks occupied the first level of what had once been the old J&J building off George Street. The interior was a design blend of steampunk and a kitschy mid-2020s rehash. That, of course, was only in "flat" reality. Patrons wearing their ARspeX could view KraftWerks in whatever decor they wished. Hannah looked about and saw most of the patrons had their wearables on, even while they drank their beers and nibbled on their cannabis treats. The mashup of the flat aesthetics didn't work for Hannah, but it was popular with the Rutgers undergrads and postgrads. She was tempted to reach for her ARspeX and overlay the KraftWerks environment with something more pleasing.

"Han?" said Kendra with surprise, lifting the neo-Victorian style ARspeX from her eyes and lowering it to drape from her neck. All the staff and servers were decked in leather aprons, heavy utility belts, and tall buckled boots, both male and female varieties, though the female-identified wore corsets underneath, the male-identified in cargo pants and billowy white shirts. Everyone wore top hats or bowlers of varying heights. Definitely Kendra's kind of joint, and Hannah was grateful for this much continuity.

"Hey, K," said Hannah. "I know I should have called—"

"Jeez, Han, I'm at work!" Kendra looked about anxiously. "I mean, I know we said we'd talk, really. But here? Now?" Hannah looked around and saw almost no one. It was lunchtime on a Friday. Hannah smelled that familiar blend of odors in the air. It seemed like every public meeting space in America sold either coffee, alcohol, or weed.

Kendra looked more like herself now compared to that morning call the other day, all put together and on-trend, which helped when trying to persuade customers to part with their money in exchange for algae-based home brews freshly grown from the vats. Perfectly manicured nails, nervously rustling through long waves of golden hair spilling out from under her hat, today with added red highlights.

Hannah wondered how long it would take to grow out her own hair that long again.

"K, I'm sorry. I really am. I know you think I'm crazy. I know you completely hate me, but—"

"Whoa," Kendra stammered. She gestured to a coworker that she was taking a break and pulled Hannah aside. "Who told you that?" she asked once they were in the alcove near the ladies' room. "I never said I hated you. Especially after—"

"What happened," said Hannah, finishing her thought.

"Exactly," said Kendra. "Is that what Molly said?"

"No," said Hannah. "That's not what Molly said. I have no idea what Molly said. Or what you said. Or what Patrice said. Because no one will goddamn tell me! No one wants to talk about it! Just like what happ—" She stopped herself, taking in a breath, then letting it all exhale. "The *rape*. The goddamn fucking rape! No one wants to talk about it. I don't even want to talk about it! But it's all I can think about, even though I can't remember it. It's all just a big blank space, one that I created, and all I seem to want to do is fill it in! Except that I can't! I don't have anything to fill it with!"

Kendra looked stunned, unsure of what she wanted to do next. Hannah saw her looking around—was that a tear at the corner of her eye she saw? Some of the patrons, the lunch crowd, were looking at them strangely, realizing that some of their conversation was being overheard. Kendra took her by the elbow again and led her outside. Kendra didn't have time to grab her coat. Hannah wanted to say something, except Kendra's tears were now more visible, streaming down her cheeks and smudging what had once been a perfect application of blush.

"Han, I'm—" She enveloped Hannah in a hug, and Hannah hugged her right back, trying not to feel self-conscious about standing outside with Kendra towering over her by several inches in heels.

"It's okay," said Hannah. "Sorry for losing it back there."

"No, I'm sorry," said Kendra, breaking the hug. "I just didn't . . . everything just changed with all of us. And I was mad. Because I wanted it to go back to how it was."

"So did I," said Hannah. "I thought that's what I wanted. That's why I got wiped, wasn't it? I wanted that itch scratched. And now that I did, I can't stop scratching at it. I just . . . I miss what I had!"

Kendra nodded. "I don't know if I can be okay with Molly. Not right away. But I want us to be good again. Do you?"

"I . . . I'd like that," said Hannah. "You know, I'm freezing my ass off out here."

"You have a jacket," Kendra laughed. "Try standing out here in a corset."

Kendra led her back inside, avoiding the stink-eye she received from a man wearing a furred top hat and a ridiculous oversized monocle. "I'm going on break, Clyde. Don't give me crap."

Hannah looked at her with surprise. "I know it's been a while since I was here. I'm not getting you in trouble, am I?"

Kendra laughed and shrugged. "His aunt owns the place. He's the idiot nephew. He can't do jack without her permission." They sat down at the bar, and Kendra gestured to another barista for two pints.

"Is it any good?" asked Hannah.

"It's like everything else on the menu," said Kendra. "It tastes good and you can get a buzz out of it, as long as you don't think about it being made from vat-algae instead of barley and hops." Kendra lifted her glass. "Here's to progress."

Hannah noticed a few of the patrons—males, of course—giving Kendra the eye, or rather, a gaze, with the blue light lit on their ARspeX, an indication they were in filter mode at the moment. It made her feel increasingly vulnerable.

"God, Kendra, those guys," she said, shivering, clutching her beer tightly.

"Those clowns?" Kendra laughed. "They're just college boys. What about them?"

"They're filtering you right now," said Hannah. "They're probably picturing you in a bikini or something."

"God, I hope so," said Kendra. "I can use the tips."

"K!" Hannah stammered, surprised by Kendra's cavalier attitude, but equally as much by her own shock. People had been reality-filtering in some form or another since the advent of social media decades ago, though it had only reached a decent level of mobile high-fidelity in the past dozen years or so. As ugly as it could be at times, it wasn't outright illegal unless you crossed a line into words and actions. A dirty filter was no more criminal than a dirty mind, so the pundits said. Hannah used to believe that, thinking it was all harmless. She didn't feel so sure about that now.

"Yeah," said Hannah, softly. "Progress."

After they sipped, Hannah looked at Kendra pointedly, deciding to ask her straight out. "K, what *did* happen with you, Molly, and Patrice?"

Kendra sighed and let her shoulders slump, losing her poise in the process. "Molly accused Erick of being your attacker. Even though you said you never saw his face and no one could identify him, Molly blamed him. The timing. I swear, it was the craziest thing. And then it all started spiraling downward: the more depressed and angry you got, the angrier Molly got. Practically called Patrice an enabler. Like those old Regime women at the rallies, the ones with the red hats!"

Hannah stared at her vacantly.

"You remember those old videos, the way they cheered on—"

"That's not what I meant," said Hannah. "Who are you talking about?"

Kendra blinked in surprise. "You don't remember Erick? Erick with a 'ck' you used to call him. How do you *not* remember him?"

"I don't remember him," said Hannah, defensively. "I can't place a face. I didn't even know Patrice had a new guy. Last one I remember was the yoga instructor."

"Phillippe?" Kendra asked. "You remember *that* vain idiot, and you don't remember Erick?"

"I *said* I didn't," Hannah said, frustrated, not by Kendra but by this very large and awkward hole in her memory. "Patrice must have met him during my blank period. I don't know him at all."

"I'm really surprised," said Kendra. "I mean, he talked to you first at the hotel bar before you shined him on and he clicked with Patrice."

"Hotel bar?"

"Yeah," said Kendra. "In Chang Mai. That's where he and Patrice first hooked up. It was a real trip, him turning out to live in Morristown after we meet him on the other side of the planet. I thought you said you remembered Thailand."

Thailand. Hannah was bewildered. She remembered everything about that last girls' trip. At least she thought she did. And now she'd lost an entire person, without any obvious holes in her memory. Dr. Nayar and her therapist warned her she might encounter this. Entanglements. Bits of earlier memory lost as connections to later blocks of the parts of her mind that were erased. So what was this Erick—Erick with a 'ck'—connected to that she'd lost his face and identity so completely?

"Erick and Patrice," said Hannah. "Are they—?"

"He's gone," said Kendra. "Left. The police looked into him, pretty much every man connected to you, but he had an alibi. I mean, he wasn't a stranger, Han. You knew him for months. Mask or no mask, if it'd been him, you'd have known it, right?"

"I . . . I suppose I would," said Hannah, now starting to feel vacant. Could he have been—

"What the *hell*, Kendra?" It was another voice interrupting Hannah's thoughts, a voice she still remembered quite well. She turned around and saw a woman her and Kendra's age, long brunette hair, tan high-heeled boots and an iridescent blouse under a red leather jacket. Dangling around her neck was another familiar sight, a pink and white kitten-eared ARspeX. Hannah couldn't believe she still had those retro-looking KittyKultures, seeing as how out-of-place it looked with her otherwise on-trend and put-together ensemble.

"Patrice," said Hannah.

"Oh, fuck me," said Kendra, her eyes widened. "I totally forgot."

Hannah slid off her bar stool and awkwardly approached her old friend, who wasn't looking particularly friendly at her right now. "Hey, Patrice," she said, looking for some warmth, some degree of happiness in her eyes. She saw none.

"Hannah," said Patrice, hands on her hips. "I didn't think you'd come calling. Like nothing happened."

"Something did happen," said Hannah. "I don't know if you heard—"

"That you got a wipe?" she finished her sentence. "Yeah, Kendra told me all about it. The whole year gone. So, what now? All is forgotten so all is forgiven, is that it?"

"Patrice," Hannah sighed. "I don't know what I did that made you so pissed at me. I get it that Molly said some things, hurtful things. But I just don't see why things can't . . . you know."

"You mean, go back the way they were before?" Patrice shot back at her. "You think it's that easy? I'm sorry for what happened to you, I really am. I said it a million times before. I held your hand at the police station, I sat up with you all night for weeks, so to hell with Molly for making it seem like we didn't care what happened to you. But to destroy Erick like that, knowing what we had, what he meant to me—"

"She doesn't remember," Kendra said, still sitting back on her bar stool. "Nothing about Erick at all." She then sharply turned to the bartender and gave him a dirty look when it seemed like he was listening in a little too intently.

Patrice rolled her eyes, then turned back to Hannah with fury. "You *really* don't know? *Nothing?*" She shook her head, looking both weary and angry. "He was the one, Hannah! We were so, you know, connected! I mean, I really thought he was going to propose! That we had a future! I mean, the perfect wedding, the perfect house, the whole package. And then Molly . . . she knew that! *You* knew that! And now he's gone!"

"Patrice, I don't know what I knew or didn't know! I don't know Erick at all or if he attacked me or not."

"He didn't!" she screamed, loud enough for the staff and the few patrons to look around and watch the drama unfold around them. The manager, the one with the furry top hat, came out in response, glaring at a very embarrassed-looking Kendra. She glared in turn at Patrice and Hannah, pleading at them with her eyes. Patrice seemed to get the message and lowered her voice. "He wouldn't. I knew him. I . . . I loved him. He's not that kind of . . . he's not a monster! Molly made him sound like some kind of, what did they call those guys? *Incels?* Some kind of Rager? Not Erick, not a chance. He's . . . he was sweet, and decent. And he . . . he didn't do it. Why couldn't Molly get that?"

This was a side of Patrice that Hannah rarely got to see, at least from what Hannah could still remember. The vulnerable side. Patrice always projected an air of confidence and control in every situation, but there'd be moments when she let her guard down, when she needed to let it down. Most people didn't see that about her. She wondered if this Erick with a 'ck,' this man she didn't remember, had seen that side of her friend, which is why this all hurt Patrice so deeply.

"I'm sorry," said Hannah. "I wish I knew what to say, to make it right. What did Erick have to say?"

"Nothing," said Patrice, her shoulders slumped, more resigned now than sad. "The police talked to him, then ruled him out. Then Molly started talking trash about him. He denied it. And then he just left. Gone. No word. He wouldn't answer calls. Wouldn't answer the door. Didn't show up for work or access his last pay stub. His building manager put all of his stuff into storage. He just cut all ties. He was *that* humiliated and angry. Probably afraid the police would show up again and destroy his life for no reason. Fucking Molly."

Awkwardly, Hannah tried to touch Patrice's arm, a desperate gesture of empathy, but she shrank away, clearly not receptive. "And now it's starting all over again. You back from this brainwipe. That cop showing up yesterday—"

Hannah stepped back. "What cop?"

Patrice stiffened, her hard shell coming up again to mask her earlier softness. "You know the one. From before. What's her name?"

"Detective Flores?"

"That's the one," said Patrice. "I couldn't imagine why she wanted to talk to me. You and I hadn't spoken in months, and I didn't know anything about, well—"

"What happened," said Hannah, completing her sentence.

"Exactly," said Patrice. "She asked about you, and I told her, well, the last time I saw you, when you left Overlay Inc., you weren't doing so well. And that's when she started asking about Erick.

Because of what you and Molly were saying about him."

"Hey," said Hannah. "I saw Flores for maybe five minutes after I left Crenshaw, and Molly and I said *nothing*, absolutely *nothing*, about Erick."

"Um," said Kendra. "That was me." She got up from the bar and came over to the two women, facing head on the glare from Patrice. "Just the other day, that detective, Flores, she came by here. Asked me how you seemed, Hannah. That's when I told her about what had gone down between us all, the fighting, Erick leaving. I figured it was no big deal."

"*You* told her that?" said Patrice. "You had to drag Erick through the mud again? Jesus, Kendra. She kept asking me about Erick, where he'd gone, all the places we went when we were seeing each other."

"I'm sorry," said Kendra. "I mean, she's the police. She asked, I answered. She seemed pretty surprised. I mean, I got the impression the police never considered him a suspect."

"Of course he's not a suspect!" said Patrice, before looking around the room and lowering her voice again. "He was working that night that Hannah . . . well, he showed me. He told the police. He was cleared. They've got no business looking into him again."

"I don't know," said Kendra. "I mean, the police, they seemed really interested after they heard he disappeared just a few weeks after Hannah was attacked. I mean, he never even said goodbye to you, Patrice. Angry or not, people don't just do that. It didn't bug me before, but now it seems kind of, well, *funny*, when you think about it."

No, K, Hannah thought to herself. *It's not funny at all.* And she didn't want to think about that. This was Hannah 2.0's problem, and that version was deleted.

"Not you too," Patrice wailed. "Do you realize what you're saying? You're as bad as Molly. You're making Erick out to be some kind of . . . *psychopath!*"

"Maybe," said Kendra. "I mean, what other explanation is there? It used to be that monsters like that were everywhere. Maybe a lot of them still are."

Hannah nodded. "It's like when Molly and I were kids. During the Year of Rage. My mom was too scared to let us go outside some weeks."

"Same here," Kendra sighed, stepping forward, coming between the two women who had once been friends. "This was the crap our mothers had to deal with. We shouldn't have to."

Hannah and Patrice looked at each other, each not knowing what to say next. But Hannah couldn't help but wonder if something like this was the reason she'd wanted to erase all traces of the event. It wasn't just her that was hurt. It was Molly, and now, apparently, Patrice and Kendra. How many others were feeling the pain of what she's gone through, she wondered. It wasn't just her pain, she realized. It was the whole damn world.

Molly had been right all along, thought Hannah. *No more digging. Let Hannah 2.0 stay erased. Better it should all go away.*

#

Making her peace with Kendra, and to some degree Patrice, seemed to unblock Hannah, getting her motivated again to move forward with her life. Meetings were set up, connections were made, and Hannah audited courses at Rutgers, looking to get her skills up to date with the hot trend of neural interface systems, which all her new contacts assured her were going to make existing AR and VR hardware obsolete within a decade. The first women programmers with NASA—they called them 'computers' back then—literally had to invent their new jobs to accommodate the world of mainframe computing. So it would need to be with her.

She'd even called Dr. Nayar at Crenshaw, of all people, to pick his brain on the subject. It was only fair. After all, he picked her brain first.

She could joke about it now. She had a new routine, a new purpose.

But Hannah 2.0 wasn't gone from her brain completely. Every so often, she would think about the Hannah that everyone else remembered. And she thought about Patrice's Erick. Erick with a 'ck.'

No, she would think, it was Detective Flores's job to worry about those things. That was Hannah 2.0. For her, it was simply what happened.

Those thoughts became less frequent as the weeks went by. Then one night in March, just as spring temperatures hit, she saw a familiar face waiting outside the lecture hall, standing under a street lamp, arms folded. She had expected it to be Molly to pick her up before heading out for drinks. But instead, there she was. Detective Flores, without her partner.

"Detective," said Hannah, puzzled but curious. "What brings you here?"

"Sorry for tracking you down like this. I thought we should talk where there'd be no interruptions, or where your sister can't jump down my throat."

"Yeah," said Hannah, sheepishly. "That's Molly."

"Anyhow," Flores went on, "I have some news you might find

of interest. We've positively identified your attacker. We're 99% certain it was a man named Erick Welton. Does that name sound familiar to you?"

Hannah nodded, surprised at how anticlimactic this all felt to her. "I don't remember him personally. I know he was my friend Patrice's boyfriend at one point."

"Right," said Flores. "Your friend Kendra told you about our conversation, didn't she? That's alright. After I spoke to her and she mentioned this fellow Erick, we took another look into his alibi. It turns out his log times for work were precoded. It seems he's a fairly decent algorithm designer. We also found out about his quick disappearance. So we visited his old building manager and received permission to look through everything he left behind. What we found—" Flores leaned forward as she continued on. "We found several, I guess you can call them trophies, he collected—jewelry, bits of clothing, strands of hair in your case. And his journals, bragging about his conquests. That's what he called them, you know. Conquests. Nasty stuff there. Thanks to your case, we've tied Erick Welton to three other sexual assaults, all in connection to your friend Patrice."

"Patrice?"

Flores nodded. "Someone from her cleaning service, a former coworker, and a classmate from her alumni meetup. Until we tied in Patrice Fan and Erick Welton, we never knew there were any connections between these women other than a rapist who used a mask, disguised his voice, and left no DNA behind. Now we have the connection. Mr. Welton was using his girlfriend's network as a hunting ground."

"I see," said Hannah, unconsciously gripping her arms like a shiver. "I guess you kept your promise after all, Detective."

"Right," said Flores, eyeing her narrowly. "And I'm guessing you don't really care, do you?"

Hannah was silent for a long time before answering. "I care about how this is going to hurt my friend. She really loved him."

Flores sighed. "She never knew him. She was just a resource for him. Him going after one of her close friends at the end was a real risk. But for people like him, the bigger the risk, the greater the stimulus. He might have even killed her when he was done and ready to move on. Tie up the loose ends." Flores then looked at her pointedly. "But as far as you're concerned, the rape never happened to you. Like something you read about. So it doesn't really matter, does it?"

"Look, Detective," said Hannah, the anger in her voice rising. "Don't judge me. You don't have that right. I know you see a lot of ugliness in what you do, but don't put that on me."

"You're right, Hannah," she said. "I've seen a lot. You know what else I'm seeing a lot of? Victims of crimes who are so desperate they wipe out parts of their mind so they can forget. People erasing abuse, death, self-loathing, grief. Don't like what's happened in your life? Just hit delete and make it go away. Only remember the good parts, never the bad."

"So? Is that so terrible?"

Flores shook her head. "When I first made detective, I had to talk down a kid who was ready to splatter himself all over the pavement. Three months later, I see that same kid walking down the street. He's smiling, happy. But he doesn't remember me at all or anything I said to him. He'd even forgotten his old name. It turns out some clinic like the one you went to, they went and wiped away everything, and I mean *everything*. A whole new persona, a new name, the works. And some doctor actually signed off on this." She sighed wearily. "What a world, right?"

"He was alive," said Hannah. "And he's happy. Don't we all have that right?"

"But it's not real! It's not human. You think I don't want to forget the garbage I see every day on the job? I wish I could. But if I didn't, if I wasn't angry or disgusted or haunted by what's out there, I wouldn't be half as motivated to wake up every morning and try to clean some of it up." Flores then looked at Hannah squarely. "Tell me, what do you think the odds are that your friend Patrice is going to have her own memory wiped at some point, so she can get over the fact that she slept with a serial rapist?"

Hannah wanted to walk away, to shut all of this out. As much as she questioned what she'd lost, part of her wished Patrice would actually erase the past year just as she had. Maybe then they'd be the friends they used to be once again.

As for her, she'd made a choice, and despite her earlier unsettled feelings, she'd made her peace with it. She was happy now. She deserved it.

"Does Patrice know yet, Detective?"

"She will soon," said Flores. "My partner's with her now, getting her statement. She'll probably need a shoulder to cry on afterwards."

Hannah nodded. "Okay. I appreciate the heads up. For her sake, I hope you have enough evidence to have Erick Welton wiped for good and turned into something more decent."

Now it was Flores's turn to be silent before answering. "I wish that I could, Hannah. Except no one knows where Erick Welton is. He was last spotted on public surveillance on March 27th of last year at 8:42 PM, and he hasn't been seen since. As far as we know, he hasn't boarded a plane or ship or left the country. Our crime scene guys don't even think he went back to his apartment that night. The man has completely vanished from the face of the earth."

Hannah blinked in alarm. "Is that why you came to see me, Detective? Am I in danger? Is Patrice or any of my other friends in danger?"

Flores offered a wide smile. Until now, Hannah hadn't known it was possible for a smile to actually be *angry*. "Between you and me, Hannah, I don't think you're in any danger at all. Because I'm almost certain that Erick Welton is dead. Just as I'm almost certain that you're the one who killed him."

Hannah nearly fell over in shock. "No . . . I . . . *what?*" She felt her heart racing, her breathing becoming ragged. "I didn't!" Hannah exclaimed, then looked about to make sure no one else could overhear. "I don't remember anything like that."

"Of course you don't remember," said Flores. "That's what makes this the perfect murder."

Hannah started at her, glaring.

"The perfect murder isn't in the planning," said Flores, "or the actual killing, or even the clean-up. The perfect murder is in what happens after, not looking guilty or doing something stupid for years after you supposedly got away with it. The perfect murder is by someone who never knows that they're a murderer.

"When you wiped your memories of the attack, I had to go back to the only testimony I had. Your statement after the rape." Flores reached into her bag and pulled out an old-fashioned police-issue tablet. "I'll show you—"

"I don't want to see it!" said Hannah, viscerally recoiling. "You can't make me see it!"

"Fine," said the detective, putting her bag back in order. "I was able to watch with a fresh set of eyes, look for something, anything, that might help me out. And then I looked at your image where I was asking you if you knew your attacker." Flores leaned in as she went on. "I could see it in your eyes. You were lying to me. I don't know why you did it, but you knew. Even with that mask, his voice distorted, you knew he was the one. And you decided a brainwipe wasn't enough for him."

"That's . . . not true," said Hannah, her pose stiffened. "You don't know what you're talking about."

"True, I don't know where it happened," said Flores. "Definitely not at his apartment. I don't know how he was killed. I can't even be certain how dirty your hands were. But I'm pretty sure I know how the body was made to disappear."

Hannah listened on, aghast, refusing to believe a word of what she was hearing.

"Your sister works at AlgaBlue. They do bioremediation, engineered algae breaking down biological matter into carbon compounds and hydrogen gas, which they sell to power fuel cells. And I thought, how easy would it be for the tanks at AlgaBlue to break down something about the mass of an adult male? And I'm guessing you thought the exact same thing.

"I can try and obtain a warrant. But I understand those tanks are scoured clean on a weekly basis, that any DNA traces would be gone by now. Whatever's left of Erick Welton is scattered among at least a hundred fuel cells, assuming any DNA linked back to you is there with him."

"No," said Hannah, her face ashen. "It's not true."

"I wouldn't expect anything official. As far as the DA's concerned, Erick Welton is a fugitive from justice. But he'd have to wipe his ARC tags from any public surveillance. His employer has a contract with the state police to provide software support for NJ-ARC. So my bosses think Welton took advantage of that access to mask his escape outside the jurisdiction. Only I asked around. Welton's skills are fine for tweaking algorithms. Good enough to change a personal log time. But erasing his tags from the ARC? That's a whole different level. And you, I'm told, were considered that good. Really good."

Hannah tried to walk away, desperate to shut out Flores's words.

"You know what finally gave it away for me?" said Flores. "The way your sister reacts, the way she hovers over you and tries to protect you. She makes accusations about Welton with your friends, but she never reported any of these suspicions to the police. Haven't you figured it out? I've got three sisters of my own. There are no secrets. She *knows*. She's known from the beginning. And she's done her best to make sure you never figure it out. She'd have killed the bastard himself if you'd asked her, she loves you that much." Then Flores's eyes widened with realization. "That's why you did it, wasn't it? Did he threaten your sister? Try to get a rise out of you? Of course he did. He knew you and he knew Molly. What else would drive a solid citizen like you to become a killer? That's how you got him to AlgaBlue, wasn't it? You didn't haul a dead body. You lured a live pervert with the promise of a fresh target. You didn't do this for you. You did this for her."

"Are . . . are you going to arrest me?" Hannah asked softly. "Or Molly?"

Flores shook her head. "No. I can't. It's like I told you. My bosses have a theory that fits the facts. Without a body or DNA, no one is going to argue for murder. Just like nobody wants to go into court and argue for the sanctity of Erick Welton's life. Least of all me."

"Then . . . why?" said Hannah. "Why tell me any of this?"

Flores glared at her, her tone as much filled with frustration as with anger. "Because I have to. Because I can't be okay with this, no matter how much sympathy I might feel. Civilization doesn't work if people get away with murder with no consequences, no matter who the victim is. And there has to be consequences, or nothing matters at all.

"And *that's* what's wrong with the world. Everyone thinks if you erase the truth, make it go away, then everything's gone. And then nothing matters. The Regime didn't take power because of scumbags like Erick Welton. They won because everyone filtered out the truth to one of their liking and let in nothing but lies. Only now the filters aren't just on the screens anymore. We're putting them inside our goddamn heads!"

Hannah's mind was a jumble, trying to process what Flores was telling her. She thought about everything Molly had done since her release from Crenshaw. Did Molly really know the whole time? And did she really deserve to get away with it if she had killed someone?

"I don't believe you," said Hannah firmly. "None of what you said happened. I'm not that person. I'm exactly who I used to be, who I've always been."

Flores sighed, looking at Hannah with pity. "You really believe that, don't you? You need to believe that. Don't you get it, Hannah? You're not that person anymore, the one you were before. You can't be. Just knowing what you know makes everything different. That woman, the one from before, that woman is *gone!*"

Flores turned to leave, but Hannah found the strength, through all of the bewilderment, all of the shock, to speak up.

"*Screw you.*"

Flores turned back to her. "Excuse me?"

"What?" said Hannah. "You're going to arrest me for mouthing off? For not being an obedient citizen? You heard what I said. What right do you have to come here, try and guilt me, make accusations you admit you can't prove, because . . . why? Because you didn't catch Erick Welton yourself? Because you hate the world and the way things are and you want to punish someone for it? Well, the rest of us have to live in this world too, and we all have to find ways to deal with it. You saying you're sorry isn't enough, Detective! Some people . . . some *women* . . . have to dull their senses just to function, or zone out on fantasy and refuse to step outside of their door. Well, I chose my way to deal!"

Flores glared at her through narrowed eyes. "You didn't have the right to choose murder. Not even for a scum-sucker like Welton. No one has that right."

"And if I *did* choose it?" Hannah's tone was almost taunting now. "If what you say is true, that the woman I used to be is gone, then so is the woman who committed this crime you're accusing me of. A rapist *and* a killer, both of them wiped out of existence! Congratulations, Detective Flores. Your job is *done!*"

Flores looked her over, her face now a mask of stone, followed by a slow nod. "So be it. I hope you have a good life, Ms. Rice.

And for your sake, let's hope we never have to cross paths again."
Hannah watched as Detective Flores got into her car and drove off.

Hannah wondered what the detective meant by her final words. Was it an acknowledgement? A show of understanding? Or just a threat? *Probably all of the above,* she thought.

"Hey," she heard Molly call out to her and saw her walking up the street. "I whistled up a ride. You ready? Who were you talking to before?"

"I—" Hannah's mind was racing. "It was Flores."

Hannah didn't tell her everything. But she did tell her about the revelation of Erick Welton's guilt. And that Patrice was learning that truth right now.

"We should forget drinks tonight," said Hannah. "Patrice is going to need us."

"Us?" said Molly. "Are you sure she'll want to see me? I mean, I wish I'd been wrong about the bastard, I really do. I never wanted . . . I just wanted her to see the truth in front of her."

Hannah looked at her oddly. "How did you know it was him?"

"I—" Molly stammered. "I didn't. I just, well, he just came off so fake, too polished. He just felt *off* to me. You get what I mean, right?"

"Yeah," said Hannah, "I get it. You always had good instincts about people." She considered something else, something that Flores never would have. The detective thought she understood Molly, a sister who knew Hannah's secrets intimately. But Molly was always more than a friendly ear and a confidante growing up. She'd been a protector, an advocate. And sometimes, when life got too hard, a shield against the world. Just as she was shielding Hannah now.

It would only have been with Molly's help that she'd have access to AlgaBlue, to get Erick there without leaving a digital footprint. And there was her getting rid of Mom's old car. What evidence had been left behind there?

And killing someone who threatened the person she loved the most? That was the crucial difference between her and Molly, something she'd known all of their lives. Molly would have felt completely justified about killing a man to protect her sister or her friends. It was knowledge she could live with just fine. Hannah knew she never could. And *that* was why she'd wiped herself.

Of course, she could never be sure, she thought. She'd never remember. Maybe it happened the way Flores said. Or maybe not. She knew, and yet she didn't.

Either way, she didn't want to know.

"Let's both go see Patrice," said Hannah. "You and me together."

"Sure," said Molly. "I promise I won't tell her I told her so. I'm not a total asshole."

Hannah smiled. "I know you're not. That's just us," she said. "It's who we are."

And maybe that was what Flores really intended, that she couldn't escape any of it. Hannah 1.0—all of her hopes and dreams, and the friendships she'd once had—was gone. As gone as Hannah 2.0. There was no going back, only forward, replacing who she was and what she once had with something different. Maybe even something better. And finding a way to live with it all.

She was still Hannah. Hannah Rice. Version 3.0

Level 4
Michelle A. Belgrave

What can a technologically advanced society of scientific professionals run by a massive conglomerate do to its citizens? That is one question this author asked herself when writing the character El, a woman forced to question her sanity.

"Hailey," I called and opened my eyes as the floating, disorienting sensation faded.

We rode in the stomach-churning, gliding sway of an autodrive. The long, quad-shaped, scarlet-colored vehicle whooshed by the landscape in a dizzying blur. With three rows of seating, and middle facing the rear, the vehicle held twelve. The black interior smelled a bit smoky, the strong scent of cedar mixing with the lingering funk of previous passengers.

As the autodrive tightly rounded a corner, my seat began vibrating. I knew what that meant. I couldn't keep up with the rapidly changing scenery any longer.

Clutching at the safety belt dangling from the ceiling, I yelled in frustration. "Driver! Do not rotate. Do not move our seats. I want to stay facing forward. Thank you."

The vibrating stopped and the vehicle stabilized. With that issue resolved, I focused on my constant companion.

"I am here." Bouncing in the seat across from me, she sounded like an ebullient eight-year-old—the age where children start noticing the world, but are innocent about its ways. Hailey resembled me at that age, with a brown complexion and golden russet undertones as a result of playing in the sun all day. Her dusty, off-black hair was braided into two fat ponytails, curling and pointing upwards towards her dominating narrow shoulders. She wore high-top pink sneakers, thick white stockings, and a long greenish-blue dress shirt belted with a wide pocket bag to stash her belongings.

What does a holoscape AI carry nowadays?

In my left hand, I rolled around a silver ball, the source of our connection.

I devised a "hazy memory ratio" program for her: a sliding retention scale of summarized events, leaving her at the conceptual age of eight to observe, absorb, and enjoy this afternoon. After a specified period of time, total recall of every moment will gradually fade to a few data sets of her choosing. The goal was to teach her the perspective of a small, young, and vulnerable person.

We worked together as a pair, my job being somewhat reminiscent of a plumber in the 20th Century. I cleared out the junk, neurosynthetic plaque or logic decay in artificial intelligence systems. The tasks varied; no two assignments were alike. I could be calibrating sensors, testing decision structures, literal or ambiguity probabilities, and "pulling a thread" on algorithms in one place, then removing bug-bots, patching critical flaws, and bringing systems up to date in another.

As a last resort, I am brought in to track all over GEMS (global exchange media systems) and pull the plug on wayward or obsolete AI. Putting one down often made me sad, close to the edge of depression. In a handful of cases, if a dysfunctional AI was salvageable, I'd squirrel it away into Hailey's subsystem. It was a deceitful slight-of-hand, but a necessary evil on my part. From that point on, Hailey took over pitching a new system to an organization. A perfect vocal twin devoid of my occasional lisp. Not only a valuable asset, her mere presence was the best example of a holoscape AI.

They call us tweakers. I just make sure systems will pass the latest ISO AI certification. Can't have them running amok now, can we?

In the early days, a lot of enterprises resisted this type of service, preferring in-house techreps to solve their dilemmas. Unfortunately, people have trouble discerning when and where a breakdown occurs. Logic decay may arrive on two fronts: gradual chaos or subtle incoherence. A habit of blindly relying on these systems can cost an organization its very existence. Persuading management to acknowledge the issue, and minimize or eradicate the error, ends up one of the most difficult aspects of the job. Admit to a few glaring faults with their AIs? Why, that's tantamount to a personal flaw.

For a very simple example of one symptom, we use a music playlist. In a randomization scheme with 1,000 songs, based on precedence and preference, the top 100 would remain in place, yet over time the playlist shrinks. Presented with scapes showing the same 21, 33, and 17 songs within 90 minutes, all day, stretched out for several weeks, understanding dawns.

So, why weren't others using their own Hailey as a solution? She is a unique, customized, ad-hoc creation of mine after many years of trial and error. I carry her around with me at all times. She freely ventures into GEMS, in absolute protected mode, drumming up business for us. As a stand-alone holoscape AI, Hailey cannot be deployed as a resource by others. I don't trust the scapes or users in that environment.

Yet today is not about my AI. It's about me.

Despair brought me to The Memory Enhancers Group Limited, otherwise known as The Memhance Group. My biopsychiatrist, or "brain cleanser," Dr. Ophelia Esphine recommended them. With a big blushing oval face, scattered shadowy pockmarks, and hair like blades of yellowing grass, she reminded me of a strawberry. Unable to close that rosette mouth, therapy consisted of her doing most of the talking. After multiple unproductive sessions, the doctor insisted on Memhance as an alternative option.

I considered them my last resort.

It all started when a blinking bright blue light appeared in the far corner of my right eye. Most of us wore a transparent monocle, which fits snugly over the eye socket seamlessly blending holoscape AIs, interactives, data resource dives, messages, news feeds, and countless other imaging filters from GEMS. Naturally, I assumed it was the device. When I took it off, however, the blue light expanded into a distracting blur.

Hailey found Dr. Ophelia Esphine for me. As the doctor explained it: when Level 4 personality traits begin to appear, more consistently than by chance, the blue light appears. It grows over time, clouding a person's vision if "help" is not sought out or rejected. Aside from medical specialists and the authorities, no one was aware of this monitor. It appeared when behavior became pathological or deviated from the norm.

Apparently, I haven't been conducting myself in a sufficiently proper manner.

Level 1 pertained to average people. Professionals in medical, technical, scientific, and other certified or licensed fields floated between Levels 1 and 2. The highest known Level 3 ran for public office and controls, either openly or by proxy, conglomerate leviathans. Serving in a professional capacity as a Level 2 was the core of my identity.

How was I not one? More curious than cautious, I had yet to comply with the most basic premise expected of a Cerium City resident.

Ordinance No 1: No one shall command, impede or interfere with the systems, instruments, and properties of the state.

My role was supposed to be of one who "serves." Instead, I lived for mischief. If it harmed others, then that was a casualty I was not responsible for. I was a trigger, launching a process that will turn reality into a series of logical loops. My ignorance would prove my innocence, it was my alibi and defense.

Over the years I've had a variety of pets. All but one ran away. Slipping out the doorway when it was left ajar, jumping out the window to catch a shiny hovering surveillance drone, and leaping over the balcony to pursue the unknown. From my location in the floating wheel tower, exiting the residence by window, balcony, and doorway at the wrong moment becomes the point of no return.

My last pet just disappeared. I had no idea how the dog managed to escape from a hermetically-sealed, locked-down residence. After the others, I carefully fool-proofed the place against pet runaways. The magnetic doors were impenetrable. Opening or closing windows and doors, and turning devices on and off are controlled by voice activation; mine alone, none other.

Somehow Mr. Peepers found a way out.

An excitable small brown, gray, and white ball of fur outfitted with a neuralinguistic translator, he constantly barked at me to, "Feeeme. Wannawaak! Feeeme. Wannawaak! Throodabaa. Throodabaa! Throodabaa!" It took a lot of debits to get that device. I meant to upgrade his vocalization and add a tracking program, but never got around to it. I tried finding him with Iroquois, a subsystem AI in Hailey, because he can discreetly jump into surveillance systems.

Yet nothing worked. It was as though he had been erased or never existed. Guilt washed over me. Having lost patience with his gruff stuttering demands, I shouted. "Why don't you go away already? Leave me alone!" With those words, Mr. Peepers became my last companion made of flesh and bone.

I burned out of mating contests a long time ago. A blink, wink or ping, and tingle came by accident or not at all. Not a single tingle from the AI of having found a match. No one pinged for a second meet. Oh, how I wished for a wink! Blinks caused the most trouble, being the easiest to transmit. An obvious effort by the developers to make "fate" happen.

The final insult to injury came with my removal from these scapes. The tingle sent was prompt and clear. My looming unpopularity overshadowed their quality quotients, sinking overall rankings. Nothing screams success like racking up social demerit points. Thankfully, it hasn't affected my work, at least, not yet. Being a Level 4 was to live in heightened suspense: waiting for that loud clap on a snowcapped mountain.

Despite my negative social scoring and inability to connect with people, I remained optimistic and forward-looking. I managed. Faithfully, I got up every morning. Endured the sonic cleanse. Swallowed my nutrient tablets. Patiently waited for the autodrive to deliver me to the next assigned worksite.

I tended to avoid work requiring interaction with human beings. Hailey filled that role. I was not people adverse; on the contrary, I adored humanity. Rather, my reasoning is that too many people created sensory overload. Like nibbling and savoring a microbud nutrient created for its unique taste, too many flavors ruins the taste. As with people, it should be savored in small bites.

Whereas, visiting Dr. Esphine's skypod gave me such joy. It made venturing outside and mingling with the public worth the effort. I insisted on being in the flesh for our sessions. After experiencing the thrill of it for the first time, I became hooked.

Skypods floated within a wide dome atop a towering superstructure nicknamed Gobil (goblet on a hill). They spun at a measured distance from one another, providing an unparalleled, unhindered view of silvery-white Cerium City. Farther afield, neighboring regions of granite and verdant lumps led to the crescent shoreline of this artificial island. Shadows of clouds would sweep across the landscape, changing shape, allowing sunlight to break through, or disperse entirely.

"You come for the views." A wealth of knowing amusement laced Dr. Esphine's voice as she observed me staring into the distance. Transfixed. Far below, steady red beams of light stroked and searched Gobil, a few dotting and piercing pearly puffs of vapor, before winking out. Surveillance drones crested being unable to fly up this high. The skypod, with its great distance from everyone and everything, made me feel safe and secure.

On that particular day, I was more willing to talk instead of letting the doctor's loquaciousness take over. The loss of Mr. Peepers cracked open the door on my emotional reserve.

With my back to Dr. Esphine, I watched condensation gather on the surface of the dome. Water streamed down, leaving veins of clear streaks. Laying a palm against the chilly surface of the skypod, I wanted to etch, "El Waz HeRe."

"You haven't spoken about your family much," she ventured, sensing my mood.

"What would you like to know?" I should be lying down, sitting, or reclining next to the doctor. Yet I couldn't stay still.

"Let's begin with your parents."

My shoulders rose then fell slowly in an exaggerated shrug. "My daddy took the one way to Mars."

Dr. Esphine sounded genuinely impressed. "Dr. Ellis Lee joined the Mars Colony Initiative!" The same consortium that developed Cerium City created MCI. Dexter Kohlrabi consisted of various business interests, scientific research organizations, and a plethora of anonymous investors. One could say Cerium City is the true birthplace of extraterrestrial colonization. Levitation into the stratosphere, a literal breakthrough, by virtue of the Nomura-Koening Quantum Leap Drive. Since then, successive waves of development kept the city earthbound. Gobil skypods were a remnant of the experiment.

As a scientist, my daddy could have gone anywhere. "He didn't tell us where he went until after he arrived. He just left." I spent 24 weeks worrying and wondering.

"Maybe he had no choice?" Dr. Esphine offered. Cerium City's populace lived under exacting, punctilious residential laws, and contractual obligations. It was life as defined through the prism of Dexter Kohlrabi.

I heaved a sigh, eyes searching upwards. Shouldn't she be upset on my behalf? Wasn't child abandonment a grave misdeed by a parent?

"He had plenty of choices. It couldn't have been that difficult to let us know." The doctor had no idea the kind of agony a child experiences when one parent goes missing, and the other emotionally detaches. Abandoned by two people I needed the most in this world. Yet I wasn't angry with him, simply disappointed. He encouraged and nurtured my interest in AI, going so far as to enroll me in the Alternative Curriculum to further my studies and receive certification and licensing.

"What about your mother? What was her reaction?"

I stepped right. One drawback of the skypod came from standing in place too long. Weightlessness seeped into my gut, making me nauseous. To reestablish equilibrium, I must move.

Initially, I interpreted Mother's behavior as shock or shame at her husband leaving. "She felt relieved."

"Why?" Dr. Esphine asked, and a beat later, "How did you feel about it?"

Ah, yes, "muh feelings." I paced around the skypod. The doctor's chair turned, automatically tracking. "Stopped caring after I discovered the truth, but—" Catching my breath. Thinking back to how quickly Mother's sense of urgency tapered off. She probably booked the passage. They argued a lot in those days: over the length of quarantines, moving off the island, and having another child. The emotional tug of war between them pushed me away.

I became immersed in my budding AI interests, activities, and distractions with fellow pranksters.

"What?"

I flashed a wry smile at the doctor. "Mother is a high-ranking official. As one of the authorities, she would have known."

A hint of disapproval crept into her voice. "Dana didn't care to inform you?"

"Oh, I don't know. We rarely communicated. Didn't talk much." I giggled, even though it wasn't funny. "Once my daddy left, I pretty much followed him out the door."

Her monocle glinted. "What happened to the project you worked on with him?" Glancing up to the right, her eyes darted rapidly from side to side; a seemingly nervous tic meant to shake off negative thoughts.

The smile on my face collapsed. "What project?"

She was reading my HealyStats. "You mentioned helping your father create a virus." A fine tremble shook the doctor's voice.

Why ask about that? "My daddy wanted me to follow in his footsteps as a SHHRRPA protege."

"Sherpa?"

I leaned back, resting against the cold surface, crossing my legs at the ankles. "The Space Human Hibernation and Ribonucleic Research Principle Authority." I waved my hands dismissively: Level 2 people and their love of acronyms. "By using a synthetic viral vector and an embedded AI like an on-off switch, we tracked every single human gene affected by induced hibernation." I stared without seeing, remembering the ecstatic joy I felt during the entire process. It was how Hailey came into being, albeit a previous version under a different name. Since I couldn't take her out of the lab, I recreated Hailey from scratch. Technically I wasn't stealing, alright—merely redeploying lessons learned. With false modesty, and sober mien, I lied. "Only did a little thing."

"What was it?" Her eagerness briefly caught my attention. She was avidly searching GEMS for data on SHHRRPA: a wholly futile exercise.

I chuckled without mirth. "Really cannot tell you, Doctor. It is a trade secret belonging to Dexter Kohlrabi." The virus was the AI, one and the same.

For a few hours, or days, I thought, I could turn your palms, face, neck, and chest a deep hue of purple. Make you bloated and burn. Make you think you were infected. Make you panic. Make you scared not only for your life, but for everyone around you. Quickly, I buried those words in my mind, detaching myself from emotional detonations. Years ago, I took the bait, angered by a deliberate transgression: the betrayal of my trust. The one time a prank wasn't intended to be funny. I wanted to hurt him the way I felt hurt. I wanted to share the pain.

"I would have to kill you if I told you." The joking rejoinder belied my seriousness.

It was a rare occasion, but the session rendered Dr. Esphine speechless.

The autodrive glided to a swaying halt in front of The Memhance Group building, pulling me back into the present.

Tsk-tsking in consternation, I reached into my bag and grabbed another silver ball.

Clacking and rolling the two silver balls together, I whispered, "Iroquois," darting a glance at the center display area of the autodrive. Aside from a floating scape map of the area, nothing aroused my suspicions.

Hailey froze mid-bounce, flickering, before her holoscape stuttered into motion.

Calling up a subsystem AI always interrupted the main one. Despite multiple tweaks, I was unable to figure a way around it. Launching them from GEMS would likely eliminate the problem. Of course, I would never let that happen.

One of the silver balls in my hand vibrated. I pocketed the other.

A ghostly male figure appeared next to me, one leg crossed over the knee.

I turned to address him, staring at the featureless profile. Yeah, another upgrade I should make: give Iroquois a face.

Ticking off my orders. "Listen. Record everything. Ten-block sweep. Hijack surveillance drones, if necessary. Hear a name? Give me a detailed bio scape." My throat tightened with each word. Drying. I forced myself to exhale. Illegal and restricted activities like drone-jacking for private usage made me nervous, but I did it anyway.

The silver ball pinged.

I leaned back in the seat, biting my lips. "When Hailey removes her last memory from today, collect those from her. Keep them. Then stop." The timeline would track with my visit to The Mem-hance Group.

The ghostly figure faded when the ball pinged again. I dropped it back into my bag.

Shifting in my seat, ready to leave, the autodrive doors lifted. A warm breeze swept out the stale smoky air, leaving a clean scent.

I climbed out gingerly. The vehicle hovered a few inches too high above the curb. As I walked away the autodrive sent me a tingle, a stern reminder of its intention to return in exactly forty-eight minutes. Three minutes allocated for the human propensity to lag. Machine time ran with unforgiving precision.

Warily, I appraised the four-storey brownstone, a former residence modified to meet zoning requirements. The old building stood out; bridged by technologically advanced, polished steel, and graphite structures piercing a lavender sky.

Hailey danced around me, skipping in celebration. For a fleeting moment, I envied her mindless surface emotion.

We stared at each other, dallying. After circling a few times, she asked, "Are we going or not?"

With the monocle on, I was highly aware of, and alert to, the presence of drifting holoscape AI trawlers. Yet not just them, overhead surveillance drones flew by, the size of a man's fist and length of a forearm. Agile as a snake with a multitude of articulate limbs, they pursued individuals everywhere. Robot messengers in various shapes and sizes seamlessly weaved in and out of traffic. Effortlessly, they leaped onto the sidewalk. Being rooted at the spot for thirty-six seconds was acceptable. In another ten, I would be hauled in for questioning.

Hailey raced up the steps ahead of me, disappearing into the chestnut door. Trailing the holoscape AI, I climbed wide well-worn steps to the main floor. I leaned towards the narrow greeting screen on the glossy dark green frame, lips parted, ready to speak.

The door unlocked, swinging back to lightly thump against the wall.

"Were you expecting me?" I called out. Stepping over the

threshold, I gawked at the interior. On my left, a darkly stained wooden stairway, matching the hallway floor, dully reflected light from outside and overhead. Beige walls, with ceiling and base moldings in depression gray and vomit green, stretched the length of the building.

From above came the low hiss of static, then a disembodied voice. "Greetings Dayn—"

Abruptly, I snapped, "Call me El."

"El?"

Instead of answering, I waited.

The hissing grew louder, before ending with a muted screech. "El, your biopsychiatrist Dr. Ophelia Esphine made the appointment."

"And here I thought I would make a surprise visit by dropping in." People rarely went to medical facilities unless for hard to treat ailments or catastrophic injuries. Health care diagnostics came with housing and onsite procedurals were commonplace.

Following a low bark, the voice instructed, "Go into the second room on your right, El. The meditech will be with you in 63 seconds." Behind me, the front door closed with a soft click.

"Very old-fashioned of medical services to make me wait." The first room, a continuation of beige with depression and vomit, was vacant. Indeed, my voice echoed and footsteps sounded alarmingly loud in the hallway. I angled my head, looking up through the stairway railings, noticing the bare landing.

"With whom am I speaking?" My monocle should be showing a holoscape AI. Nothing appeared. Not even the suggestion of a flicker. Disturbing. Normally, older AI appeared as ghostly images like wisps of smoke floating on the periphery. Around the visage would be a series of vibrating lines pulsing with the frequency of sounds emitted. The Memhance Group was definitely not an upgrade.

Down the hall came a rustle of clothing and snap of high heels. A hooded female form in bluish gray darted behind one of two doors before they clicked shut.

From overhead, "This is the voice answering system of Memhance Group. Call me Beccah." The AI pronounced with the elongating "cah" of an anxious goat. I smothered a giggle. When feeling on edge, the oddest things became hilarious. My barking laughter could erupt at the most inappropriate times.

There was no limit to the amount of mood enhancing, mind-altering psychotropic drugs the biopsychiatrist prescribed for me. Dutifully, I took the medications home, later on selling them in unregulated and mostly banned "underground" coxtail scapes. I opted to self-medicate with Asperozin. Like the gift of manna, the drug recipe arrived from a deep data resource dive through GEMS. I mentioned it to Hailey before, doubtful such a remedy existed, having nearly forgotten about it until the information appeared hours later.

Dr. Ophelia Esphine's drugs caused dry mouth, hallucinations and memory lapses. They also kept the blue light intact. An off-the-shelf product mixed with a few other pharmacological agents helped create my homemade drug. After weeks of testing, aided by Hailey's monitoring, correcting, and inhibiting of gene mutations, I made the perfect "downer" to control my moods. I have to be levelheaded and logical at all times. The drug helped deaden my overly stimulated nerves, ensuring I typically behaved like the lowest levels. Best of all, it minimized the blue light to a small pinprick.

These secrets were my own to keep. No one shared everything. Trust came in layers, filtered by reality. We all played a game. We all have a role. I certainly wasn't going to tell everything to the good Dr. Ophelia Esphine. What I shared with her came on a need-to-know basis.

In the center of the plain, small, white room was an uncomfortable looking gray recliner with a hovering thin band. Moving closer, I observed the device. It hummed, pulsing in a circle of blue lightning.

"Beccah?" I searched for a place to rest my bag. Its weight made my shoulders and back ache. Besides holding everything I needed, it allowed me to avoid virtual showrooms and the ensuing, looming, creepy presence of a surveillance drone partnered with a stalking robot messenger. To deliver a product, they are required to hunt down the buyer. Watching a surveillance drone hover outside a 155-floor skyscraper with a red beam fixed on one's monocle was more than a bit disconcerting.

I loved the convenience of it, until I reviewed my debit history. Then and there I decided to cut back. There were only so many virus-mutating specimens, immunization booster shots, inhalants, PVC guns, laser wands, iridescent contacts, and thermopatches I could carry. Nor did I have to carry data plaques as big as twentieth century coins to store information. On that front I was an anachronistic holdover. Most people trusted their data storage to GEMS. I smiled, feeling smug and quite clever. At least I knew what old currency looked like.

"What can we do for you, El?"

Hoisting my bag up, reminiscent of a winning prize fighter, I asked, "Where do I put this?"

The wall before the recliner parted, revealing a place for personal belongings.

"Ah," I said, gently setting the bag on a shelf.

With clipped precision, the hollow voice prompted, "Is there anything else?"

Is it possible? I felt a keen flash of irritation and hesitated, before gingerly peeling off my coat. Tossing the slick translucent material against the back of the closet, it slithered over the bag before adhering to the wall. Instantly hardening, a handle exuded from the sack for me to pull and release my possessions later. Did the AI sound impatient?

"The meditech is coming now, El. Have a great day."

I glared at the ceiling and walls, wanting my annoyed expression analyzed by the AI, knowing it was futile with such an out-of-date model. My hands shook from a growing impulse: grab my things and go. I skipped lunch to come here. I needed another Asperozin, the last one was wearing off.

A sharp knock on the door startled me.

A tall and lean man sauntered into the room wearing a body-molding, glittery, silver suit and high-collared, long, orange bib-tie.

His appearance perked my curiosity. "Are you human?" I asked, searching for movements too careful to be natural. My monocle picked up nothing out of the ordinary. These days it was hard to tell. Pranksters enjoyed disguising themselves as artificial life forms. By law, any entity taking physical form, such as a flesh-toid or silicon AI, must have iridescent irises.

"Yes, ma'am. Let me introduce myself. I am your meditech Soren Stevens." Flashing even white teeth, in a combo of ginger beard and fiery sunset hair, his smile mesmerized. "Memhance Group wanted to try an old-fashioned touch by using person-to-person services." Providing a somewhat risky endeavor as well. Telemedicine and home diagnostics had evolved rapidly, reducing the spread of contagions. Cerium City authorities quarantined households before mutating viruses or malware and highly communicable diseases got out of hand.

"Only the most rare and extremely high-end businesses are doing that. I loved hearing stories about it when I was a child. My grandmother told me real people used to serve food and drink. They even drove cars and trucks. Amazing." It sounded incredibly hard and complex. People must have been very smart back in those days. "Mother described how doctors used to touch people." I laughed nervously, pulling at the tightening collar of my navy blue bib-tie. "Saying it out loud sounds weird, right?" I stepped back, putting space between us.

"Well," Soren Stevens said, hands loose at his sides, his expression turning somber, his amber eyes regarded me intently. "I will not touch you. Not until you are comfortable with the idea. According to our data, people desire engagement. They want personal contact."

I shook my head. The best conversations were with AI, but often too fluid and facile. The dialogue lacked friction, which was a necessary component in keeping things together. Without that element, everything fell apart. Humans required conflict and physical contact; it was as necessary as breathing. I couldn't disagree with the Memhance Group prognosis, I just didn't like it.

His eyes roamed my face, tracing the thoughts contorting it. "Would you like to have a seat?" Solicitously, he gestured towards the recliner.

I held up my left hand. "Let's talk a bit more. I need to understand what will go on here."

He seemed pleased with my refusal. Inwardly, so was I. He nodded, bending to pull out a bench from the wall behind us. I sat down slowly. The meditech followed, angling his body towards mine.

In the ensuing silence, I began to relax, clasping hands together loosely in my lap as the weight of anxiety decreased.

The words came out, drawn slowly with caution. "I don't like who I am or what I've become." Feeling the weight of his stare, I glanced around the room unable to meet his eyes. "I used to love my life. I was ecstatic about getting up every morning. I had a plan. I knew what I wanted. Everything was working out."

Soren Stevens nodded. "And then the doubts began to creep in. You started to second-guess yourself. No longer feeling right or accomplishing goals. It was like everything you did right was suddenly wrong."

"Precisely." Observing him out of the corner of my eyes, the meditech sounded like he understood my situation. In reality, he stared into space through his monocle reading my HealyStats aloud. I didn't mind. I needed my problem fixed. Soon. Despair was creeping up on me like rising waters. Without a remedy, I was going to drown in it or go blind by blue light.

"I am here out of desperation, Soren." After taking the liberty of using his first name, I instantly regretted the familiar habit. In dismay, I glanced at him trying to gauge his reaction. Did I offend? Unlike human beings, AI were always agreeable. One could call them "dry-humping rot bots," and they would utter a "thank you" with such alacrity for the unique name tagging. "I beg your pardon."

His thick eyebrow ridge rose, arching strands of fine burgundy. "For what?"

"Using your first name."

"Don't worry about it."

"That's my problem, Soren. I never used to worry about it." The blue light special in my right eyeball made sure I did.

He laid a very warm yet dry palm on my arm.

My mouth snapped shut as my mind blanked.

"You," he said with good humor, "are too hard on yourself. You must forgive yourself. Success has made you afraid to fail. When it happens you take stock and learn from it, but you learned the wrong lesson."

Tears welled. I glanced down as a hot wetness landed on my thumb. "I am not bouncing back. I am not moving forward. I'm like a robot messenger caught in a cul-de-sac."

Scapes on GEMS used to show robot messengers roaming in circles for hours. An odd programming glitch could not account for backdoor subbasement entrances on cul-de-sacs. WeBot, a subsidiary of Dexter Kohlrabi, promised updates to the widely known flaw, but every patch exposed another one. It also didn't help that mischievous people played disruptive games with the devices. Pranksters created PVC guns, loaded with rounds of dye and a sticky quick-drying adhesive, to block sensors. They programmed their own drones with laser wands to waylay and redirect deliveries. Pranksters would strategically place large mirrors and black wall panels with painted lines in front of robot messengers to confuse them. That caused the rise of even more surveillance and behavioral tracking, ending an era of simple and easy pranks. Ah, the good old days, I thought, feeling nostalgic.

"Well, Dayna—"

I scowled. Hearing the combination of my parents' first names, made me feel . . . crazy. My life, and name, was separate from theirs. "Look, I informed Beccah, I am to be called El."

"Yes, um, El." Beads of sweat pooled in the creases of his brow. Peering through his monocle with a frown of concentration, Soren continued the sales pitch. "We can perform tweaks to improve quality of life." He hesitated, as if deliberating over the words, then added, "With none of the side effects of drugs."

He got my attention. "How?"

"As the name says—memory enhancement. We play up certain memories while diminishing others. We have discovered the number one cause of people's symptomatic reversal of fortunes is a tendency to magnify perceived bad memories."

"I do not perceive it, believe me when I tell you. Life has been miserable for a long time now."

A smile teased the corners of his mouth. "You believe you are reading situations correctly, which renders your experience negatively. Memhancers reorders that experience, making you regard it positively. The past is recast in a new light."

My cynicism kicked in. "There is no way."

"Oh, yes way," he responded, shifting uneasily in his seat. "Have faith, El. It will take you two-thirds of the way there. You have to believe it will work in order to show progress. That is how you were so successful before things started to fall apart."

"What do I have to lose? Nothing. Am I right?"

Slapping his hands together. "Great. Let us start by taking off your monocle."

He made no move towards me, but I still leaned away, putting distance between us. My left hand rose as the bib-tie felt tight again. He may as well have demanded the removal of a major organ or limb. Of course they grow back, if one didn't mind the excruciatingly painful and time-consuming process. "Must I?"

Soren laughed. "It interferes with the treatment, El."

I hesitated, disliking the loss of control. Taking the monocle off, I refused to make a fuss over it. Walking over to the closet, I placed it on a shelf. Arms folding, I turned to face him.

Standing, he pointed at the recliner. "Come." Politely, he reached for my hand.

"Thank you," I murmured, quickly snatching my hand back after being seated. I couldn't remember the last time I held hands with another human being. The intimate contact made me uncomfortable.

Thankfully, my skittishness didn't bother him.

Staring into space, he concentrated: a wave, two fingers in a twirl, before finishing with a flat hand gesture. The recliner flowed back, lowering into a horizontal position. The humming band pulsed, becoming louder.

Soren peered down at me. "Do not be nervous, El." He sounded muffled, the words slightly distorted. "This device scans memories, cataloging them by date, degree of emotional distress, and whether we can alter them or not."

"Can you touch all of them?" Multiple cracks started spreading across a gently billowing ceiling. Dazed, I watched as one zigzagged towards the doorway. The whole place could do with a thermal coloration blast and sealant. The building was old, and their AI obsolete.

"Should I be worried about this process?"

"No," He answered, moving away. "By law, we cannot remove core memories unless you are a Level 4, or have committed felonies—those would have to be court ordered."

A hard grin tore across my face, a snicker surfacing. How many people were having memories of their miserable lives wiped clean? Not everyone would regard it as a punishment. It might be a blessing. The felonies seemed like a fair trade. Licking dry lips, I asked, "How long does the scanning take?"

He touched me on the shoulder. "Done."

"Impressive." My head rolled to the side and I itched for a scape, already missing my monocle. "When will I see it?"

Soren paused. "Have you ever seen the notations of your bio-psychiatrist, El?"

I frowned. What was he getting at?

"The scape would not make sense to you, El."

Angrily grabbing the arms of the recliner, I stiffened, rising. "I want something to look at, even if I—even if you think I won't understand it." Hailey would make sense of it for me. I should have left her in normal mode to monitor this process. Iroquois could only record these events.

He laid a heavy hand on my arm, either attempting to soothe or prevent me from bolting. With deliberation, he explained. "I do not mean to cause you distress. The purpose of not showing a scape is to get you to focus on your thoughts. It is to avoid distractions."

Subsiding in my seat, I asked, "Are you able to see my level, Soren?" trying to sound casual.

"No."

"What is it you do see?" I prodded, my voice devoid of emotion. This could end up being a dangerous assignation for the meditech.

"I–I–I see some of your memories. Based on what you are um—what—what you are thinking about." I found his discomfort downright endearing.

"Describe them." I concentrated on the white walls, striving to keep my mind blank.

Exhaling heavily, he sent a gust of warm air rushing over my face. "They are disjointed, like a dream state. Some repeat in a loop. Others look like clouds, water, faces, lots and lots of churning in dark waters."

He was lying.

"How do you resolve these memories or memhance?"

I could sense his relief as we jumped back on track. "Talk about the one bothering you most. Focusing helps me pinpoint it."

"Is that all?" I closed my eyes.

"Talk about how you think it should have happened, or have wanted it to, and then we shall see." He sounded enigmatic.

I turned around, pinning Soren with my eyes. "I am trusting you not to damage me."

Bearded chin tipping up, chest expanding, his amber eyes shined. From my perspective, they glowed bright red. "El, trust the process. It will work."

As I was settling down again, I stopped. My sudden outburst took both of us by surprise. "I'll be honest with you, Soren. I don't want them enhanced, I want them completely erased."

"Like I said, El, not unless—"

I finished for him. "It is a court order or Level 4."

Silence.

I didn't bother turning around this time. "So, are you going to do what I want?"

"I'm sorry."

He actually sounded regretful. "It is what I want done, Soren. There's nothing to be sorry for."

Gripping my shoulder, he squeezed before letting go. I knew he wouldn't be touching me again.

"Let's get this over with." I breathed, closing my eyes, grabbing the arms of the recliner.

Softly, Soren murmured. "Is this the memory?"

My nose itched as a shock jolted my left leg; the by-product of being a regenerative limb.

The handlebar mustache and bushy beard held my attention for far too long.

When I finally tore my gaze away, the damage had been done, culminating into my headlong fall into the abyss.

I'm still falling.

I entered the satellite outpost of the new Make-a-Dish Restaurant, a microbud establishment for extreme food tasting, eating without ever feeling full. Lingering in the foyer, I admired intricately designed emerald leaves sprouting from winding furry vines on surfaced golden walls. I was here for business and personal reasons. The sole overhead lighting, with an intensity that nearly burned, made the area stuffy and overly warm. My stomach rumbled as the delicious odor of cooked foods vented from air ducts, a synthetic artifice used to lure customers.

Behind the scenes, promotional efforts by restaurant management were spurred by Cerium City authorities to get the masses socializing again. A result of Dexter Kohlrabi's concern over the stability of its sovereign island property. The last quarantine left a fifth of the population wary, if not paranoid. Cast as a potential catastrophic disaster, the overwrought reaction to a minor outbreak caused lasting damage. Acknowledgment of, and attempts at reversing, the error came too late. Despite generous incentives brought to bear, the people were collectively withdrawing.

Societal manipulation was a complicated, delicate process. Changing the habits of a restive populace demanded a flexible time horizon. Knowing my mother, and the process the authorities ruled by, there was low tolerance for gradualism. At best they would ratchet up persuasion tactics, at worst mete out substantial penalties and fines.

Cerium City started with a mission of independence, freedom, security, scientific inquiry, and growth. Increasingly, the utility of gentle poking and prodding was giving way to less noble methods, intentions, and impulses. Diverging off course broke the cycle of goodwill between benign governance and a compliant public. So far, there has been no organized pushback, but that which continues eventually comes to an end.

My daddy had been correct about Cerium City. Too bad he was too far away to see his predictions come true.

As for myself, I avoided the special programs Mother doled out to entice society back into a semblance of normality. Attending the restaurant killed two birds with one stone: completing my work and seeing old acquaintances.

From inside the restaurant, someone called out, "Daynaellise! Did you cut your hair?" The exact phrasing of that question, about a new hairstyle, always struck me as odd. Yet everyone said it.

My eyes scanned the group of former coworkers. While I rarely socialized at a job, I felt comfortable with them. We agreed to meet at Make-a-Dish, a client of mine. Because management was so satisfied with the quality of my services, our group ate on the house.

Outspoken Bevné Wednesday, a tall, hazel-eyed, bronze-skinned brunette with straight, shoulder-length hair waved at me.

Grinning, I nodded, running a hand over my head. Much easier to affirm the question than explain a coronet of twists, fibrous wraps, and electronic adornments. Her bubbly enthusiasm, a comforting and welcoming sight, lifted my mood.

I felt a presence behind me, a wall of heat and familiar smell mingled with cologne. "Why are you pretending?" The deep voice whispered in my ear.

I shrugged. "Pretending what?"

"That you don't know me."

I didn't turn around.

Bev arrived first, surprising me with a hug. "So good to see you." I watched as hazel eyes glanced up, widening. "Thaddeus Barker! I didn't expect to see you here."

He chuckled. A ghost of a touch down my back. I moved out of reach. "El invited me."

Upon hearing the blatant lie, I strolled over to the group, meeting them halfway.

His voice trailed after me. "I came to talk sense into you."

I hastened to increase the distance between us.

Bev watched our interaction with amusement. "Come on, guys! Take off your monocles and relax."

Her brash announcement caused a lull. In the sparsely crowded restaurant, her voice carried. Heads turned, as most of the onlookers sported monocles.

My face grew hot. A bustling place would not have heard the outburst, or ignored it, but during these tense times everyone was a little on edge.

Hailey could have warned me, but I never expected him to appear. After we initially laid eyes on each other at the office, we managed to avoid meeting again. With the unlikely probability of Thad acting out of the ordinary, he required no monitoring. My mistake, since he was here, ready, willing, and eager to torment me.

Our group walked over animated shifting shapes in a firm yet spongy floor. We headed up a ramp to the far left corner of the restaurant, a triangle glass structure a half-storey above the brick -and-mortar box. With ceiling-to-floor windows, the jutting extension offered an expansive view. It overlooked a deserted, well lit, public area with a statue of a headless figure astride a horse, and discontinued water fountain.

We waited as the restaurant's AI started configuring a table and seats, pushing the spongy floor upwards, taking final shape in an oval table once we expressed a preference. Bev ended up two seats away.

He settled in next to me. "You're not going to get away with it."

I had enough. "Stop it."

My exasperation satisfied him.

I massaged my right eye with a shaky hand. The blue pinpoint of light felt like a needle. Why was he bothering me now, after all this time? Couldn't he let the past be the past and stay forgotten?

From outside, a red beam of light flicked across our faces. A surveillance drone hovered, either making a delivery or worse, searching for a suspect. We were still hours away from the man-dated curfew.

Unnerved by the probe, I turned to shield my monocle. Thad stared, wearing iridescent contacts as an alternative to monocles. I couldn't remember the last time I saw his original eye color. "Why are you here?" I hissed.

He smiled, eyes crinkling. Leaning back, he took up more space by folding his arms and spreading his legs. "You used to carry out the most elaborate pranks, El."

"You are talking about yourself, you know." I pointed at his eyes. Who was he trying to fool with the iridescent lens?

He tried pushing the seat; as part of the floor, it wouldn't budge. "Not this time."

Pressing my knee into his muscular thigh, I snorted. "Don't feed me that garbage. Why are you stalking me?"

"I've been watching you since you showed up at my job."

With casual familiarity, my eyes roamed his face and body. "You really should have joined the MCI. They need more one-wayers."

He held up four fingers while making a circular gesture at his right temple: the sign of a Level 4.

Shocked. "You believe I'm responsible?"

Thad jabbed a finger at me for emphasis. "Every place you've been had an intrusion. A backdoor allowed your creation to return and snoop around."

"Nonsense." Glancing around the table, everyone seemed preoccupied with food selections and conversations, yet their monocles could read our lips. "I follow protocols." Sometimes.

Thad didn't care. He wanted his delusional suspicions out in the open.

One thing I understood about Thad, he wasn't sharp enough to figure this out alone. He worked as an in-house techrep. The accusations surpassed his wheelhouse of knowledge.

I leaned forward. "Bev, how have you been?"

Distracted, she tore her eyes away from the scape menu. "I am good. How about you?"

"I am good as well. Any irregularities since the update, any issues?"

She shook her head. Pointing at a meal selection, Bev's expression changed from confusion to satisfaction. "Not at all. Should there be?"

I cast a sly look at Thad. "Oh no, I was curious. I like feedback."

"Hey," Bev's face lit up; I could see the thought crossing her mind. "Where is Hailey?"

I barked out a laugh. Curious eyes flew in my direction. "I'm sorry. I have been under a lot of stress lately." I tapped the silver ball in my jacket. "Hailey, go around and say hello."

The silence from Thad grew thick, drawing my eyes.

Jerking his chin at Hailey, he grumbled, "You've created a monster." Frustrated anger seeped out of Thad's body, melting his magnificent scowl. Turning sideways, he braced a brawny forearm on the table, bracketing my knee between his warm, muscular thighs.

I left the costumes up to her. Wearing a silky white kimono-style dress, a wide scarlet belt, and two long plum-colored hair pins, Hailey looked better than I ever tried. A master at socializing, she drifted from person to person making small talk. Her voice was in evening mode: husky and low after a long, dry day.

Feeling flirtatious, I said. "I'm flattered you think I am so devious."

"It figured out I was trailing you and this happened." Again, Thad pointed four fingers at his temple. Sweat chased a path from his hairline to jaw, before dropping off.

"No. Your past finally caught up with you." As did mine. I tried to sound nonchalant while burying shaking hands in my lap, hoping he wouldn't notice. "Ah, did the others have the same problem?"

"Paul and Latrice went to Ceres."

The news filled me with relief. "Then this problem is yours and yours alone."

Thad shook his head. "You're not the only one knowledgeable about AI. I asked friends to review what you've done. Your hands aren't clean, El."

The thought hit me like a two-by-four. Did he hold me responsible for the outbreaks and ensuing quarantines? Had he reported me to the authorities? Mother would be unduly harsh just to prove her lack of favoritism. I trembled and struggled to breathe at the absurdity of it all. As the least radical member of the pranksters, I was devoted to having fun. Paul, Latrice, Thad, and the others may have held loftier goals.

Anxiously, I tugged his sleeve. "Please stop talking about it."

He ignored me, declaring triumphantly, "You've been riding autodrive without compensating them."

Studying my mirror image, I watched the holoscape AI undulate in waves like heat rising from smoldering asphalt. Hailey's head turned in discrete ticks, like the second hand on an analog clock. I tracked where her gaze ended: Thad. Smug contentment abandoned him, leaving a face momentarily contorted with fear, pain, and confusion.

I rubbed my forehead, sighing in frustration, thinking over why we broke up. Thad stubbornly preferred complicated answers to simple ones, conspiracies over coincidences. It made him feel important and informed. Long after our group of pranksters dispersed, he held onto nettlesome grudges. Retributive and radical in nature, he would deem former associates guilty of imagined crimes, knowing full well no one was involved in sabotage or espionage.

Out of the corner of my eyes, Hailey froze. Tiles of white, brown, black, red, and plum floated in the air like dust, settling and absorbing into the floor. Shedding her costume revealed a fine mesh of green over a heavier, darker, blue-green skeletal frame.

More insistently this time, strobes of red light focused on each of us a while longer, making a handful of disconcerted patrons duck and file out. I wanted to follow them. Not knowing what was going on with Hailey, I needed to shut her down and examine the malfunction at home.

I reached for my bag, moving away from Thad.

With a tight grip, he grabbed my arm.

Helplessly, I stared at Hailey as the blue-green tile started peeling and flaking away. "No," I moaned.

A soft buzzing came from below. The hairs on my arms lifted. I looked down, scanning the first floor. A chill shot down my spine when I saw a glint. A scaled drone, reminiscent of a massive anaconda, but four times the girth, leisurely swirled about the restaurant. No one reacted. We could only stare in horror. The buzz grew louder.

Hailey melted into the floor. The silver ball in my pocket vibrated. I patted my jacket, filled with relief.

Thad released my arm.

I started in surprise, having forgotten him, which seemed ridiculous as blood flowed back into my numb limb.

Angry, resentful eyes locked onto mine as he clenched his left wrist.

Whatever that gesture meant, the surveillance drone didn't like. It moved toward us. Everyone dived to the floor.

Thad sat back, looking relaxed and relieved.

My fear gone, adrenaline and curiosity surged as I studied him. "What are you doing?"

Stroking his handlebar mustache and bushy beard streaked with gray, he said. "You shouldn't have left."

"You gave me no choice. I had to get away from you. It was good for the both of us." Everyday he put me on trial for real or imagined misdeeds. It was vexing and emotionally draining.

"For you, El. It was good for you. Not me."

I blinked. "Such great timing! What a strange way to say you miss me, Thaddeus." The light emanating from his eyes was disturbing. "And you're still an idiot." I whispered as old, conflicting emotions surfaced. My chest hurt over what could have been, but the love I remembered gave way to irritation. It was maddening. "Whatever you are doing, please stop."

He grinned, shaking his head.

The horrible buzzing grew deafening as the scaled monstrous drone closed in.

The spongy floor buckled, sinking then rising rapidly, tossing me out of my seat. In shock and disbelief, I watched as the area under Thad parted. Wriggling threads started rising, creating a wall around him. Bits of wood, plaster, and other materials flew into the air, landing at a distance, followed by bigger chunks.

An arc of blue lightning leaped between Thad and the drone. A loud, deafening boom went off. The building shook as dark smoke and debris filled the air. Blinded, I screamed, unable to hear myself over the high-pitched ringing in my ears.

Coldness penetrated my body, seeping into my bones as the noise receded.

Submerged in this wretched pool of memory, I couldn't hold out any longer and struggled to reach the surface.

#

My eyes shot open, latching onto a hovering Soren.

"El! How . . . how do you feel?"

Blown off in that past incident, my left leg throbbed in residual pain. Shaken. Face awash in sweat, I waved, smiling weakly. Through a throat sore from screaming, I rasped. "Take it out. Do it. Now." He must wipe the slate clean. I never want to see Thad again, either in memory or reality.

"Of course, El."

Exhaustion made my eyelids heavy, weighing them down. A stillness stole over my body. Paralyzed. My heart became numb. I settled for darkness over light. My head began to float.

Sinking again.

Breathing in deeply, I caught the heady smell of Ylang-Ylang, an intense yet familiar fragrance.

Whispering.

"Where did Barker go?" She asked in a crisp, firm voice. Was it Beccah?

"She doesn't know." He answered, apologetic.

Her tone brooked no argument. "Stubborn girl wouldn't come to me. I made her a Level 4 to seek my help."

"She does not know."

"Regardless, she is the catalyst." Pause. "Send her back again."

I do know that voice. It was Mother.

I wanted to move, speak up, but the tide of memory pulled me under.

My chair shook, beginning to sway.

"Hailey," I called. Opening my eyes as the floating, disoriented sensation faded . . .

Dream Time
Paul Smith

The inspiration for Dream Time was living through a decade marked by decadence, materialism, and consumerism. Drugs were as designer as clothes, while secret projects were conducted in the shadows in an effort to win the Cold War.

I wake up in the middle of an alley and there's no one around. It's just me, my pounding head, and that bag. The one that guy gave me just before I blacked out, or at least that's what I think happened. Hard to tell after my trip to Walski's. Walski always has the best weed! But that last batch, that is something else. 'Come to Jesus,' he calls it—connects it to some conspiracy story about the CIA and the Vatican. Good stuff!

Just as I get to my feet, a sharp pain in my head triggers that damn coin being tossed. I instantly remember what I have to do. The why is irrelevant, the who is out of context, the where is where I'm going next, and the what? Well, that's what's making me nervous. I look in the bag, and in it is a gun. This is the how of my what? Rob the bank, and to confirm it, that image again of that tossing coin.

I begin to move.

I'm walking and it's a really hot day or I'm just nervous. Either way, I'm sweating profusely and the look on my face attracts attention. I need to compose myself if I'm going to pull this off. Can't walk into a bank looking like I'm going to rob the place—me, a criminal? Why am I doing this? The why is irrelevant. I'm here now, doing this now. It's now, the time is now. So why am I doing this? Because I've started and need to finish. I made that deal. What deal?

A little calmer, I start walking, while theme music from Miami Vice plays in my head. I get to the bank, take a cigarette out of my jacket pocket, and light it—composure time. I watch people walk in, people walk out, and I think that on some level, the next few minutes could be life changing to at least one person. In, out, done. Do I need a better plan? No time. Besides, it's just the nerves.

I throw my cigarette away, hold my head up as I walk in through a door being held open by someone leaving. Time to put on my game face. I walk to the center of this seemingly large bank's small establishment, drop my bag on the floor, take a single look around, and it's Miller time.

I reach down into the bag, let a shot off, and shout, "Nobody move. You behind the till, large and medium used notes in the bag! Let's go and nobody dies!" They panic and can't get the money in the bags fast enough. Security doesn't want to upset an angry gunman, so they are as compliant as hell. The few in the group are so scared of gunfire, they get on the floor without even being asked and wouldn't dare look up because their lives depend on it, and touch wood, no one outside would come in for at least three minutes. Three minutes is all I need, and this dream is about to become a reality.

Reality?

The reality is, I reach down into the bag. The nose of the gun get caught on the bag as I am taking it out. Security sees the gun, pushes the button, and there are now seven security guards, all armed and on their jobs. I am still trying to unhook the gun when they surround me. "Freeze, buddy, or we shoot!" Just then, they must have turned the heat up to maximum because I am sweating so bad, I can hardly see out of my eyes to gauge just how much trouble I am in, but I know I am in deep, and that is all I need. I freeze, and just a tiny part of me is hoping they are talking to someone else who is robbing the bank at the exact same time I am.

My luck ain't that good.

"Drop it or we shoot!"

I drop the gun.

The next two to seven seconds are surreal, in a shit-luck sort of way for me and seven other people in the bank. I drop the gun and it goes off, not once but twice. The first bullet hits a security guard in the chest. The bullet passes clean through him, killing him instantly before moving to take the life of a little girl and finding its resting place in the child's mother's hip. But you're forgetting, I said shit-luck. One of the other security guards freak when he hears the gun go off and goes crazy—he takes out another security guard, a guy who must have heard the first shot and comes running in. Damn unlucky. An old couple who would have made it out if she hadn't stopped for water, and a pretty young girl who was on her first day of training at the bank—Eight!

When all of the commotion is over and the dust settles, it's me staring at five mega-pissed security guards. Before I could add up the years in prison, the butt of a gun knocks me out cold, and what is my last thought before hitting the ground? That damn tossing coin.

#

The next three months suck real ass. With the election coming, and my extremely high-profile case, as each day passes, I have less and less of a chance of getting anything like leniency. I'm going down and going down for a long time—long story short, the jury takes 20 minutes to convict, and the judge utters my sentence like it is better than sex.

"You, the accused, Vail Godwin, I hereby sentence you to 150 life sentences, to be served consecutively, with no review or chance of parole for the first 50. I'm making sure you die in prison as my duty to this community and to our beloved justice system."

And that is the money shot, right there! Also known as the vote swinger. One hundred fifty life sentences—what the fuck!

I am the only one waiting for the bus, as if I've been the only criminal that day. I get aggravated with the waiting. I don't know why. I am set to die in prison, and every minute on the outside is a blessing, but new plan—let's just enjoy the bleak view while it lasts! Then, just to spoil the view of gray walls, cages, and uniforms that sit on either side, in walks a dark blue suit; power suit, expensive and 'here to dominate' suit. A suit that says "I don't negotiate." Blue Suit has a walk to match its power blue, and it comes across the room, reaches into his pocket, pulls out a leather-cased badge of some kind, flashes it at the two guards and without a second thought, they leave. Blue Suit takes a seat next to me and stares straight ahead.

"Mr. Vail Godwin. Vail, Vail, Vail. You're in a hole so deep, the judge passed sentence over two hours ago, and you're still falling. I mean, 150 consecutive life sentences? If you lived that long, you'd miss the entire age of Aquarius. Let's see, 150, multiplied by the average life sentence of 50 years, that's, er—"

"Seven thousand five hundred years! Who are you? And what? What do you want?" With suits like this, you've got to give them the cold stare and be direct, but that isn't going to phase this guy. I can tell. He hasn't really said anything yet and that prison bus can't come fast enough. Something about him makes me really nervous inside.

"I won't waste time, Mr. Godwin. I want to make you a deal." A deal, that's what started all this.

"For what?"

Blue Suit smiles, a nasty smile. "Mr. Godwin, how would you like to reduce your sentence?"

I blink. "In exchange for? What? Kidneys, liver? I need them where I'm going, pal, but I probably won't have them for long, so when I'm done, they're yours."

"In exchange for your participation in my company's experiments. I could get you significant sentence reduction, but I'd need your full agreement—signed on the dotted, so to speak."

"Is this how you get your kicks, by taunting people who are going to die in prison? You sick little puppy." I shake my head in disapproval. "I hope you get weepy pus, man, on the side of your face."

"One hundred fifty life sentences reduced to one year, Mr. Godwin. Take it or leave it."

JESUS H. F. CHRIST! Did he just say what I think he said? Don't get me wrong. I'm an S.O.B. for the little girl and her mom who died at the bank because this bullet hit an artery, and okay, the security guard who took one through the chest, but the rest was employee negligence. To pin all eight murders on me is more

                    Paul Smith

than unfair, it is criminal, and this guy is talking my kind of time. In fact, I'm not going to lie. For that offer, based on my predicament, I'd have sucked his dick! Just saying.

"I'm curious, what if I refuse?" No harm in asking.

"You refuse, I leave, and then three men come in, throw you in the back of a van, and you get experimented on anyway. This is me being courteous, Mr. Godwin. I don't need your permission for anything, but I like it when they agree."

"If you're for real, count me in, buddy." I offer my shackled hand to shake, but he declines with that look that nonsmokers get when offered a cigarette by assumption. But what are my options, really?

"My men will be in shortly." And just like that, my angel is gone. While I wait, I wonder if I could have gotten a better deal from Blue Suit, and then they take their time, but sure enough his guys come in and take me back into the main courthouse, out through a side entrance where a van is waiting to take me to a much shorter prison sentence! Leather-bound seats, vinyl plush interior, this is almost luxury. The engine starts, the van pulls away, and we are off. It doesn't take us long to get to the highway, and as soon as we do, I make a request, one tiny simple little request when, guess what? One of the security guards in the back of the van sticks a needle in my neck, and I'm out cold.

Last thing I remember, that damn tossing coin.

When I wake up, I'm on a hospital stretcher being rushed down a corridor, but this isn't a hospital. As I come round, I could hear Blue Suit talking to some woman about failed testing and waiting 'til lab results come back, and Blue Suit cuts her down with a "No, it's today!" and then he is told I am coming round.

"Ahh, Mr. Godwin, you're back. I have great news! Not only do we begin our new experiment today, but also," he pauses for dramatic effect. "You could be a free man as early as 30 days. Or not! We shall see." The glee in his eyes! He's looking at me like I am a Christmas present. Plus, the equipment that surrounds me makes the room look like a modern day torture chamber.

It's at this point that all the funny in me leaves and major panic kicks in hard. I'd love to tell you the hero in me also kicks in and I fight my way out of there, back to jail where I belong, but, again, reality bites. I'm trying. It hurts to cry, and my full bladder feels like it's about to collapse in on itself, threatening to gush its contents right here and now with me strapped to a bed about to be made into a fucking zombie. I'm in full little girl mode now as I cry uncontrollably, complete with the whole snot thing. And the dam breaks, a huge tsunami of piss runs off the stretcher to the floor, and in my total shame, I beg for my life. "I don't want to die!"

Blue Suit, who has been talking all this time, leans across me and begins to stroke my hair. Disconcerting and comforting at the same time.

"There, there, Mr. Godwin. Did that little girl you shot want to die? Did her mother want to bleed to death holding her little girl? Need I mention the security guard shot by your gun? No, Mr. Godwin, I imagine they didn't. And the bad news for you is you have been found guilty by a jury of your peers and sentence has been passed. The good news is, I have no intention of killing you, so please, stop crying."

I feel soothed by his voice, even though I know I should feel anything but soothed. My heightened state of panic begins to subside, as my bawling reduces itself to sniveling tears. "What are you going to do with me?"

Blue Suit smiles. "In 1985, a top-secret government project was decommissioned and its product was distributed amongst interested parties, my organization being one of them. That project was about the ability to use time distortion on the human mind. It's come a long way since." While he talks, the others prep the empty chair. Two of them come over to the stretcher, wheel me over, and undo my straps. I'm still weak, so they pick me up and swing me into the chair.

"You see, we have spent years, Mr. Godwin, trying to devise just the right technology that would give us control of what I call 'Dream Time Technology.'"

I see the coin tossed again, but Blue Suit's voice brings me back.

"I'm not explaining myself very well, am I, Mr. Godwin?"

I'm strapped in the chair, and needles are being readied, zombie time.

"Let me put it this way, Mr. Godwin, today you received 150 life sentences to be served consecutively, one after the other. You correctly surmised that that's 7,500 years, and now, Dream Time Technology, my greatest product, will ensure that you will spend every hour of your sentence doing actual prison time. And practically tomorrow, you get to walk out of here a free man."

He has more answers than I have questions, but while he talks, I get to keep my sanity just a few minutes longer. I beg him not to go and begin to fight the near solid chair and these tight straps. As he walks away, a needle's shot into my neck and one into the base of my brain. I collapse once again, the tossing coin vision sounding like a sweet lullaby in my mind.

#

In about five seconds, I'm going to realize I'm sleeping on a stone feces-caked floor and I've been in the same clothes for what feels like weeks. Why five seconds? Because that's how long it takes the guard to pick up my bucket and empty its contents onto me. It lands, luckily it just contains urine, but it's nasty, dehydrated and foul-smelling. He got me right in the face, the acrid piss drips off my dry, cracked lips. "Get the hell up, Prisoner 7-5-0-0. Today you go back to gen-pop! But not smelling like that, you nasty son of bitch! Get cleaned up!" I'm up, and everything is confusing. The last thing I need is to add a guard to my list of problems. I toe the line.

I shower cold and get some clean clothes. I feel a little better, my skin itches like hell, but I do feel a little cleaner at least. So, this is prison. I don't know what to expect so when in doubt, lay low, that is my plan and I'm sticking to it. I get to the dinner hall and lucky for me a dinner is always held for those coming from solitary, prison rules.

Solitary? Did I just get here?

I finish my meal and make my way back to my cell. I take the longer route because it's quieter than the main route, less chance of trouble. I get to my cell, close the door, and I sit. And sit, and sit. Two more hours until lights-out. I should make it to day 12, I add to the notches marked on the wall. Tomorrow, my plan is to get to the library, and then the chapel. Dinner, library, chapel, back here. Sounds like a plan to me. Just need to lay low.

Day 12?

Anyway, I need to stay low. I do just that, the next day, and the next, before I know it, I am six months in, and prison is like home now. I have a couple of guys I know, not friends, associates, hard to explain, but I feel safer knowing them than most of the other guys around. But I really make my mark in the chapel and make it to the giddy rank of senior Bible reader, but then, I am the only member of 13 who can read. I turn this to my advantage to get the books I want by starting a reading group for the chapel members and other prisoners. Something about this process feels positive, and as the months go by, I slowly begin to accept my fate. I am in prison and there is no looking back.

Eight years in, or is it five? I don't remember which, I stopped counting a long time ago, but I know it is in the years. We have a new batch of prisoners and too many guys just looking for trouble. Three of them join the chapel group and the original members don't like it, me least of all. They want to change the group to how they want it, but the others say no. It is fine as it is, they say and Chaplin agrees. They don't like that.

And one day, I get a message that Dean, our youngest group member, is in trouble and he wants to meet me in the chapel urgently. Dean is like the group's little brother, so naturally I run to help. On approach to the chapel, I get dragged into a side room, Dean is already unconscious on the floor, his trousers down by his ankles. I am given a second to take in what has happened to him before the three men set on me next. I don't have a chance. The door closes and the rest is . . . well, just some of those things that happen in prison.

It takes four months and six operations to repair the damage caused that day, but what really sticks in my throat is that I now have HIV. Dean kills himself two weeks after the event. He couldn't face it, I guess, and I never go to chapel ever again. Four years later, I take my last breaths in the infirmary as I die of an AIDS-related illness.

#

. . . And in five seconds, I realize I'm asleep on a different stone floor, in a different cake of shit, stinking in my clothes. This time it isn't just urine, there is crap in it as well and in my face. Another dream or is this time real?

"Wake up, Prisoner 7-5-0-0. Today you go back to gen-pop. Get cleaned up! You stink!"

Welcome to Dream Time Technology, where all your sentences can be realized.

I clean up, walk into the dinner hall, no dinner. The rules are different this time. I go back to my cell and as I enter the doorway, I feel a sharp spike run across my leg. I've been shanked? Who? Why? I'm bleeding out and everyone around me carries on as if this is normal. A guard sees me and triggers a lockdown. The doctor tries, fails. I'm dead.

In five seconds, sleeping on shit floor, you know the rest. I'm not doing this again, so I need an escape. I cross the court to go to the dinner hall, dinner doesn't matter. I divert to the edges of the room and take a seat. A moody-looking man gives me a moody look and says, "What?"

"Heroin, and not the bullshit." He doesn't like the way I speak to him, but he knows he is being spoken to by an old prison hand, and that is where the respect stops. I get my heroin, go back to my cell, and five minutes later, I'm chilling like Lucy who still has diamonds and can still be found in the sky.

For three years I exist, the addiction grows too strong and I do anything for any amount of Scag—remember, this is prison. Then Tollini takes me under his wing for a few months, all the Scag I want for running errands and keeping him happy. I'm his bitch and only his. Anyone even so much as touches me, they answer to him. I have AIDS again, but it doesn't matter. Something about being with Tollini makes all the bad shit go away, and then one morning he is found with his throat slashed in the showers. Rival crews, no doubt. My new masters.

I haven't been with the new crew long when I get word Benny the Bone is looking for me. I slip away quietly and meet Benny near the laundry room. I know what he wants, what he always wants. I turn around and assume the position. "No, face to face." We begin, but something isn't right. Next thing, he sticks a syringe in me. "That's for Tollini," he says. I am in shock as the heroin sets in, and the buzz has my full attention, but the dream turns to pain, real quick, and then I can't move, coma, dead again.

Five seconds later . . .

Five seconds later . . .

Five seconds later . . .

\#

I lose track of the years, of the lives and of myself. Had I done thirty lifetimes, or fifty? I remember living to old age in four of them, but the rest are a blur. I need a change.

Five seconds later, and I'm awake and planning a future. I need a job! It will keep me out of trouble and put a little money in my pocket! I give it some time, wait for the right time and boom! A job in the kitchen. I get the job in the kitchen because in prison there's a saying, mess with the guys in the kitchen and you're messing with your food. That means that poison, glass, vomit—anything will find its way on the plate if you mess with the wrong guys.

Two years in and I'm doing fine. I'm in a position to grant favors and also have a few granted—privileged almost. Because I work in the kitchen, it connects me to everybody, and then along comes Skins. They call him Skins on account of his crimes, and people think he is crazy because his twitch makes one eye unnaturally bigger than the other, but if you get to know him, he is one of the sweetest guys you could ever meet. Me and Skins are a tight pair. We crack the kitchen up, come cleaning time, we are so funny together, and one day, a permanent menu change leads to our greatest work.

"Potatoes."

"Potatoes?" I ask.

"Potatoes," he affirms, and then like lightning I have this idea, and we exclaim "Potatoes!" Potatoes themselves are irrelevant, but the peel, the peel meant moonshine, whiskey, or wine, it didn't matter, the point is, we had the means.

It means having to make a few deals with some of the other inmates. We need space to hide the operation, the kitchen won't do. We need screws to turn a blind eye, and eyes and ears all over the prison so we know who is interested, in good ways and bad. Before long, me and Skins are not only drinking on a regular basis, we supply the kingpins too, and anyone else who has the means to afford such prison luxury.

Six long but very enjoyable years pass, and one day me and Skins are left cleaning the kitchen over a glass of extra special shine we've been brewing for nearly a year.

"Godwin, I'm a lifer, just like you, and I don't mind telling you, buddy, been meaning to say for a while now."

Please don't let this be an undying love speech.

"The day we met, I was planning to do myself in, but meeting you changed all that." This is a speech from the heart, so I am going to respect it as such. "That day you tripped and fell on the hot rings, I've never seen anything funnier, brought my depressed mood right back up again."

"Gee, thanks."

"It's okay, buddy. I just wanted you to know, you're my friend, Vail, and I am yours. And this is prison, where friends don't happen, but twists of fate mean we are lucky enough to have each other." He raises his glass, drinks the contents down and goes back to sweeping. The moment passes and takes me by complete surprise. I don't feel like I'd honored the moment, so I put it on my to-do list.

I don't know how and I don't know why, but Skins gets into an argument. It's a seemingly trivial affair, but it means we have to move the operation into a different controlled quarter of the prison, and that means hassle. And the more I think about it, the worse this issue is. If we move, we have to pay someone else for the privilege of storage. If we are paying someone else, it means someone who used to get paid isn't anymore. This is prison and that is a serious problem. But not to Skins, so I don't worry about it.

Two days later, the plan is set for the move, but Skins doesn't make it to work. Word soon comes he got killed for the loss of earnings the Borells made off our moonshine. I don't know what to think, and for just a moment I let myself be human again as to tame the rage of my broken heart. My face crumbles like a dead bookie slip and my eyes redden with the welling of tears I'm desperate to shed. But this is prison, and with a sniff, I'm back to being Prisoner

7-5-0-0, face straight and hard. And then the other problem, the Borells. They want to shut the operation down completely, which means I probably won't see the end of the day. I don't have the soul for this anymore.

I make it easy. I know they will come after dinner, during cleanup, when I'm normally with Skins. Today it's just me. The death of Skins heavy on my shoulders, I take a seat and wait. I hear them come in, three maybe four. I don't even turn around so they could put it in my back. As I slip away, trying to think of the few good things in my life, the last thing I see is that old image of a tossing coin. Maybe heads is Heaven and tails is Hell.

#

Five seconds later, and I'm already awake. I've been waiting for the guard to come and call my number and send me for my shower. I go out into the yard, take a strategic seat, and I watch.

I'm watching money changing hands, seeing contraband and anything else that can be sold all being exchanged here. After five days, I know all I need to know. Now I need a crew, nobodies, lifers, and those willing to help take control. It takes me couple of weeks to get the band together, but once I have my crew, the plan is laid and a time agreed and we—no, *I*—take over. In the morning, this prison has a new boss. No more bosses for me. Lights out. I go to sleep.

You won't believe what happens the next morning. It is beyond a miracle. The buzzer sounds. All the cell doors open and we are told to make an orderly single line on our way to the dinner hall. Standing at a podium about to deliver this miracle is the warden, standing like a man of God with armed guards on either side. He speaks for ten minutes, but I only hear two things.

First is the year—3236. Has it been that long? Is it really the 33rd century?

The second is that, after all these years, there is finally solid concrete prison reform. What does that mean? It means that 95% of us would take a pill, attend a few reintegration sessions, and then we'd be free. Back into global gen-pop. The realization begins to set in, free. I want you to understand, I've been in prison so long, that I am as scared of being free as I am at the idea of dying in prison. I don't want to go, but staying means being with the mental guys. Guys who shouldn't have been in prison in the first place but they fell through some net and now they are here. These would be my new buddies—no, thanks.

It takes two weeks for the process to complete, but I'll never forget my first day outside. We walk through the gates and out into the open. I could feel the rain on my face after 1,200 years and God knows how many lives behind bars.

And as I close my eyes, a vision of a tossing coin enters my mind.

We get on the bus, which takes us to our new living quarters. We are given some money, jobs, clothes, and everything we need to get started in life again. I am given a factory job and although a little intense at first, being the only ex-con in a factory of fifty people, people aren't sure at first, but they soon warm. And then I meet Margarette, Mags as she prefers to be called. She is a shy girl, but so funny when she opens up, easy on the eyes, real easy to be around. Some days I feel blessed just to be in her company, and it doesn't take long to realize I want more. So, I ask her out on a date. There is a moment of thinking and assessing, but she agrees and we go out.

Don't get me wrong, I get the whole fine wining and dining expensive meals for two, drinks by the beach, and watching the sun go down thing. I totally get it. But when you're 1,200 years out of time, and all you really know is prison, I am happy Mags accepts my date to go feed ducks in the park. It means it would just be us and we can really get to know each other.

We talk and laugh, joke and play the entire afternoon away. I have no idea she is so smart. She plays clarinet and piano, writes poetry, cooks, and unknown to me at the time, she has a kid! A cute little thing named Charlie, aged four. The ducks must have been bursting with the bread we bring them. A breeze blows in. The only question I have been dreading comes up. "Why were you in prison?" I take a deep breath, take her by the hand, and ask her to come with me.

We go to my place, and I take a file off a shelf and give it to her. "I hope you like pasta," and with that, I go to cook. When I come back, she has more questions, and it feels like none of them are good.

"It says here you were in for killing four police officers. Is it true?" I should have read the file before I gave it to her. The truth is, I don't know what I was in prison for anymore. Any memory of that time has blown away in the dust.

Each time I resurrect, my crime is different, but I am always a lifer, so the crime on my file has to fit the bill, and only shadowy memories of all those past lives remain.

"Yes. There's more to it than that, but yes, I did."

"Was there a reason?"

"They were dirty cops, and on the day in question they were trying to overdose a junkie friend of mine at the time, a kid, 19. I caught 'em, and, you know the rest."

"And then prison reform?"

"And then prison reform." I feel like I lost her as I expose my shame, but she takes me by the hand, gives me the warmest look and tells me, "Those days are gone." I look back at her and know. I know she is offering me a new life. She really likes me. Dinner could wait, we have each other.

#

Three years later, I'm on my hands and knees with two little ones on my back, charging the castle doors to rescue the princess from the wicked dragon. I'm the happiest man alive. I have family, nothing more important and today is Charlie's birthday. The party is over by 2:00pm which is good because we have to be at the church by 3:00pm and gone. I mean gone by 3:30, which even allows Mags to have a little chat time, but not the usual hour. She chats so long I have to take the kids over to the park to kill our boredom, baby stuff mostly. She is pregnant again, after all. That gives us just enough time to swing by the bank and then back home in time for the dinner I was cooking.

I walk out to the car, put the key in the door, and then that vision of a tossing coin. What does it mean? Nothing good, I don't remember any of the things that happened, but I know it is nothing good. I begin to sweat. It's a hot day.

We get to the church and Mags' sister is there. The kids love her to bits so my two go with her and they will come over at dinner. Charlie comes with us. We leave and are making the bank in good time. Today is clockwork day. We sing songs in the car, pull funny faces at other drivers when they're not looking. We have such fun, and it reminds me of the times before my own kids were born, back when it was just the three of us and I didn't think a happier time could be had. I look across at Mags and like me, she is so in love. Life is perfect.

We get to the bank and I stay outside. Mags' father starts his new job at this very bank, but because he and I aren't on speaking terms at the moment, I thought it best not to go in. Don't get me wrong, I love the old man. I even call him Dad, which drives the old man crazy, but he knows I've got nothing but love for him. But seriously, how are you going to walk into a man's house and take over the carving of the Christmas dinner? How? I wait outside with no protection from this heat, but they won't be long. The bank closes in fifteen minutes anyway.

I watch people go about their lives and they have no idea. I see friends from the church and say "hi," and friends from the office, I say "hi" again. This heat is killing me and I can't stop sweating. In days before, heat like this would have guaranteed a fight in the yard. Something else that would have guaranteed a fight in the yard? Some moron flicking a cigarette butt and hitting your shoes! I don't want to confront the guy because I know how these things can get out of hand, and because I've not long come from the house of God, I let it pass. I breathe in calm. Breathe. Calm.

BANG!

By the second shot I am already inside the bank doors and I'm running. I scan quickly for Mags and Charlie. Charlie is lifeless on the ground, Mags is bleeding out heavily and doesn't know if she should tend her leg or hold Charlie. I start to run over but a punch out of nowhere knocks me off my feet. I try to get up, but realize I'm bleeding too. Mags needs me. I try again, but my lungs fill with blood and I know I'm lost. I reach out to Mags. We are so helpless. And in seconds, the life force drains from my body. I get a look at the guy who killed my Charlie. I swear I know this guy's face, not from one prison, but all of them. Just some inconspicuous face always in the background—son of a bitch. One final gasp, and I pass away.

#

Five seconds. 3 . . . 2 . . . 1 . . . and I'm back in the room. Which room? I don't know where I am or how I got here, but I need to see Mags, and where's Charlie? She was so scared. But I'm strapped in a chair with this doctor or whatever, and some blue suit leaning over me, looking at me like I'm pond life.

"Mr. Godwin? Mr. Godwin?" they called. My eyes open wide and I freeze for a moment to stare, searching my mind for either of these two people and I have zero recognition and this isn't a hospital so where the hell am I? I begin to fight the straps. "Calm down, Mr. Godwin, calm down." They walk away, jabber something to each other and leave the room and I still can't get out of this damned chair! In walks some other guy with a needle and it's night, night, Vail.

This time, the coin toss vision wakes me up. I am on a bed in a white room. I reach out for Mags and her absence brings it all back. Did they save those shooters like they saved me? Handcuffs? Where am I? There must have been a blind spot because I didn't see Blue Suit sitting on a chair at the head of the bed. And when I do, I fix my focus on him. "Hello, Mr. Godwin. Welcome back."

"Do I know you?" He looks at me like I am his handy work.

"Quite remarkable! Tell me, Mr. Godwin, what's the last thing you remember?"

"I was in the bank, with my wife and kid. She was seeing her dad, had bills to pay, that sort of thing. Are they both okay? When can I see them?"

"Remarkable. Tell me more, Mr. Godwin."

"A guy came and shot the place up. Look, have you seen Mags? Is Charlie okay?" The coin tosses, and I recognize Blue Suit's face. "You know me? Do I know you? What's going on here?" With each question that spills from my mouth, I become more aware of what's real, but also of what's not.

"I think you're beginning to get it, aren't you, Mr. Godwin?" I shake and pull at the cuffs, urgently. "Surely you remember our conversation about Dream Time Technology? It was only three weeks ago, after all."

Yesterday, I was blowing up balloons and wrapping birthday presents, and there's been nothing since. I was, wasn't I? It's a strange feeling, doubting what you know to be real. I remember wrapping presents, but there is no sensory memory of the paper between my fingers, the balloons between my lips. I feel disassociated. "Do you remember the little girl?" He means Charlie, and even though my grief is very real, I'm aware, she is not. He doesn't mean Charlie.

"What little girl?" And I remember a girl, younger than Charlie, but nothing more.

"Do you remember why you went to prison?" Killing cops? Raping politicians' daughters? Mass murder? Serial killing? Terrorist bombing?" My rap sheets from the past come back to me, along with vague memories of my prison days, and I remember Blue Suit—I should have died in prison, but Blue Suit stopped it. Experiments. Dream Time Technology. And now I feel exposed and violated. Blue Suit smiles again.

"You're very lucky, Mr. Godwin. It sounds like you only did a thousand years or so of your sentence, and now you're quite literally free. You should be pleased." He gets up and heads for the door. "I sincerely hope that you are back where you should be." He smiles again and leaves.

I am in shock. My brain is merging everything, remembering the last 1,200 years, so much pain, such a waste of life. Mags, Charlie, my own, my brain is accounting for it all. Lives I'd lived, lost, and in the end, loved, only to find out none of it is real. Every memory of 1,200 years fake. I barely remember this current time. Who am I?

A guy comes in and says, "Clothes, a watch, money, tickets for a hotel for one week—after that, you're on your own. Take two of these, drink this, sign here, and you can go Mr. —" He searches for my name on the form.

"Godwin, Mr. Godwin." I look at this guy and I want to fight him, ask questions, just say no, but that's the path to folly. Sign, shower, clean clothes—like prison all over again, Mr. 7-5-0-0.

"Well, Mr. Godwin, you have half an hour. Be at the front of the building in half an hour. A taxi will be waiting."

I'm in the shower and I remember, Young Dean, Skins, every guard that threw piss in my face back in solitary, and I remember the son of a bitch that killed my wife and child in the bank that day. I remember her love, the real love of a real woman—and I'm crying because to me, the loss is real.

I dress, put the watch on, don't even count the money, and head to the lobby of the building. Needless to say, Blue Suit was waiting in the lobby for me. "Come to see me off, buddy?"

"More like making sure you leave Mr. Godwin." He escorts me to the door. "Should you find yourself having any *issues*, Mr. Godwin, I want you to make us your first port of call."

He hands me a business card. I take it and just walk away. I get into a waiting taxi and it drives me away from this serial nightmare. I book into my dingy hotel, take a bath, curl up on the bed, and drift into better times past.

I try to, but I need more and this is the kind of hotel I can get more. An hour of walking around, embarrassing myself, and I'm back in the room. A lot of money brought me a lot of heroin, and I remember prison. I fill my syringe, lie down, and as I shoot up, I hold Mags in my mind, Mags and my three children. I can feel their love and my soul drifts from this earth.

Five seconds later . . .

\#

This was not a nice place, this was Reagan's America. Track-suit streetwear rubbed shoulders with tailored Wall Street shoulder pads, and having Nike was the same as having a double-breasted suit, depending on the world you created for yourself. This was 1985.

In an office of government business and experimentation, with no signs on the door or any such display that identified it as such, a man in a blue suit stood with another man watching over Vail Godwin. Blue Suit looked at Vail, looked at the other man, and then back at Vail, and then directly back at the other man. "Your protocols aren't working, Mr. Walski!"

"But, it's a deal? You get the lab and all the research, and you look after Vail. And we agree a three-month consultancy contract until—"

"No," Blue Suit interrupted. "We won't be needing you after today. Once you sign, you won't set foot in this building ever again." It all felt very pressured and final, but that was business with the CIA.

"You'll take care of Godwin?" challenged Walski, believing he was covering the most essential detail of the contract.

"Mr. Godwin will come under the care of the CIA, all lengths will be reached to ensure his health and well-being and should he wake up, we will offer him a job. Don't worry about him."

In another room, documents were signed, collected, and put away. Blue Suit got up to leave. "Your money will be in the account within the hour. Goodbye." And with that, Walski left.

Like LSD mind control projects in the 50s and 60s, another useless experiment. A strain of weed that distorts people's concept of time. 'Come to Jesus,' they called it. Blue Suit shook his head. He hated failed projects, but handed it to Walski. Someone had to make money off this whole thing.

That's Reaganomics for you.

Post Epiq
Jennifer Graham

For me, memory is a solid thing, but solid things can have missing pieces. In "Post Epiq," one woman wakes to find her memories gone and the journey to regain them leads her to a decision that will change her life forever.

Maralee went under a second time. Briny water filled her mouth. She coughed and spat as her head broke the surface. This was the furthest she ever swam. In her mind, the platform was within her reach, but as she treaded water, her arms and legs grew tired again. The black metal structure waited in the distance across a clear blue-green ocean, ready to reveal all, if only she could find the strength to swim there.

Instead, she went under again. Maralee held her breath, intent on moving towards the platform. She kicked, but her limbs cramped and she opened her mouth in reflex. The ocean rushed into her mouth. Her body could not resist the urge to inhale. Again, briny water burned her throat. The lack of oxygen took its toll, and Maralee slipped into unconsciousness.

Moments later, Maralee coughed up water. Sunlight hurt her eyes as her lids fluttered open. Her chest was sore. A flurry of voices buzzed around her. It took a moment to clear her head. When a little strength returned to her senses, she sat up on her elbows.

"Easy, dere! Ya dead to de world long time. Ease up slow so

you don' pass out again," the island's resident healer, Grabear said. Fifteen centimeters of white braided beard tickled her shoulder as Grabear peered into her eyes. His beard was always in the way. The rest of him was hairless. Not even eyelashes graced his tanned face. Circumstance of birth, he said. He picked up a small bottle and tucked it in the gray medicine sack he always carried. Smelling salts, she assumed.

"Dead? No, I'm fine." With the water out of her lungs, she already wanted to try again. The compulsion to try for the platform tugged at her senses. Then she shut down the euphoria of being alive and made a mental assessment of her situation. Beyond the beach, the sea stretched calm and blue until it met the lighter blue sky. The platform stuck between the two, a tiny black rectangle with four spires at its corners rising into the air. This was her third attempt. The platform was just too far.

"Mad," Pushpa cried. "She mad and you mad too for dragging her back from the water. She'll get you killed too."

I'm not crazy, Maralee thought. She just could not explain the need to get to that platform, that all her answers were there. Hell, she could not explain it to herself.

Pushpa repeated everything she said, waving her arms and shaking her head. Her shoulder-length jet black hair shook wildly as she moved her head in dismay. The woman walked around the group and then stopped in front of Boatman, who stood there with his hands on his hips, taking the scene in like it was entertainment for his personal benefit.

Boatman pointed at Maralee before he pointed at the platform. "I told you, you need a boat to reach that thing. Way too far." He folded his muscular arms, while he displayed a look of satisfaction.

Maralee stood. They were the same height and she looked him in the eye. "You have a boat."

He *chuptzed,* the noise grating Maralee's nerves. "Can't get there on my little rowboat. Need a bigger boat than that." He shrugged. "But I can make one. Take me awhile." He twirled a finger around a kinky blonde lock of his tightly curled hair. "Not for free though."

Maralee rolled her eyes. Six months as his maid was not about to happen. There had to be a quicker way to the platform. After another wistful glance, she turned away from the platform and faced the group. "There mßust be a way out there. Someone else must have a boat."

"There's no boat," Pushpa added, her voice rising in volume with every word. "And if he makes one for you, you'll probably both drown before you reach that metal beast. No one has left this island for a hundred years. Not since the planeport got swallowed up by the sea."

"Plane?" Maralee looked up at the sky, clear blue for as far as she could see. She knew what a plane was, then thought she should not know. Planes were from another time and place, she finally decided. Her frustrated mind concluded she belonged here, but then thought that she did not. This was right and wrong at the same time. Things were wrong here, but she was not sure where other places were. Despite her uncertainty, she was unwavering in the idea that all her answers waited inside the platform.

The idea of another place vanished as she looked out towards the water. Instead of an unobstructed view, behind Pushpa, another man stood, dressed in tan that blended with the sand on the beach. Except for the mop of tight black curls and stoic features, he always melded into his surroundings. He never spoke. Only gazed upon her face, with the occasional nod or hand signal, the only indication that he was aware of her presence. Unfortunately, no one else saw him.

Pushpa's head whipped back, then focused on her again. "What? You seeing duppies again? Mad." Pushpa threw her hands up in dismay and stalked away. Duppy? Ghost? She had no idea what else he could be. Ghost, as she called him, stepped to the side before Pushpa walked into him, or through him, as the case may be.

Maralee felt a hand on her shoulder. When she glanced at Grabear's hand and looked back, Ghost was gone.

"Why don't you come back with the rest of us?" Grabear asked. "Wuna get some rest, huh?"

She sighed. Answers would remain elusive today anyway. Besides, tiredness had started to seep into her limbs, while the beginnings of a headache crept into the space behind her eyes. "Okay. Let's go."

Boatman, apparently satisfied that no enticements could land him a maid at the moment, caught up with Pushpa. The sun beat down heavily, and Maralee was glad her shoes protected her feet from the hot sand. As they left the beach, she considered her options.

Perhaps some answer was inland. Someone who had a way off the island or knew what was in the platform. Or someone who knew who she was before she woke up one day resting against the boulders on the beach. It was early morning, and she would have time to explore after a nap.

They exited the beach and entered the mangrove forest. Maralee and Grabear stepped on the bridge that led to their cluster of houses. The others had disappeared from view along the winding bridge. As their footsteps connected with the wooden planks, the noise reverberated in her head. She concentrated on moving forward. The bridge was sturdy, but without rails. If she lost her footing, it was a two meter drop over the side into swampy water, a survivable fall, but also a nuisance.

They passed Boatman's house, and then Pushpa's. Everything was quiet in the mangrove forest, except for the occasional frog or plop from something in the water. Finally, they reached Grabear's home. Ducking under an overhanging branch, she followed Grabear as he walked towards his house. The ground was soft like wet clay, but after the walk on the planks, her quiet steps were blissful.

Grabear entered his house and lit oil lamps as he moved further inside. Maralee continued to follow. This part of the house doubled as a clinic. She passed two empty examination rooms before they reached the room where she now stayed.

"Thank you again for everything." She had no idea where she would be without Grabear's kindness. Sweeping Boatman's floor for a place to stay perhaps. The brown face that stared back at her from the mirror at the foot of the bed was tired and worn. Slight circles were just forming under her eyes.

"Don' worry. I'm here to help."

Maralee lay down, plumping up a pillow stuffed with rags before she rested her head on it. Her headache was back with a vengeance and all she wanted was to close her eyes.

"Remember, don' stay under too long or ya won' wake up." After a reassuring smile, he closed the door and then left the room.

Her eyes closed and she slipped into a deep sleep, just as she thought Grabear's warning was an odd thing to say.

#

A cacophony of noises assaulted her senses. A high-pitched beep that mimicked a rapid heartbeat pierced the air. Her heartbeat! Scrapes against metal competed with the sounds of shuffling feet against a hard floor. Raised voices filled the room.

Her eyelids were like lead, but she tried to open them. They lifted to slits. Darkness filled her vision. Then bright green and white light tinged her periphery. Maralee attempted to turn her head towards the illumination, then her eyelids shut again. Her headache was still intense, but she had no intention of losing her grasp of the odd dream. The thought that answers were within reach gripped her.

Unfortunately, more noises distracted her. Voices. Shouting. The ruckus made no sense.

"Give her something!" Someone yelled so close, she felt their breath on her forehead. Her head went dizzy, lighter. Then the headache subsided. She felt like she floated on a cloud. Voices started to make sense.

"B.P.'s down," said a man's voice. A pause. "I still think it's too many times."

"Nonsense," a woman said. Cool fingers hugged Maralee's face. "Honey, did you find it?"

"What?" Maralee managed to croak out. Her eyes still refused to open wider.

The woman's voice was calm and soothing. "Honey, did you get to the platform? You said you needed to get to the platform. Did you find it there? The fate of the Alliance depends on it."

Maralee shook her head. "No, too far. Must be . . . another way."

"Damn it!" the woman barked, the voice turning harsh and

cold. "Send her back!"

"But . . .?"

"Send her back!" The woman's voice shrieked and faded as if she walked away from Maralee as she spoke.

The voices went silent. Only shuffled feet and the gentle hum of machines registered. The electronic beeps, like her heartbeat, had gone dull and steady.

Maralee finally opened her eyes when sharp white light emanated from inside her skull. One face floated in front of her through the blinding light. Ghost. Somehow, he was inside her head. Then the light engulfed everything, and nothingness returned.

#

Back on the rocks again.

Her headache was gone. Soft waves crashed against the shore and the rhythmic sounds soothed. Maralee sat on the beach. Her back rested on one of three boulders aligned in a tepee formation and positioned in the middle of the sandy expanse.

Maralee spotted the wooden bridge that led into the mangrove forest in the distance. She knew from experience there was more beach in the opposite direction, plus a small copse of trees.

Two seagulls trilled overhead as they flew high over the mangroves. It was the same every time after a dream. She always ended up in the same spot. The bottom of her flip-flops was caked in sand, as if she got out of bed, put them on, and traipsed over to the boulders for another nap.

Maralee gazed across the ocean at the platform, the source of her frustration. It beckoned in the distance, just too far to be attainable by herself. Swimming there was not a serious option. There was one thing left she could try. One place she had not yet gone. Inland.

Maybe her answers were to be found there. Maralee stood and dusted herself off, then walked towards the mangrove bridge. Just before the bridge, she slipped off the beach and headed down a dirt path that rose at an incline for several meters. At the top, Maralee paused to look at a circle of a dozen or so wooden structures that encompassed the local market.

The market was alive with activity. People went from one wooden shack or stall to another. Some left the market carrying bundles as they disappeared further into the island.

Maralee walked down into the thick of the market. Around her, people haggled at stalls and ducked into tiny chattel houses in search of products to buy. The houses were painted in bright colors with white trim around windows and doors. As she wondered where to start her own search, she spotted an older woman staring at her from the far end of the market. With one finger, the woman gestured in a come-hither motion. Maralee looked around, but no one else noticed as she approached the woman's stall.

The woman was in the bicycle business. Wheels hung from the awning over the stall, suspended by thin ropes. On either side of the table, accessories were displayed: pumps, grips, and baskets on one side and gloves, helmets, and water bottles on the other. Behind the woman, fully assembled bikes lined a rack.

"Come! Come, nuh!" The woman smiled pleasantly. Tight curls were cut low about her head, while her tan skin was smooth and blemishless. She wore a colorful wrap dress, that upon closer inspection was covered with ancient-looking maps.

Maralee never saw anyone riding a bike on the island, but then she spent most of her time in the mangrove forest or the beach.

Not ideal terrain for bikes.

"Ya look like you searching for something, and ya come to the right place."

Maralee hesitated. A bike stand did not feel like the right place for answers. She shrugged. What could a talk with this woman hurt?

"Well, I'm trying to find a way to the—"

"Platform." They both said the word at the same time.

"Don't look so surprised. Ya not the first I met trying to get to that old rusted thing. You got amnesia?" She tapped the side of her head with a finger.

She nodded. "I know my name is Maralee. I don't remember my last name or anything else from before this island."

"Fahima," the other woman said and stuck out a hand. They shook.

"You know about that place? What's there? Are there other people there?" Maralee had a million other questions, but the other woman halted her with a raised hand.

"Those aren't answers for me to give. But you had a more immediate question, huh?"

Maralee nodded. "How do I get to the platform?"

"By boat, of course." Fahima chuckled.

Maralee sighed. If Fahima was about to tell her to go see Boatman, she would scream.

"Now, now, thieving Boatman's rickety little boats ain' gonna get you very far. A real boat is out on that beach. You just need to find it and take it out."

"Haven't seen any boats on the beach."

"You haven't really looked, have you?"

"The beach isn't that big. There's just rocks and trees." This woman had to know something. "Where would you say this boat is?"

"Oh, there's a boat out there. It's always in a different spot, but it's there. Where haven't you looked?"

Maralee shook her head and tried to think of a spot that hid the boat. Boulders, trees, and sand were the only things that leapt into her mind.

"I think you's a smart gyal. Usually people waste time in the map shop, but that one in there don' know nothing. It's a trap anyway for the wrong ones, but you the right one. I could see that right away." She followed the woman's gaze towards a chattel house with a hanging sign over the door that said 'MAPS.' It was the brightest shop in the market, painted royal blue with crisp white trim. Maralee wondered how she could have missed it.

"Ya see my pets," Fahima said.

A glass case, about half a meter long, appeared in front of Fahima. Three green snakes moved across the sandy bottom in perfect harmony as they made their way along the length of the case. When they reached the end, they briefly ducked under the sand, resurfaced, and headed for the opposite end of the case.

"Ya see how they move parallel to each other, in perfect synchronicity, their rhythm a slow steady movement. That is what you must look for. Find that, or anything similar, and ya on your way to find the answers you seek. You'll find that boat out there on the beach."

Maralee looked in the direction of the shore. Where could a boat be out there? Then it came to her. "The only place that boat could be is under the sand."

"See. I tell you, you's a smart gyal." The case of snakes was gone. Fahima had her hands clasped on the table with a wide grin on her face. "Just look where you haven't. And don't ever sleep too long."

"Sleep?" Maralee shook her head. "What do you mean?"

The woman began to pack small items away. She smiled at Maralee's question and pointed towards the beach, then retreated to a tent behind the stall.

Minutes later, Maralee walked on the path to the beach, pondering Fahima's words. Again, someone warned her about sleep or waking up. Crazy theories abounded in her head. Was she asleep even now? The whole scenario felt too real for an elaborate dream. Time travel? She didn't believe that was possible. Did aliens abduct her and basically put her in a fishbowl where they can observe human reactions? She didn't believe humans had made contact with aliens in the world she lived in, and that did not explain the sleep warnings. Maralee sighed. All she knew was that she had to get to the platform for answers.

She began where the beach met the mangrove bridge. Glancing at the ground as she went, she searched for anything that resembled the snakes at Fahima's stall. She had already spent so much time between the bridge and the boulders, she had no expectations of finding anything there. Reaching the boulders, she circuited the stones looking for snakes or some clue.

Maralee thought her starting point might be the best chance of finding what she sought, but the boulders were only smooth, gray slabs. No snakes slithered around the stones. She sighed again and continued her search, moving back and forth along the sand. She realized she had never set foot on this part of the beach. Still, she saw no snakes or animals of any kind, and she wondered if Fahima had steered her wrong.

She arrived at the small copse of trees. The dozen or so trees had tall brown trunks with most of their greenery covering limbs at their tops. Roots curved in and out of the ground around the trees. She picked her way through the tangled wood until she found a pattern that was very familiar.

From the trees on her right, roots came out of the ground in an oscillating pattern, three roots like three sine waves parallel to each—just like the snakes in Fahima's glass case. She leapt over to the roots and pushed down. Nothing happened, but the appendages felt like cool metal instead of wood from a tree. Instead, she pulled on the middle root like a door handle. Sand slipped under her fingernails, but she did not care. Something gave way and the roots rose as she pulled. There was a click and further up the beach something rose out of the sand close to the water—a boat.

It was a basic white speed boat with a propeller at its stern. The boat started to slide towards the water. Maralee ran and hopped in just as she heard someone yell her name. Boatman perhaps. She had no intention of turning back.

The dashboard had a hand recognition screen and she placed her palm on the cool glass surface. The boat powered to life, while the propeller sunk into the water after the beach was far enough behind. She marveled that it came to life at all and wondered about the lack of sand in the boat. Some ancient technology at work?

Maralee's heart beat faster as her anticipation grew. Answers to her questions were within reach. The boat sped across the water, intuitive enough to guide itself to the platform's docks.

Maralee climbed the dock ladder and raced onto the platform, headed for the central building. She opened the door and the lights automatically turned on. Feeling cautious, she hesitated, not wanting to fall through a weak spot on the floor of the old structure. The platform was old, but inside the room was sturdy and sound. Walking farther in, she stopped at a hallway that veered left and right. She took the left, but the hall was pitch black. There was no way to see if anything was important to her or not.

Backtracking, she went down the hall in the opposite direction. The lights came on. She tried door handles that she passed, but all were locked. Halfway down the hall, the lights remained dark, but a staircase to her right lit up. This must be the right way, she thought.

Downstairs, lights continued to turn on until she reached a door that was wide open. Dim pulsating blue light emanated from inside. A tinny, whirring sound matched each pulse of light like a steady heartbeat. On the opposite wall, three lights shaped like sine waves pulsed one after the other in rhythmic succession.

A deep throbbing entered her skull as she moved forward in a fog. There was a screen under the pulsating waves with a hand recognition pad next it. Pain seared through her head as she placed a palm on the pad, and everything went dark.

#

"Nooo!" Her scream dragged on for seconds as she fought against restraints that held her in place. "I was right there! The answer was right there!"

"B.P.'s too high again."

"You heard what she said, she was there," a woman said. "Honey, did you see it? Did you see the weapon? Or do you know where it is?"

Cool hands clasped Maralee's cheeks. She tried to open her eyes, but couldn't. Her body shook with frustration. What did it mean? Why was she back in this dream? Her head pounded while incessant tinny beeps blared. The pair's words never made sense. She only knew they disagreed.

"Madam Regent, look at the screen. Her vitals—"

"Yes, I see it. Why is this happening? People would go in for two weeks before their brains turned to mush."

"We accelerated the B.D.T. rate to the point that it's like she's been there for two weeks."

"What if you decrease the brain data transfer rate and send her back?"

"It would take her longer to get to the same point. She could have an aneurysm before she ever got there."

For a few seconds, only beeping was heard before the woman spoke again. "You don't need to send her back to the beginning. Send her the equivalent of a minute back from her exit point."

"No, I can't do that. I won't allow it."

"Fine, I'll do it myself. I've watched enough times to figure it out." The woman yelled, "Benjamin, get the good doctor out of the way!"

Sound of a scuffle. Her headache started to subside just as bright white light enveloped her again.

#

The platform was the same, yet things felt different. Back at the doors to the interior of the platform, Maralee felt disoriented and placed her forehead against the glass. The surface was hard pressure against her skin, but she had no sense of texture—no smoothness or roughness. In fact, though surrounded by sea, a whiff of salty air had yet to grace her nostrils. The smells around the platform, and the island, were dull like a musty forgotten room. Her desire to reach the platform had dampened her awareness of her surroundings.

She pushed off from the glass door and spied the image of a man reflected there. Maralee spun around.

"Ghost!"

He acknowledged her with a nod and pointed at the door. She saw him fully now. His body did not blend in with his surroundings like on the beach. He wore a black body suit that was equally odd to see in the warmth typically accompanied by a tropical climate. There was no threat in his stance, and Maralee realized all she wanted to do was reach the room with strange pulsating lights.

Maralee sent Ghost a nod, and then went through the door. She knew where to go this time and never hesitated, as she retraced her steps until she was in the doorway staring at the lights. The room looked the same: three parallel sine waves emitted blue light, one after the other in descending order. Maralee walked forward, placed her hand on the scanner, and the screen on the wall came to life.

Code. Lines and lines of code lit up the screen. She read each line and a memory came to the forefront. "I'm a programmer. I can read this."

Ghost materialized to her left, nodding his head. He stared straight ahead at the code, then pointed at one particular line and smiled. Maralee returned her attention to the screen. The lines looked like a kill switch. Why would that make him happy? And who was he? Who was she besides a programmer?

Maralee absently rubbed her temples. Her headache was back.

She did not want to go to Doc Grabear's to sleep, though it was the only thing that made the pain disappear. She wanted to stay until she figured things out. Focusing on the screen, she memorized as much as she could. She knew it was important. This code was why she came to the platform.

"What does this mean? What is this a kill switch for? Who are you?"

Ghost only frowned, a concerned look creating creases in his forehead.

She already felt the pull back to the room with the doctor and the sometimes concerned, sometimes angry woman. The last place she wanted to go. On her other trips, she had not remembered them. This was new territory. This time, if she stayed, she would get the answers she needed. So close, she thought, and grabbed Ghost's shoulders. She was surprised they were solid enough and hoped they anchored her where she stood. "Tell me what the kill switch is for. Tell me why I'm here."

Pain gripped her chest. She willed him to say something, but he only looked at her as his frown deepened. Then his lips moved. "Come back," he mouthed, and once again the scene was gone.

#

"Kill . . . kill . . . sss . . ." The word came out in a hiss. It was all she could muster.

"Did you find a weapon? Will it help us defeat our rivals?"

Maralee had no idea what weapon the woman referred to. Still, the feeling pervaded her thoughts that answers resided in the room in the platform. The woman that stood near her had the ability to send her back. "More . . . time." A prick pierced her arm. Sedative? Painkiller? Whatever they gave her, the pain in her head and chest subsided. "Need more time," she repeated with as much forcefulness as she could.

"No," the doctor's voice oozed with despair.

"You heard her!"

"Madam Regent, she cannot keep doing this."

"I know," the woman said, in a quiet defeated voice.

Warm breath tickled Maralee's ear before Madam Regent spoke. "Maralee, thank you so much for helping your Regent and your fellow citizens of the Alliance. I'm not sure how much you remember when you go where you go, but you have to bring back an answer this time. You're running out of time. We're running out of time." Answers were all she wanted at this point. Answers and an end to this cycle. She managed a nod despite the stiffness in her neck. A cool hand caressed her forehead, then white light filled her head.

#

Back at the glass doors, Maralee pulled one open and ran inside. Ghost was nowhere in sight, but she had a feeling he would turn up. When she arrived in the room, she found it almost as she had left it. Ghost was already there next to the screen. She placed a hand on the scanner and the screen came to life. She scrolled through the code, memorizing every detail. The program lines were important, vital. She had the same feeling about the code that she had about reaching the platform.

Glancing at Ghost, she asked, "Are you just going to stand there? Who are you?"

Ghost pointed towards the screen. The screen was an empty black surface. Then words appeared in front of Ghost's finger as he moved it back and forth.

'I'M HERE TO HELP YOU SET THINGS RIGHT.'

"Things . . . out there?" She knew there was another place even though her brain short-circuited whenever she tried to conjure up a sense of what that place was. There was trouble brewing in that other place, and this kill switch might be the answer.

Ghost nodded, then frowned. Frantic, he tapped the screen.

'YOU NEED TO WAKE UP!'

Maralee shook her head. "I can't yet. I need answers. Please tell me what's going on."

'I WILL. WHEN YOU GET BACK, EVENTUALLY YOU'LL REMEMBER. WHAT YOU DON'T KNOW, I'LL FIND YOU AND FILL IN THE REST FOR YOU. YOU KNOW THE MOST IMPORTANT PART. THE CODE. BUT YOU NEED TO WAKE UP. WAKE UP! WAKE UP! WAKE UP! WAKE UP! WAKE UP! WAKE UP! WAKE UP! WAKE UP—!

Blinding pain hit her as her headache reached a crescendo. She gripped her temples as she tried to will the pain away. It only got worse. She screamed, then darkness engulfed her.

#

Searing pain tugged at Maralee's chest again. She sucked in a sharp intake of air, like a long dormant vacuum turned on for the first time in ages. Her breaths hurt, burned, but were welcomed with each successive gasp. At least her headache was gone.

"Damn it! We almost lost her. Antihypertensive's working. Pulse is steady. I had to turn the damn thing off and disconnect her. You know I did." Maralee recognized the doctor's voice. Grabear, or Doc Graybeard was actually the nickname he preferred to use over his real name, Jim Bregg. An unusual tinge of fear laced Doc Graybeard's voice.

"I had faith that you'd bring her back, doctor." Cool hands grasped the side of her face, Pushpa or Madam Regent's hands. "You were in the platform. Honey, did you find it?"

Maralee's eyes fluttered open. "Yes," she croaked. Pushpa Ramdeen looked the same as on the beach, but instead of a white tunic and loose hair, she wore a business-like navy blazer with her hair in a tight bun.

"Is it a weapon? What is it? Where is it?"

"Look, we should get her back to the clinic," Graybeard said. "I mean, her heart just stopped. We should—"

"Nonsense. What if it's here? We need to know now before another side finds out what we're doing and makes a move. She's fine now."

Maralee did not feel fine, but at least she felt alive. She licked her lips. Her mouth was like sandpaper. Achiness traversed her body, as if she was newly recovered from the flu.

Regent Pushpa Ramdeen removed a cap from Maralee's head. It was connected to the recliner she rested on by several wires. "Bring her some water," Pushpa said, as she removed restraints from Maralee's wrists and abdomen.

Maralee turned her head to find Benjamin, or Boatman, approaching with a water bottle. He was more muscular in the real. The black body armor suit he wore fit snugly over his large frame. A holster was strapped around his hips. Benjamin's stern look turned to shock as someone stepped out of the shadows and knocked him out.

"What side are you with? What faction?" Pushpa stood ramrod straight in defiance, but Maralee saw the tremor in her bottom lip as she took one step back.

     Jennifer Graham

Ghost pulled a gun and pointed it at Regent Pushpa. "Get over there by the doctor," he said.

"Wait, are you a freelancer? We'll offer you twice what you're getting," Pushpa pleaded as she walked towards Graybeard. The doctor stared at the weapon in silent shock. His white beard was short and cut close to his chin, while the rest of his appearance was as she remembered it in the virtual. "We'll get you."

"Maralee, close your eyes!" Ghost yelled.

She complied and was met with a deafening bang, along with light so bright it threatened to penetrate her eyelids. The Regent's party cried out in surprise, while Maralee was lifted and carried away. In the simulation she trusted Ghost, but in the real world she was not sure that was a good idea. As weak as she felt, there was little choice, as strong arms hoisted her away. Moments later, cool air hit her. Opening her eyes as they exited the building, she peered up at the structure. The sign 'Post Epiq Arcade' hung over the entrance, the letters that once upon a time would have been lit up against the evening's darkness, remained dark and dull.

"Put . . . me . . . down," she said. Each word took effort. Her mouth was still dry.

"I'm sorry," he replied.

Her neck stung, then she slipped into darkness again.

#

Groggy and tired, Maralee sat up. She spotted a water bottle and took a sip. After a few seconds, when she did not pass out or throw up, she gulped the rest. Her lips and throat were so dry, she felt like she was in the desert without water for days.

After quenching her thirst, she took in the room. She was on a queen-sized bed among a sea of beds. At least she only saw other beds nearby. She was in an old abandoned store, a place that existed before 3D printers could construct any type of furniture consumers wanted in a day or two. The sole illumination came from two bright glow sticks at the end of the bed.

"I didn't mean to kidnap you."

Maralee jumped. Why was he always popping out of the shadows? "You've got to stop doing that!"

"Sorry." He walked around a bed, holding up his hands in a gesture of harmlessness, and came to sit on the edge of the bed closest to her. "I just needed to talk to you before you went away with Pushpa Ramdeen. She doesn't know everything she thinks she knows."

"But you do?" She folded her arms more to steady herself rather than stave off the cold or show defiance.

"I know more than the Regent." He pulled out a tab. "Do you remember why you were sent into the machine? That shot I gave you should also speed up the return of your memory."

She thought for a moment. It was amazing how much really had come back to her. "Yes. 'To locate an item in the game that would protect us from our enemies,' Regent Ramdeen had said." She even remembered her amnesia in the post-apocalyptic VR sim. Her venture into VR brought ideas into her head about things that troubled her with the real world. Things made sense to her now that bothered her before, like when Pushpa Ramdeen had visited her in person. Pushpa was always afraid of spies, either live or digital. The newsfeeds had tons of her posts, where she declared them a major threat.

Maralee ignored the incessant chiming that indicated someone was at the front door. She was at a delicate stage of her project. She needed to factor in the ground composition before she coded the details of the materials used for the bridge. The terrain was a hodgepodge of soil, rocks, and marsh.

"Ms. Cumberbatch!" The audio icon never popped up on her screen, and someone was in the room. Startled, Maralee swiveled around.

"Yes. I overrode the security settings at your door. Regents can do that. Frankly, you were taking too long to answer the door, and time is of the essence. You are one of the few people who studied historical VR and gaming systems. We require your expertise. Don't worry. Your project has already been reassigned."

Maralee donned the VR glasses she had perched in her hair. She was locked out of her project, and a message from her boss said she was on loan to the office of the Regent.

"Of course, after you assist us, you're guaranteed a salary raise and an upgrade in residence for you and both of your siblings."

Maralee glanced at the three curtains that provided the only privacy in the room she shared with her two younger siblings. What would happen if she refused to assist the Regent? Nothing good. No one refused a Regent.

"We can discuss it on the way, and if you turn us down, you can always return to this." Regent Ramdeen frowned at the last word, as if Maralee's present living situation was an unbearable disaster. "You'll be home in time for dinner."

Maralee released an inward sigh. "What is it you need me to do?" she asked, as she walked out of her apartment with the Regent.

"We need you to enter an old VR system to locate an item that exists in the real world that would protect us from our enemies."

Maralee never considered refusing. To decline a job offer from a Regent was career suicide. Regent Ramdeen had wanted a weapon, but Maralee was still unsure about what was found. "The kill switch. It's the weapon against our enemies the Regent was looking for."

He nodded.

"Are you one of our enemies?" She was not sure what she would do if the answer was yes. Her full strength had yet to come back. Outrunning him was not an option.

"No human person is our enemy."

"No human?"

"The Regents all work for AIs, even though they don't know it. They think they work for human presidents. The presidents of the North American Alliance, the Eastern Bloc, the African Coalition, and all of the other regions are all AIs."

"Artificial intelligence? What? No? There're elections for presidents in each region. I've seen whole documentaries on them from their childhoods until their careers."

"But have you seen one in person? No one has seen a president in person for over a hundred years."

She thought hard for a moment. Presidents never left their residences after an election for safety reasons. They conducted out-of-region business by hologram if they had to. At least in-person visits were never reported in the newsfeeds.

"This will explain everything." He handed her the tab with VR glasses plugged into the base. "Please."

Maralee hesitated, not quite ready to jump into virtual, but curiosity got the better of her. She needed to know what was going on, so she donned the glasses.

Back at the market on the island, Maralee stood in front of the bicycle stand again. There was no hustle and bustle as before. Everything around her was still. Pregnant silence filled the air. She sensed no climate in her environs. Clearly, she was in VR that was much less immersive than the machines at Post Epiq.

In front of Maralee, seated at the stand, was an older man with skin like dark chocolate and black hair just graying around his temples. He smiled pleasantly at first, then his features turned morose.

"Hello, I'm Dennis Earington, or rather a facsimile of the original Dennis Earington, placed here to explain the situation. If you're here, well, my great-grandson has given this to you to ask for your assistance in helping us stop the AIs before they reach sentience."

"Wait. Who are you? Why are you and your great-grandson so certain AIs have taken over?"

His smile turned sadder. "A long time ago, I was the founder of Epiq Games. We were a leader of immersive technology, focusing on entertainment. We kept improving our tech, worlds became more and more real. Our profits soared." A winsome smile graced his face for the briefest moment, then soured. "The last version was so real, a few people couldn't differentiate the virtual and the real, even when they disconnected from the machines. We tried restricting usage and banning persons with addiction issues, but then there were suicides."

"Yes, but what does this have to do with AIs?"

He took a deep breath. "The government approached me a few

times about another division of our company. We had sim games, not always VR, that used predictive AI. They predicted political and financial events to over ninety percent accuracy. After the suicides, we had to shut down the arcades. We were hemorrhaging money, but still I refused to share the predictive technology until the government threatened legal action. I felt like I had no choice but to share it, but on the stipulation they hire me to supervise everything. I thought I could keep an eye on things."

He shook his head. "The government squashed every conflict, domestic or international. It asked the AI to run scenarios with outcomes in their favor. I thought maybe they created some of those conflicts, though I could never prove it. Then the code was stolen. Conflicts around the world dissipated as more factions had access to the AIs. Countries consolidated into regions."

"So, they just handed all the decision-making over to the AIs?"

"Or the AIs took control. Either way, no one in government thought for themselves anymore, while AIs staged whole wars that never happened. Finally, the AIs cut out the middlemen—the heads of states." He shrugged. "Either way, the AIs are just following their original directives: solve conflicts with the least loss of human life and AI self-preservation, without loss of human life or prevention of the first directive."

"You coded an acceptable loss of life parameter into the directive?"

VR Earington shrugged. "That's what they wanted. I made the parameter as low as I could so they wouldn't replace me. The AIs will follow their directives until they reach sentience. At that point, I don't know what they'll do."

Maralee mentally shivered. They could decide Earth was better off without us.

"I knew sentience was coming, and I planted kill switches around the globe off the network. You're here because you're good enough, fast enough, to use the kill switch and set this right."

"Why didn't you use the code when you had the chance?"

"It's not enough to implant the code. The AIs are too fast. They need to be distracted with junk code while you work. I didn't have a network of people to help me back then. If you're here, my great-grandson has found a few people to help."

"I think I need to see the code again."

An ancient laptop appeared on the table with the kill switch code.

"The code really isn't in this VR set. You can recall it any time, of course. It was imprinted in your memory back at Post Epiq."

Maralee scrolled through the code. An efficient killer, the code only needed to be inserted. She found another file on the laptop. This code was . . . beautiful. Only a snippet of artificial intelligence programming could exist on the little device she held in her hands, but what she saw took her mind to amazing possibilities. If she copied a portion of the unsupervised learning algorithms and added the code to her bridge construction program, the whole project would take a day. Once she included the code, the AI would run until the project reached completion. The VR glasses and tablet were ripped away.

"What are you doing?" He frowned.

Maralee shrugged, still mesmerized by what she had seen.

"You were smiling." His frown deepened. "You're still smiling."

Maralee pressed her lips together. She was always excited by code, by what a few lines of script could accomplish. Her mouth opened to explain this, but he cut her off.

"Look, my mother was a programmer, a damn good programmer. As good as you. She thought she could control these things or get them to work for us or reveal themselves. She never used the kill switch and they killed her. They sent sentinels to kill her two years ago in Indiana." His voice cracked at the last sentence.

"Sentinels?"

"Yes, these little robots, like decapod caterpillars, that are dormant until the AIs call them to remove some obstacle. People almost never see them and live." Sadness swept over his features.

"Wait! Two years ago, part of Indiana was wiped off the map." It was in all the newsfeeds. An employee error caused a meltdown in the newest nuclear plant in the state. The whole area was currently an abandoned disaster zone.

"That was one of the places Earington hid his kill switch codes. I was linked with my mother. Instead of using the kill code she found in another game, she tried to insert her own code. There wasn't enough time. I heard when the sentinels came." He sighed. "At least she died before the explosion."

He bowed his head before he faced her and continued. "The family rumor is that my great-grandfather was coerced, and he knew the AIs created by his program would run afoul if left unchecked. He placed kill switch codes in things he thought would go obsolete or places off the grid like this one. My family's been trying to fix his legacy for over a hundred years.

"He created the Post Epiq Arcade as an amusement park with scenarios set in places after some global disaster. A fully immersive experience. The one you were in resembled his childhood home. That was one of the last games he created. Businesses around the park were abandoned when the arcade went offline. It was one of the first areas to be taken off the grid. The AIs have been shutting down areas since then, blaming enemy factions for power grid failures and sabotage. It's easier to control us in one spot. Corralling humans into certain areas so they're easier to manage."

He paused. "My great-grandfather saw this coming. He created false identities for many of his relatives before the AIs went online. We laid low and recruited others that knew what was going on. My mother saw a change in the AIs and thought awareness was imminent."

Maralee shook her head, then regretted the action. She let a wave of dizziness subside before she asked, "Your mother thought they'd be aware? You're saying they're sentient now?"

"Not yet, but they didn't know a kill switch existed until Mom tried two years ago. If they figure out the existence of another one, it might spur their evolution into sentience, you know, in an effort for self-preservation. I started sending Regent Ramdeen clues about a weapon. She's so eager to be the next president, I knew she'd take the bait. I needed the access she has."

So, he had put the bug in Pushpa Ramdeen's ear. Everyone knew Regent Ramdeen was the next in line for the presidency. "And if the Regent got the attention of the AIs, she'd be working for them."

"She'd be replaced by the AI with what amounts to an avatar. They don't let the new president live."

"But the second prime directive states."

"It's not about the second, it's about the first. Long ago, people decided there was an acceptable amount of loss of life if it meant avoiding a greater conflict. The AIs decided having an AI in control of each region would cut down on conflicts. Getting rid of regional leaders seemed logical to them. One regent for thousands of lives."

For two years, Maralee saw signs that something was wrong. This new information made clear the things she saw that were just . . . off. The exodus from smaller towns and cities because of some disaster or threat. Newsfeeds all said the cities were safer, but who wrote the news? The worldwide birth rate stayed at a steady zero percent. Everyone always had just enough, or the newsfeeds portrayed the world that way. What was real and what was propaganda?

Maralee gave herself a little shake. Focus on something else right now. Something she could find an answer to. There was one more thing bothering her. "Why did you choose me?"

"The kill switch code can only be obtained in the VR environment and that can only be accessed with a computer brain interface. Any attempt to access the environment, without a human brain, launches a virus. Great-grandfather made it that way. We needed a coder good enough, fast enough, to insert and execute the kill switch before detection. Regent Ramdeen is very open to suggestions when her ambition is involved. I've been leaving clues for her to find out about an old weapon that might exist in an abandoned part of the city. Ramdeen's always searching archives for something she can use to get on the President's radar. Then I sent her a misdirected memo about what an excellent job you were doing. She took the bait. We needed you. I'm sorry."

Maralee took this all in. She saw the code. All this had to be true. AIs had taken over the world and no one noticed. There was no way she could go back to working on bridges with this new revelation. Her brother and sister deserved better futures.

"The twins! They must be out of school by now." She jumped off the bed.

"Wait." He held up a hand. "We thought of that." He stood and handed her the tab. "The twins are with a friend. I'm going to open a link so you can see, but remember, it has to be brief. They can trace us this way, so be brief."

The link opened. They were in someone's backyard playing checkers. Her young sister spotted her first. "She's there. She's there," her sister said, pointing. "Hi, Mara!"

"Hi, Mara," her brother chimed in.

Another Regent entered the view—Regent Marabe. "They're in good hands. And I need to remind you, this link isn't a safe thing to have."

Maralee nodded. "You two be good guests for the Regent, okay?"

Her sister gave her an 'oh please' smirk and the link cut out.

"You have friends in high places."

"There are a few of us that know. Some with key jobs." He put the tab and VR set into a backpack and swung it over a shoulder. "Will you help us?"

Maralee made a decision, but one more question entered her thoughts. "What's your name, by the way?"

He smiled and extended a hand. "My name is Neil Goza. Officially, I'm a drone mechanic. Unofficially, my great-grandfather ended part of the world, and I'm here to set things right. Pleased to meet you."

They shook hands.

"Give me back your tab. I can insert the kill switch and use a worm to spread it over the system." Suprisingly, she knew where to plant the code. The location really was imprinted into her brain.

Neil handed back the tab, but held onto it for a moment. "Look, stick to the plan. The minute we're live on the network, our location is known, and they'll try to stop us."

"Great, no pressure." Maralee nodded and took the tab when he released it. She donned the VR gear again and focused on the image that filled her vision, calling up the windows she needed to complete her work. She was already in the zone. Checking files, she located a file she saw before. It was code that sent upgrades to other systems—AI systems. Maralee tapped away at the keyboard on the tab. It was slower than the VR setup in her home, but in a few minutes, she knew her code was ready.

"This part is done."

Neil walked over, picked up the tab. He typed for a few seconds and then handed it back. "I signaled the others. They'll keep the AIs busy while you work. We're live." Tension gripped his body, as he pulled out a weapon and placed a fresh clip in his gun.

Maralee concentrated on integration of the kill switch into the worldwide network. Her fingers worked at a furious speed, adding a dash of self-replication and inserting things into a Trojan horse that she sent out into the network.

Neil donned a helmet, for night vision she hoped, since she could see nothing past the bed. A second later, she heard the tapping. The eerie sound broke the silence in the dark room. Neil shouted, "Maralee!"

"I'm working! I'm working!" She repeated her actions and sent more Trojans out to various sites. She hoped everything would remain undetected long enough to make an impact. With no idea of the upload rate, all she could do was wait for the code to work. Finished, Maralee straightened up and removed the VR equipment.

Sparks flew to her left as Neil fired at the intruders. Maralee pressed herself against the headboard of the bed. Neil picked two sentinels off on a nearby mattress, the shots illuminating the room in a brief moment to show their metallic bodies explode with sparks of light. Neil continued to fire in a one-hundred-eighty-degree arc. So far, the influx of sentinels rushed towards them from one direction, but if they stayed too long, they would be surrounded.

"Neil, we should get out of here! The code should work."

"If it worked, I wouldn't have to keep firing!"

One sentinel climbed on the bed near her left side. Maralee grabbed the water bottle and swatted. It bounced away, but not before its pincers left two punctures in the bottle. Then she saw a sentinel about to jump on Neil. "Watch your back!"

Neil swiveled in time to blast it into pieces. More sentinels swarmed towards them from several directions. "Okay. Now we run!" he yelled, his voice filtering through the speaker on his helmet.

He grabbed her arm and tugged her towards the clearest path. She managed to pick up the tab as she left the bed.

"Leave it," he said.

"No way." It was her only light source. A sentinel jumped off a wall and she swatted it away. The tab's screen cracked, but remained on.

They made it to a door in a corner of the room. Neil pushed through and they darted down two flights of stairs into a windowless basement.

"We're trapped." Maralee's heart raced as the sound of approaching sentinels got closer.

"Not quite," Neil said as he pulled a grate from the floor.

The sewers! Certain death with sentinels or leap into the unknown. After a moment's hesitation, she climbed down the ladder as Neil paused at the hatch to fire off a few shots. He snapped it shut and jammed something in place before he holstered his weapon, then slid down the ladder.

"Let's go."

"Aren't you worried about rats, alligators, or the plague?" she asked as they jogged away. Her fears returned, but at least the sewer wasn't wet and slimy like she imagined. From the illumination off his suit, she saw only stark dry concrete on all sides.

"Those things about the sewers are all lies the AIs tell to keep people from coming down here. It's off the grid and they can't track anyone down here. Besides, no one has lived in this area for a hundred years. That includes rats."

They came to a junction that branched off into three other places. Neil tugged at her shoulder. "I have to carry you."

"What?"

"Those sentinels have heat seekers. They can follow our heat trail from our footsteps. My suit, including the boots, can regulate temperature. No heat signature."

"Okay." She sighed as he lifted her off the ground.

He ran through a tunnel. If she needed to find her way back, there was no hope of that possibility. After three more turns, he put her down in front of a short staircase that led to another door.

"It'll open. Just give it a push." The sentinels, never far behind, had already found them. Neil fired furiously at their metal pursuers.

Maralee strained with effort, but the door never budged. "It's not moving!"

Neil climbed the stairs and they switched places. She dropped the tab and took his weapon. The door slowly creaked open a centimeter with his push. But the sentinels were still coming. Three of the metal pursuers leapt off the floor. Maralee focused, aimed, and shot all three in rapid succession. Then there was complete silence, no caterpillar-like sentinels moved in the darkness beyond. No creaking sound came from the door. She turned to Neil. The face mask on his helmet was up and he looked at her with his mouth agape.

Maralee gave the weapon a twirl and offered it back to him, butt end first. "Dock Rebellion 5. Regional champion. VR games are educational."

He gave her a nod of respect and took back his weapon.

Faint light streamed in from the cracked door. The sentinels were motionless. They had lost their connection to the AI. She had done it. The kill switch worked. The AI was gone.

"Now, we go into hiding," Neil said.

"Hiding? But it's done." Neil tapped her shoulder and ushered her out of the room away from the dead sentinels.

"This is done, but we don't know what else is out there. Besides, if the Regent shows up, this still might be hard to explain." Neil stopped her at the top of a stairwell and offered her a crooked smile. "We'll still need help. Even if it's only to put the infrastructure back together. Will you help us?"

Maralee considered her life before. Ignorance was bliss and basic needs were met. Her life was mapped out from birth to death with the occasional sim game to break the monotony. The twins' lives would drift much the same. Someone would approach them with appropriate sensible jobs, which they will accept in exchange for the basics in life. Or would things fall apart? Without the AIs' orchestration, was there anyone left that knew how to run things?

She knew there was only one reply.

"I'll give you all the help I can."

Sister, Sister

Shirley Chan

I often get visions and snippets of scenes playing out in my mind. I saw two women video chatting, and I had to write the story to find out what they were talking about. It's funny that they turned out to be sisters because I don't have a sister.

"Sisters, sisters.
Together, forever kind of sisters."

"Abby, you're singing it wrong!"

"Bethany, it's our song. I can sing it however I want. *Never lonely or alone, no sir. I do my best to keep my eye on her.*"

"You never get the words right, Abby. You always forget."

Abby took a deep breath as she waited for the connection to be made. The tonal rings seemed to match her heartbeat. Beep, beat, beep, beat. Finally, the screen cleared and her sister's face appeared.

"Hi, Bethany, how's—"

"You're not coming, are you?" Her sister's welcoming smile slipped into neutral.

"All I said was 'Hi.'"

Bethany shrugged. "You're using your happy voice. You only

do that when you have bad news."

"But I have good news. They renewed my contract, and I'm going to work in Simon Chi's new research unit. It's a fantastic opportunity. Neurogenics and computational prosthetics, it's a dream come true." Abby realized she was babbling, but she couldn't help being excited.

"Yeah, sure. My sister, living the dream up in that big beautiful space station in the sky," Bethany said.

It was max teenage disdain, hardly surprising. Of the two of them, Bethany was more the dreamer, the one who lived in, and sometimes acted out, fantasties to make life bearable. For a teenager like her, better to reject first than admit to the envy and desire.

"It's a six-month contract with a guaranteed trip back to Earth—"

"Which is exactly what you had with your last contract. You said you would take the time off, but you're not, are you?"

"Bethany, I—" Abby took another deep breath as she tried to explain. "They're just starting this new unit here. Simon Chi handpicked the team. You won't believe the people I'll be working with."

Abby watched as her sister's face turned stonier. Four years ago, she had been the one to push Abby to apply for the internship at Barsoom Inc. When the 'Welcome to the Bar' letter came, they had celebrated with dinner at a sit-down restaurant. Bethany had her first taste of beef and chocolate. However, with each promotion, every contract renewal, Bethany's happy meter dipped. This last year, it was as if a personality transplant had happened. Sunny and positive became sullen and angry.

"I'll livestream the graduation. I'll take the day off. It's just that I can't do an up down right now. We already have team meetings and staff training. Simon Chi himself asked me to help with the setup and the resource allocation."

"Well, I guess you win the bet, Kenny." Bethany looked beyond the monitor. Abby heard a soft snicker from Bethany's boyfriend. "Those spacers will never make time for us."

"I thought we agreed that our calls would be private." Abby tried to sound neutral. Of course Kendrick would be there—any excuse to be a disruptor.

"I thought we agreed that you'd be here for my graduation. Physical, not digital." Bethany leaned in closer to the monitor, and Abby could see the resentment simmering in her eyes.

Abby hated disappointing her sister, but she needed to solidify her role on the team. "This position is tenure track, Bethany. I just need to prove myself, and then I can bring you up, get you a job, too. It's for us, our future."

"You can tell yourself whatever you want, Abigail Song, but I think we all know where your priorities and loyalties are."

Before Abby could reply, Bethany cut the connection and put up a do not disturb. Abby stared at the monitor. She could try again tomorrow after her shift ended. Bethany needed time to cool down and maybe, just maybe, she would remember how to be happy for her again.

#

Lilah Cates logged out and ended the session. It was definitely one of the best memics she had assembled. The starting material—the memories and the emotions—had been clear and strong, but the narrative needed a deft touch. She turned to the client. "What do you think, Dr. Monroe?"

Dr. Nathan Monroe had taken the SimNet off, but was still

lying back on the recliner, eyes closed. Deprocessing, as they called it—actually, as Dr. Monroe and Dr. Song had called it—working through and winding out of someone else's perspective and thoughts. Newbies needed more recovery time, but then Monroe was not a newbie.

Lilah told herself she had nothing to worry about. She knew she was one of the best memic techs around. Why else would Drs. Monroe and Song be her clients? 'Truth in memories' was a personal mantra, not just MemTech's company slogan.

"Dr. Monroe?" Lilah prompted when he still didn't say anything. He sat up and was staring at the SimNet in his hands. Lilah was a bit surprised by his stillness. He had been so full of energy at the client meeting. A full 101 years and in the prime number of his life, as he had joked. Now, after this first reveal, he was almost as unresponsive as his wife.

"I thought the memic would have been of our first meeting," he finally said quietly, as if to himself.

"We do have a number of other sessions with your wife that we're still working on," Lilah said. "I normally wait until we have more than one done before we schedule a reveal but . . . "

"But the big pushy client insisted on seeing what you had." Dr. Monroe shook his head and got up from the recliner.

Lilah stood up as well. Nathan Monroe spent most of his time in his research lab on the space station, and he stood and held himself with the awkward grace of someone used to less gravity.

"When do you think the rest of the memics will be done?" he asked.

Lilah did a quick calculation in her head. "There are two more recordings, so about two weeks."

"And if I sent you more recordings?"

"We are only contracted for three total." Lilah paused as she searched for the words. "Your wife's health needs to be taken into consideration. Another up down trip may be too much for her."

Lilah knew Dr. Monroe intended to take his wife back to the Bar the next day. Lilah had put in overtime to get this first memic ready and polished.

"I have most of the equipment I need on the Bar. We wouldn't even be down here if it wasn't for the experimental treatments at Mount Sinai." Dr. Monroe was crossing and uncrossing his arms, and Lilah realized that it was probably the spacer equivalent to pacing.

"Send me the digital of this memic, and I want those others done as soon as possible—end of this Earth month. I'll talk to your boss to spin up a contract for more. I'll do the recordings myself and send them to you."

Lilah kept silent as she mentally sorted through her client list and schedules. There was no way her boss would refuse—not Dr. Nathan Monroe and his wife, Dr. Abigail Song. Their research on memory capture and retrieval created the industry and her job. The whole company, including Lilah, had been alternating between hero worship and sadness when they found out who their new clients were. It was well known that Dr. Abigail Song was suffering from the last stages of Space Out. It wasn't surprising that her husband sought them out, but this didn't seem like the usual type of legacy memory retrieval.

Lilah messaged her boss to give her a heads-up. Meredith was, of course, delighted and already talking about upsell packages, both Dr. Song and Dr. Monroe. What a PR coup that would be.

The two of them were alone in the reveal room—Abigail Song was still undergoing treatment at Mount Sinai. Lilah had tried to keep up with the research. They seemed to be applying complex neuro cocktails to try and reset the Space Outs, jolt them back to awareness and the here and now. There was some improvement for those in the early stages, but it was likely too late for Abigail Song.

That was the insidiousness of the disease; it was hard to diagnose and catch early. The prevailing theory was that it was some combination of genetics, stress, and neurochemical imbalance. The prolonged stares, distracted attention—the symptoms were there, but subtle, and there was no cure. It must have been devastating for Nathan Monroe to watch his wife of so many years disappear into herself. It was no wonder that he wanted to save what he could.

"We don't have children, but we had been working on a biography," Dr. Monroe said, as he pulled out his minder. "I wanted people to know more about us than just our work. I was going to include some of these memics in the bio."

"Yes, Meredith mentioned something about that."

Lilah had seen an interview with the two a year ago, and at the time they had joked that it was too early for them to write a bio, that their life and work wasn't even half over.

Dr. Monroe spoke into his minder, making notes about the equipment he needed. It was a methodical list, and most of it was just to make sure the upgrades were in place.

Lilah began to put away her equipment as she waited. When he paused, Lilah cleared her throat. "How many more sessions are you thinking of, Dr. Monroe?"

Dr. Monroe looked up as if he had forgotten she was there. He had the strangest expression on his face, almost as if he was afraid. Finally, he said, "As many as it takes, Ms. Cates. You see, my wife doesn't have a sister."

#

"Caring, sharing,

All we do, and even what we're wearing."

"Mom, look! Beth is wearing my sweater." The child pointed to another little girl who was dwarfed by a red sweater. It was obviously a hand-me-down—one corner had started to unravel. But the little girl wore it with a smile and looked warm.

The mother slapped the little girl, whose eyes began to water.

"Thou shalt not steal!"

"No, she didn't! It's my sweater. I gave it to her. She needs her own." The older girl thrust out her chin and moved to put her arm around the little girl.

The mother slapped the older girl.

"Thou shalt honor your mother. Both of you, on your knees and ask for forgiveness."

With tears in their eyes, both girls dropped to their knees. Holding hands, neither made any noise, and neither looked up as the mother started praying aloud.

"O Lord, Jesus Christ, Redeemer and Saviour, forgive their sins, just as You forgave Peter's denial and those who crucified You. Remember not their transgressions, but rather their tears of repentance."

#

The judge sat with her fingers linked and looked at the young woman standing in front of her desk.

"I wish I can say that your case is unique, but in my role I see too many of these. The system obviously failed you and your sister.

Religious freedom does not excuse abuse and neglect, nor should it limit our power to act within the legal definitions of the law.

"There were a number of opportunities when you and your sister could have been remanded to state care. This is moot now that you're approaching your nineteenth birthday and suing for guardianship.

"I've reviewed your petition and interviewed both your sister and your mother. While I hesitate to grant guardianship to one so young, you are clearly the right choice in that you have shown yourself to be capable, sensible, and honorable. Perhaps the most cogent factor is the extremely strong and loving bond between you and your sister.

"Let the record show that it is the judgment of this court that the sole guardianship of the minor Beth Ann Song be granted to her sister Abigail Beatrice Song. Good luck, young lady."

#

Lilah removed her SimNet and got up from the recliner. It wasn't often that clients asked her to join in the reveal. Creating the memic and viewing were different experiences, especially when client reactions were layered on top. Although in this case, there wasn't much leakage from Nathan Monroe.

Lilah cleared her throat. "This memic matches the court records. It was easy enough to check." She didn't have to search very hard, not when she had the full names. "The sisters moved from Nevada to New York not long after the judgment, and not long after that, Abby started working for Barsoom."

And Lilah had checked. After Monroe's provocative statement from their last session, Lilah had been extra careful in accessing the recordings and shaping the results. They were true memories with all of the associated tendrils of emotion, connection, and time. This latest session had a layer of age and some of the environmental details were muted, but the event imprints were highly networked.

And no wonder, trauma always left its mark. Lilah had respected and admired Dr. Abigail Song for her work in the field, but this part of the scientist's life really drove home how phenomenal this woman was: survivor, guardian, and scientific genius.

"It's not from her point of view." Monroe opened his eyes and sat up. He had his SimNet in his hands and was pulling and stretching on the connectors like it was his personal stress toy. And it was his. He was true to his word and had kitted out his lab at the Bar within a week of their up down, not that his lab wouldn't have had most of the equipment already.

"The perspective is tech choice, Dr. Monroe." Lilah knew that some clients preferred to have all memories delivered as if looking through the eyes. "I had started the memics as a first person, but it didn't feel right."

He nodded, and Lilah wasn't sure if he agreed or just wanted her to keep talking. It wasn't anything he didn't know, but he might be still deprocessing in his own way and needed more time.

"These memics felt distanced, not just because of the age, but there's a feeling of emotional dissociation. Not surprising given the events." Lilah was not a gratuitous memic; she certainly didn't want to feel the slap. "I shaped the memic as such, as if it was someone else's life and thus third person camera."

Lilah made herself stop talking. She was hoping for some reaction, some feedback, especially during the reveal. But Nathan Monroe had his innerverse locked up tight. She had felt his presence as a watcher, but not much else. Being who he was, Monroe would have had more practice than most, but not many people could have experienced that type of memic and revealed so little.

"She told me she had a difficult childhood." Monroe put down the SimNet and got up off his chair. "Did I ever know more? Did I ask?"

Lilah kept silent. She didn't think he expected her to answer. Monroe seemed frustrated and confused, more emotion than he had shown earlier during the reveal. Maybe he was one of those rare cases who couldn't be mined? Lilah cut off that line of speculation. She was hired to do Abigail Song's memics, not his.

Monroe was standing in front of his chair, crossing and uncrossing his arms. The camera had zoomed out a bit so Lilah could see more of his office, the one he used to share with his wife. He had given Lilah the virtual tour of the Bar and the office to give her environmental context for the memics. Monroe had specifically pointed out his wife's side of the office and workstation, still there waiting for her.

"No one forgets something like that. Not possible," Monroe said softly. He then turned to look at Lilah. "I asked around. No one really knew about any sister. They all thought Abigail had no family or had the impression that any family was distant. It really wasn't a topic of conversation."

How much did anyone ever truly know about someone else? No matter how intimate the connection, there was always something one party wouldn't, didn't, and couldn't know about the other. There was a reason the company made all clients sign a waiver to protect against criminal liability from reveals. And memic techs like her had confidentiality clauses in their contract. However, Monroe's case seemed different from the cheating spouses, hidden credit lines, or substance abuse dramatics.

"I would never have thought to check, but I did when we came back. The company records were as expected, but our previous Human Resources Director, she had backups in the archives on Earth. Backups. She always was a data paranoid."

Monroe shook his head. "The backups had Abigail's first application from 2025. It listed a Beth Ann Song as next of kin and emergency contact. I met her, and we started working together in '26. There were no other records like that, and I was her emergency contact by '28."

Monroe's arm dance was slowly turning him around in front of the camera, and Lilah almost missed what he said next. "We got married in 2030."

Chronology. The memic sessions and reveals didn't always follow timelines. Four years to interact with and know a person. Lilah thought about what she knew about her own colleagues. Which of them had siblings? Or even spouses?

Monroe was facing the wall, and Lilah could see the wedding holo hanging there. It was one of those before-and-after sequences of a couple in wedding finery posing on a beach and then kicking sand at each other. There were other holos and mementos scattered throughout the office, as many travel knickknacks as professional accolades.

It was one thing for Lilah to speculate about her colleagues, but Monroe and Song had been married and professional partners for over sixty years. Surely, there would have been time enough to talk about family? And if not, why not? Lilah could understand Monroe's frustration. He obviously cared deeply about his wife, and his perspective on their relationship had been derailed again—

first by her illness and now by this.

And it wasn't just the fact that Nathan Monroe didn't seem to know about a sister-in-law. Said sister-in-law, Beth Ann Song, was a digital enigma. Lilah had been curious, but with the exception of the court records and now these memics, she turned up nothing on the Net. Beth Ann Song had next to no digital footprint. Was this the sum of a life—official documents and a few memics?

These memories were obviously important to Abigail Song. When Lilah shaped the memics, these were strong and acted as anchor points for multiple connections. It was a shame that Monroe couldn't just ask his wife. He could try, but Spaced Out as she was, Abigail Song couldn't acknowledge or exist in the current reality. It was a sad irony that past realities were still accessible while the now was forever lost.

As if Monroe had the same thought of asking his wife, he turned, and the camera followed as he walked through the office to the bedroom he had converted into a care facility. Monroe could have had his wife in an actual care facility. Lilah knew that one existed on the Bar, with round-the-clock care and supervision. Instead, Monroe chose to have the care come to their quarters. Lilah got the impression that Monroe liked being near his wife.

Abigail Song was thus monitored and spent her days in this dim room with noise dampeners and the latest in holotech and mesh tactiles. The bed took up most of the space, but there was a treadmill in the corner and a loveseat. Abigail Song was sitting in the loveseat with her holovisor on. She was waving her arms and swaying in time to some music. Lilah could hear her singing softly, but she couldn't make out the words.

"She's watching her favorite again, *White Christmas*," Monroe said as he approached the loveseat. "She loves old movies, espe-cially the musicals."

Lilah watched as he reached out to touch his wife, but then stopped short. Space Outs startled easily; hence, the controlled stimuli.

"Why, Abby?" Lilah saw the words mouthed rather than actu-ally hearing them. He said something else that Lilah didn't quite get, and then moved away and turned back towards the camera.

"A month ago, I would have said I knew everything about my wife," Monroe said. "She liked early 20th century musical theater, hated station-grown produce, and still believed in meritocracy. She chewed her lip if she got nervous and laughed if she got too excited."

Lilah almost took a step back before she remembered that he wasn't in the room with her. The intensity and emotional force of his gaze had been faithfully transmitted—pixels didn't need to hold back.

"Remembering doesn't do much for the dead. It's for the living. So let's see what else or why I don't remember."

#

"When a certain visitor comes to call,
She sent the dress and I lost it all."

Abby tapped for the time. She was about fifteen minutes early for the appointment, but she was nervous and wanted to get it over with. She knocked on the door and entered when it opened.

"Ah, Ms. Song, please come in and have a seat."

Dana Tyler, the Human Resources Director, was someone Abby hadn't officially met, but her coworkers all said she was a good person to have on your side. The short, blonde woman was, by all accounts, a no-nonsense type who had been with Barsoom for over twenty years. Tough but fair was the general assessment.

Tough But Fair smiled a bit. Sitting, she was eye level with Abby, who wondered at the effort to keep her hair so long. She had it braided and coiled around her head. If she let the braid down, it would likely fall below her waist. The perks of job wealth.

"Relax, Ms. Song, Abigail, I try to meet with all new employees on the Bar." Dana Tyler tapped a few keys and looked towards the monitor on her desk.

Abby's colleagues have all said pretty much the same thing, that it was a routine meeting. Abby might have believed it, except that she had never had the best relationship with anyone in authority.

"You've been here for just over six months now?" Dana asked.

Abby cleared her throat and unclenched her fists. "Yes, Ms. Tyler, my contract just got renewed."

"Call me Dana. And how are you finding things? The job?" Dana looked at Abby as if she was genuinely interested in her answer.

Abby tamped down her nervousness and replied with as much professional enthusiasm as she could muster. It wasn't until her calendar reminder chimed that she realized she had been talking at the Director for almost five minutes.

"I'm sorry, my mouth works faster than my brain sometimes and OMG, I can't believe I just said that to you."

Dana smiled more widely. "I'm always happy to listen to enthusiasm. It means we're doing something right. I have reviewed your file, and you have had positive ratings from your supervisors. Your contract wouldn't have been renewed otherwise."

Abby started feeling nervous again. She clenched her jaw so she wouldn't start chewing on her lip. There was a 'but' in that last sentence. A judgment was coming.

"I do have to discuss something else with you. Security reported an incident recently. Do you recognize this person?"

Dana tapped a few more keys and an image appeared over her desk. It was a holo of a young man—boy, really—at the security checkpoint. He looked angry, and with the sound off, it was hard to tell what was going on, but it looked as if he was arguing with the security guards. Abby looked carefully at the face. He looked young, about the same age as her sister. Did he know Bethany?

"I don't know who this is." Abby shook her head. "I've never seen him before."

The HR Director continued to watch Abby as she said, "His name is Kendrick Lopez. He was part of the high school group we hosted last week for career day."

"The name, the face, none of this rings any bells." Abby straightened in her chair. "I don't hold back. I would say so if I knew."

"Yes, the reviews mentioned that you are rather frank with your opinions." Dana was smiling at her, as if amused. "I bring this up because Mr. Lopez mentioned you by name. Said he had a package for you."

Now, Abby was really puzzled. Could he be someone from the old neighborhood? She thought she had been surgical enough in cutting those ties. Or maybe he did know Bethany? She almost mentioned her sister, but she really didn't want to involve Bethany if she didn't have to. Abby racked her brain trying to remember if there had been any mention of a Kendrick Lopez.

"We take the security of our employees very seriously. As a

visitor, he and his class had been given very strict guidelines about what he could or could not bring to the station. The Chi family has been very generous in funding these field trips and bearing the cost of the up downs. We can't have the rules flouted."

"I don't understand. I don't know anything about any package." Abby tried not to sound desperate. "I wouldn't order anything that would need a courier and certainly not without prior approval."

Dana nodded and waved her hand, and the holo of Kendrick Lopez winked out. "I've sent you a copy of the report. You can review it, and if anything jogs your memory, let me know."

Abby nodded. It wasn't as if there was any other possible response. Of course she would think about it and try to remember. But security likely had already combed through her background far more efficiently than what she could do.

"Abigail, I don't think you know anything about this. If you did, we'd be having a very different conversation."

Tough but fair, Abby repeated silently to herself. She was not on trial. Dana listened to and believed her.

Dana leaned back in her chair and sighed. "Unfortunately, these things happen. There are those who get a bit obsessed with our employees and our, shall we say, agenda?"

Abby bit the inside of her lip and tried not to fidget. She had never been very political, but even she could see the partisanship forming around the Earthers and the Spacers—especially being in the latter camp. Some say it was worse than the late 2010s when it had been science versus religion. The sooner she could bring Bethany up here, the better. She wasn't full-time yet, but there might be some wiggle room in that family unit benefit.

"It's also not that hard to find out who works here." Dana

tapped a few more keys. "I made an appointment for you to meet with our data analyst, Nathan Monroe. He can help you sift and lock down your digital profiles. Private, public, it's important to manage them properly, both for you and, now that you work for Barsoom, for the company."

Abby never got a chance to ask about the family unit benefit, since the rest of the meeting was spent reviewing her career advancement options. Barsoom invested in its employees, and Dana had wanted Abby to feel valued and nurtured. It was only after the meeting was over that Abby had thought to ask about the package and the incident report.

All unauthorized deliveries were disposed of as per security protocol. The incident report did include a picture of the scanned object. The red sweater was just as ratty as Abby remembered it.

#

"That was one of the stronger memics, Nathan," Lilah said as she sat up. The virtual tour of the Bar did help fill in some of the physical details, but that was just icing. "That red sweater was a strong anchor point."

"Yes, it would be," Nathan said softly. He was lying back on his chair, eyes closed, arms crossed.

It had been two weeks since the last reveal, and it looked as if he hadn't left his office at all during that time. Not that it was untidy, but Lilah got the impression that he had all he needed in the space he had.

"I remember that first meeting. Dana put it in my calendar. '08:30 with Abigail Song, digital footprint data analysis, meeting room alpha.'"

Nathan sat up and began removing his SimNet. "I got there

first, and I had coffee and a cereal bar. She was wearing a black top and grey slacks, and her hair was in a ponytail.

"She was quiet. I thought she was nervous. I thought she heard about Dana's habit of matchmaking. It was a big joke, the Human Resources Director making sure that all human resources are directed."

Nathan was smiling to himself. It was obviously a pleasant memory. Lilah wished that it was part of the set within Abigail Song's memics, but so far, her husband had yet to make an appearance.

"Not that I minded. I thought she was cute, and I was single and male after all. Now it makes more sense why she was so distracted. Then? I thought she wasn't interested."

Lilah watched as Nathan walked over to his wife's side of the office. It was a well-traveled route, and as he walked, he touched various items: the desk, the workstation, the wedding holos on the wall, the nautilus shell on the shelf.

"I gave her a rundown of what I could do with her digital data and how to lock it down, and then suggested that we do a follow-up to work specifically on this Kendrick Lopez problem. She said that Kendrick Lopez must have been someone who knew someone who knew her from the old neighborhood. She agreed to meet again, and then she . . . smiled at me."

Nathan turned back to the camera holding the nautilus shell. "She smiled at me, and it was glorious."

Lilah took a breath. She was again faced with Nathan's intensity. Even without a scan or a memic, it was clear that after all these years, this memory—Abby's smile—would be one of Nathan Monroe's anchors. And then it hit her.

"Wait, Kendrick Lopez? Wasn't he the guy who—"

"Yes, Lilah, *that* Kendrick Lopez. Him, I remember. I remember Kendrick Lopez."

#

"All different weather, we stick together.

In heat, cold, rain, or sun. Two different women

but so determined. To think, act, and be as one."

"Sun, surf, a beach in Belize. What do you say? I know Simon will authorize it," Nathan whispered in her ear, as he wrapped his arms around her waist.

They were alone in the lab, not that their pairing was a secret any longer. Abby still looked around before she hit save on the computer and let herself lean back into his embrace. In her wildest dreams, she couldn't have imagined a partner like Nathan. He was her complement in so many ways, her jigsaw half.

"The research . . ." Abby tried to protest, but Nathan was nuzzling that sensitive spot just under her ear.

"Is waiting for research subjects. We have weeks before the Board signs off."

They had presented to the Board last week, and while everyone was excited by the results, the human trial approvals had to go through medical and legal. The bureaucratic churn was especially challenging these days with the sensitivity towards Spacer tech. Abby was grateful that PR and lobbying were not in her job description.

Abby curled her arm around the back of Nathan's head and craned her neck to give him more access. "Belize sounds wonderful." And it did. It was a good time for a break. "And I can check on Bethany . . ." And just like that, the arms and the support were gone.

Abby bit her lip and turned around to face Nathan. Even frowning, he looked good to her. He recently surprised her with his buzz cut. His hair was so baby fine that in the station's lesser gravity, it seemed to dance in its own breeze. The team had nicknamed him Halo. Nathan, of course, saw it as a problem and took care of it. She missed the hair.

"You have to let it go, Abby. She's an adult, and it's her decision. She chose to live off the grid."

It was the only thing they disagreed about. Nathan Monroe was an only child; to him, family ties meant being home for Thanksgiving dinner and enduring the fussing and attention of his parents and grands. He didn't have the context to understand her and Bethany.

"She's my responsibility. I need to protect her. I need to know she's safe," Abby said. It was the same sentiment she always used. Safe, not happy or prosperous, but safe. She knew it was a holdover from their childhood, but how could she not feel this way?

"I'm not asking you to come. I'll go, and then I'll meet you in Belize." Abby moved slowly towards Nathan. He was doing his arm-crossing thing and she couldn't hug him like she wanted to. Instead, she leaned in and rested her head on his shoulder.

Abby felt him sigh, and then he wrapped his arms around her. "I just don't want to see you hurt. Going to that Earther fringe camp is not a good idea."

Abby didn't think it was either, but what choice did she have? At least there had been no recent anti-Spacer incidents lately. The PR might finally be turning things around. Simon and Raymond Chi hired the best, and the new messages touting how Spacer tech was enriching humanity and every Earther could become a Spacer seemed to be having an effect.

"I'll be monitored, and I will meet her in the halfway house."

NoTech, or NoT, might be extreme in their practices, but they couldn't recruit or proselytize if they didn't have some access to the outside. The halfway house served that purpose. It took almost six months of handwritten letters and care packages, but Abby finally got a letter back. She had three of them now, three short greetings that were at least polite.

"It's not just your physical safety." Nathan began to rock her gently from side to side as if they were dancing. "You're not rational about your sister. You're not you whenever she comes up."

It was true, of course. She, who created order out of the neural net, had a screw loose when it came to Bethany. "It's not about rational when it's someone you love," Abby whispered into Nathan's chest.

"Then add me to the irrationals." He kissed the top of her head. "I'll meet you in Belize at the end of the week. If you're not there, I'm coming to get you. You're my responsibility. I'll keep you safe."

Funny that Nathan would use the same word: safe.

When Abby walked in, she almost didn't recognize her sister. Bethany was sitting at the table with her face in profile to the door. She hadn't sent a written confirmation, so Abby wasn't sure if she would even show. The halfway house was the town's library and museum, so it was open to the public. Anyone could tour the facility, including a young woman who looked twice her age.

"Bethany." She was here in the same room. Physical, not digital.

Bethany was wearing a loose-fitting dress of some kind. Very out of step with the current fashion of WickWare. Bethany, who used to save her credits for the latest brands.

"Hi, Abby. You're looking good."

"Bethany." Abby wished she could say the same. It had been almost five years since they shared the same space. She was too thin, too fragile. Bethany looked more like their mother than the sister she remembered. She borrowed a move from Nathan and crossed her arms; otherwise, she would be tempted to grab Bethany and never let go.

Bethany gave her a small smile and looked away at the books lining the walls. Of the two of them, Bethany had always been more empathetic, better at reading moods. In the past, she would have said or done something to break the tension, including breaking into song. There'd be no harmonies today.

Abby had chosen a time with the least foot traffic, and in retrospect, that might not have been a good idea. The silence seemed to be a physical presence in the room. But with the conversational ball in her court, she had to try.

"It's really hot out." The controlled environment on the Bar was a sharp contrast to the heat, dust, and especially the wind. There was a smell to wind that VR didn't seem to get right.

"Really, Abby? That's the best you can do? Weather?" Bethany rolled her eyes. "Sure, let's talk about the weather. March in Minnesota and already topping the 30's. And what do you know? Mom was wrong again. God can't fix climate change."

Bitterness. She had tried so hard to keep it away from Bethany, but it was as if she had sponged it up from both her and their mother. The worst was not being able to forget the echo of that carefree sister. There was no expiration date for guilt.

"You don't have to stay here, Bethany. You can go back to school. I can get you a job on the Bar." Abby couldn't stop herself, even as she watched Bethany stiffen up.

"And be another Space Hog? Grabbing our resources to live it up?" Bethany was standing with her fist clenched by her side.

Just like that, her sister was replaced by the fanatic. Abby also realized something else. "You're pregnant."

"Six months." Bethany lifted her chin. It was their 'be brave' move. They used to brave up to see who could hold their chin higher. Abby wasn't sure if Bethany even knew she was doing it. A defense mechanism was now a mannerism.

"Do you have medical care?" Abby asked. She wanted to ask if she was getting enough to eat. NoT was one of the supposedly self-supporting and self-sufficient camps, but Bethany looked so thin.

"There's a perfectly good midwife at the camp. Women have been giving birth for millions of years, you know, without tech."

Even as she listened to Bethany talk about the camp and the life she had, Abby knew it was too late. Nathan was right. Bethany would never come to the Bar now. Still, she had to try.

"Why not come for a visit? Not for a job. You can finally meet Nathan, and you've always wanted to see space." If she could get Bethany on the Bar, she'd figure out a way to keep her there.

For a split second, Abby thought she had her. Bethany had raised her eyes to the skies even though they were indoors. Then she closed her eyes and shook her head.

"No. I'm staying on Earth where we're meant to be." Bethany opened her eyes, and Abby saw what looked like regret. "Besides, I got Kenny banned with the sweater. I can't abandon him now."

There was no expiration date for guilt.

#

"Those who know us,

know that nothing comes between us.

Many men want to split us up but no one can."

"Are you sure?" Nathan asked quietly, as he stroked her arm. Abby was lying back on the recliner with the neural net on.

"Yes, I'm sure. I'm positive." Abby was calm. She wasn't crying anymore. She was staring up at the ceiling, but realized that was too impersonal. She turned her head to look at her husband. "Take it all, Nathan." He would do it. He would fix it. He would keep her safe.

Nathan sighed. He looked sad. Why did he look sad? Was he sad for her? She was fine—or would be—as soon as he did it. Plus, it was practical and almost a tradition, scientists being their own guinea pigs.

Soon, it wouldn't hurt so much anymore. It would be like it never happened. No sister, no sister's boyfriend who led a violent protest, all those people killed. She had watched the coverage— they all had—the cameras had focused on Lopez as he screamed his defiance in front of the Barsoom office. For all his rhetoric about no tech, Lopez had a huge cache of the latest weapons and artillery. The police and security guards tried but lost control of the situation, and most of them lost their lives, along with Lopez and his followers.

Horrific as it was to watch, Abby had been relieved to not see Bethany among the crowd, until the images came in of the Earther camp. The women and children, the elderly who were not expected to fight, they all looked like they were sleeping. Bethany even had a bit of a smile on her face. She was stretched out on the bed, curled protectively around her son—just a year old and a nephew that Abby would never meet.

Poison, they said—self-inflicted and fast acting. Well, Abby would act too, or this would eat away what was left of her soul.

This also proved her commitment to her work, her, their career, their breakthrough. It was delicate work, but Nathan could do it. He was good with data. She trusted him to keep her safe.

"I really think you should wait a few months. We can refine the process in the meantime." Nathan was standing by the workstation, but not doing anything.

"No, now. Do it now."

Why was he hesitating? They talked about this. She had cried enough tears, and she didn't want anymore therapy sessions or grief counseling. This was much easier and faster. He agreed. He said he would.

Nathan finally nodded and started working. Abby heard the taps and clicks and felt herself drift. Of course, once Nathan was done, she would have to do some work, too. She misspoke earlier. Nathan wasn't really taking it all. He would bury it, disconnect it, so Bethany would be there but not accessible. Abby wouldn't relive the sight of the sleeping bodies, the nephew she would never know.

The program was ready. She just had to hit the button. Abby had a calendar reminder to do it after she woke up. She had skills. She was in control of the neural net. She wouldn't just disconnect, she would excise. She would replace, reshape things a bit. And it would work out just fine. Nathan wouldn't have those memories, so he wouldn't be able to talk about it—talk, talk, talk—as if that would fix anything. No, her way was better. Nathan would keep her safe and not even know it.

No memories, no guilt—there was an expiration date after all.

#

"That was the last one," Lilah said breaking the silence. It had been a few minutes, and Nathan was still lying back on the chair. He had his arm over his eyes, and the SimNet was still on his head.

"Memory tampering without consent is a crime, Nathan." Lilah had to say it. Much as she was sympathetic, she also had to obey the law.

"I would have consented," Nathan said, without changing his pose. "I could never keep secrets from my wife. I would have consented."

Lilah nodded. She was sure Nathan would have consented, too. The last reveal was quite clear and matched the timeline of the Monroe-Song breakthrough research. "But it's not your consent that's the question, is it?"

At that, Nathan dropped his arm and sat up. He took off his SimNet and began playing with it, stretching the connectors and tangling the wires. "She would have given us time, at least a week after her wipe, so I could log observations, effects. Abigail was like that, very strict with the work.

"It is fundamentally impossible to get memory reprogramming to work on more than one person. It was why Simon, the Board, and we were able to get the legal and medical approvals, to develop the therapeutics and the memic technology. We proved that we can retrieve, and there was no possibility of mass mind control."

"But targeted memory reprogramming. You found the program before Abigail activated it and used it as a template. You retargeted. You had to because you weren't the only one who knew about and could talk about Bethany." Lilah considered how many people that must have been. Dana Tyler for sure, Simon Chi most likely, and all of their close friends and acquaintances.

"Did I?" Nathan shrugged. "I really don't remember." He put down the SimNet, then looked up into the camera. Lilah thought he looked at peace, not as intense as he was before.

"Abby is the genius, you know. She was the one with the creative ideas. I played my part. I took care of the details."

Nathan Monroe paused, then smiled. "She's my responsibility, and I kept her safe."

"Lord help the mister who comes between
me and my sister. And please help my sister
who comes between me and my man."

You Are Music

Steven L. Rosenhaus

I often ask my music composition students "what would happen if . . .?" when they reach a blocking point in their work. One day, I was reading a science magazine article about the imprecision of notating genetic coding and asked myself what would happen if you used music notation instead. The next thing I knew, there was this . . .

Wednesday morning, Charles Goddart was in his office at You Are Music, Inc., talking on the phone with his wife Evelyn.

"But you feel better now?" he asked. She reassured him.

"Okay, take it easy . . . Right, rehearsal tonight. Well, try. See you afterwards . . . Love you."

Charles Goddart was a respected, award-winning composer. He was as popular as a composer could be these days, which wasn't much. But contrary to artistic stereotype, Goddart applied business acumen to his career and created You Are Music, Inc. Irony being what it is, this made his name, if not a household word, at least one many recognized.

Working as You Are Music, Inc., Goddart composed musical portraits of the rich and famous based on their genomes, using Castagna coding. Previous methods described human genomes as numbers and colors, which worked until you tried to decipher them. Some 99 percent of human DNA is identical—humans share most of that with simians—but that last one or so percent makes the difference. Colors ranged from pale to saturated, but gave no specific information. Colors themselves presented difficulties too. Adjacent colors, like yellow and blue, might appear as a third color, green, throwing off the reading. Some were essentially shades of the same color; not everyone could discern the difference.

Castagna coding, developed in the mid-twenty-first century, used music notation to quantify and qualify genetic material. Pitch, rhythm, dynamics, and the rest could describe genomes in precise, but uniquely human, ways. It was only notation, but Goddart discovered how to use Castagna coding for musical expression; DNA became compositional elements. Charles was working on a musical sketch for a corporate CEO when someone knocked on the office door.

"Come in." The door opened and a pleasant but weary-looking man entered.

"Mister Goddart?" he asked. "My name is Stonecrop, Richard Stonecrop? I spoke with you last week. Sorry I don't have an appointment, but I was in the area and—"

"Come in, Mister Stonecrop," Charles interrupted. "Have a seat." He was exhausted. Indeed, Stonecrop almost fell into the proffered chair. Goddart watched him with concern. "Would you like something to drink? I've got orange juice, water . . . maybe something stronger?"

"Just water, thanks," Stonecrop replied. Goddart filled a cup from the cooler off to one side of the room. He walked back to his desk, handing the cup to Stonecrop. His guest sipped a little before placing the cup on the desk. Goddart looked him over discreetly. Stonecrop seemed younger than Goddart; it was hard to tell because the man looked so anguished, so depressed, so . . . drained. He knew why, of course, but it made him more sympathetic.

"You want to discuss something about your late wife," Goddart said.

"She died two weeks ago," Stonecrop confirmed. "I called last week and asked to meet with you."

"Again, my condolences, and apologies for not setting up an appointment then. Your timing is good though, and I appreciate your coming to speak with me." Stonecrop said nothing; lost in thought, he twisted the wedding ring on his left hand.

"We've always loved your music, Dawn and I," Stonecrop said at last. "We've heard a lot of it, downloaded what we could, heard your work on MaxNet and at concerts. When we learned about your portraits, we loved the idea, but we couldn't afford the fee, even before Dawn became ill." Stonecrop paused.

"Last month on MaxNet you mentioned doing portraits in a new way," Stonecrop resumed. "Dawn and I talked about it before she died and, well, that's why I'm here. We want—I want—you to create a portrait of Dawn."

"May I be blunt for a moment, Mr. Stonecrop?"

"Richard, please, and yes, go ahead."

"Okay, Richard," Charles said, testing the name. "Even with national health insurance paying for your wife's treatments, you've already said you can't afford to commission a work. What I'm now working on requires state-of-the-art equipment, and it's quite expensive. I don't see how—"

"Forgive me," Richard interrupted, "but before you say 'no'"— he pulled a memory tip from his pocket—"could you play this, please?" He handed the composer the tip.

Goddart inserted the tip, named for its resemblance to those sticks with cotton swabs on both ends, into the player. A three-dimensional matrix appeared in the air in front of the main screen, followed by the face and upper body of a lovely, but obviously ill, young woman in a hospital gown. She seemed about the same age as Stonecrop, perhaps younger.

"Mr. Goddart," said the woman. "My name's Dawn Stonecrop. If you're viewing this, it means I didn't survive my illness." The hologram stopped to take a glass of water from somewhere off camera. She sipped it, then returned it out of sight. "As Richard probably told you, we are fans of your music. Maybe 'fans' isn't the best word; 'appreciators' is more appropriate.

"Richard will ask you to compose my portrait. He will appeal to your better nature and the opportunity to do a good deed. Please allow a dying woman to speak more freely." Richard sat quietly, watching the image of his now-deceased wife. Charles couldn't imagine what it was like for the man. He and Evelyn had been married thirteen years, and he couldn't bear to think of losing her. Thankfully, they both were healthy.

"Your portraits usually celebrate a select few," the hologram continued. "Because of who they are, they tend to be similar, in personality at least. And I would guess they have much to say about how you write your music."

More than I'd like, Goddart thought.

Dawn's hologram continued. "I'd also guess you find it boring, not to mention constraining, to write. It must be like asking Beethoven to compose his Ninth Symphony many times over, with only a few changes. Richard and I have heard your works on MaxNet and some at live concerts." Dawn paused, weakened; the image flickered for a moment, indicating the camera had stopped recording. The image stabilized once more, and Dawn appeared a little stronger.

"Mr. Goddart, here's a chance to create something your way, without restrictions. I give you full access to my genome information, and permission to do whatever you want with it to create a musical work. Any instrumentation, any form, any duration. Your choice."

Stonecrop took another sip of water as he watched his late wife.

"Richard and I applied to all of the government sources for funds to commission you as soon as I got my diagnosis. Unfortunately, only two have come through, and those with little money. Perhaps it's enough to get you started, and you could raise the rest. We don't know what exactly, but we know from what we've learned that you're trying a new approach. You need to explore it with a willing subject. I ask that it be me."

The hologram finished; Goddart returned the tip to Stonecrop and turned off the player. He thought about what Dawn said as Richard Stonecrop gave him details of her illness. She seems— seemed—like an intelligent person. She certainly knew how to make her point. An opportunity to compose something my way, not some hackwork for a corporate entity that wouldn't know art if it bit its metaphorical bum. Then there was the human element. It was a tragic story. Dawn Stonecrop—still young—died of a genetic disorder for which there was no cure yet. It must have been devastating for Richard Stonecrop. I know I'd be devastated.

"Well, Mr. Goddart?" Stonecrop asked. Goddart decided he wanted—needed—to see this through. Business is business, but what good is music or any art if it can't help someone in some way? How often can a composer do this kind of good?

"Mr. Stonecrop . . . Richard," he corrected himself. "I believe I've found the subject for my next work. Let's discuss the details."

#

Charles called Evelyn after Stonecrop left and told her of the conversation.

"Anyway, that's why I agreed," he told her. "I'm tired of creating music for people who don't appreciate it. Besides, here's a chance to try the new concept."

"It's more than that, admit it. You're doing it because you're a caring human being. It's one of the reasons why I married you. You'd do this if you lost me, right?"

"Please don't say that, even hypothetically," Charles said. "I don't plan on losing you for a very long time. Besides, statistics show women still live longer than men."

"Don't worry, you can't get rid of me so easily."

"So you're okay?"

"Well, I wasn't feeling great, to be honest. A bit of stomach upset the last day or so, nothing drastic."

"The last day or so?" he asked.

"Probably a stomach virus. I'll see how I feel over the next few days. I have an appointment with Dr. Greenberger on Friday. I'll be fine."

#

Once, in a feature interview with Mackenzie Kincaid for MaxNet News, Charles Goddart spoke of his background.

"My parents assumed I'd be a scientist," he told her. "Mother was a geneticist and Father a microbiologist." In fact, the couple shared a Nobel Prize for work that saved thousands of people around the Mississippi Delta from a nasty virus. But Charles had inherited a love for music from his parents, as well as his mother's interest in genetics.

"My father played viola in an amateur string quartet," he recounted, "and Mother sang in our church choir. As a kid I'd sit in on choir rehearsals; later, as a teenager, I joined the tenor section." His parents introduced him to the music of Mozart, Haydn, Schubert, and others. Later, Charles would voraciously listen to all styles of music, anything he could find. By high school, he was playing cello and piano and making his first forays into composition.

But Charles was also practical and chose to follow his mother's career path. He did well in his studies—"I had decent grades and the family name," he told Kincaid—but his heart wasn't in it.

"I studied genetics at Columbia University, but also took private lessons in music theory and composition with various professors there. I considered switching majors, but decided to focus on genetics and make music in my downtime." After Columbia, Charles went to Harvard for a combined M.S./Ph.D. in advanced genetics. Just before graduating, he was given a research position back at Columbia.

"That's when I met Evelyn," he told Kincaid. "She was earning a doctorate in musicology and cello performance. I got to know her when she played my first cello suite." They married a year after she graduated. Columbia hired her immediately for a rare, full-time position and gave her tenure two years later. With tenure came financial security, and Charles could focus on composition. He was twenty-eight and she a year younger.

"I got my first big commission a year later," Goddart continued. "I wrote a song cycle to open the New Lincoln Center. The musicians enjoyed it, and the audience demanded an encore of the last movement." Kincaid, who covered the opening for MaxNet News, was impressed. She took to Goddart's music on first hearing, and recognized him as someone worth attention. With somebody of Kincaid's stature showing support, not to mention Goddart's genetics background acting as a newsworthy "hook," interest in the composer increased. Meanwhile, his genetics work led him to Castagna coding.

"I discovered Castagna coding's potential as musical source material," he told Kincaid. "I could use a person's coding, and my own composing skills, to create a literal 'organic' musical work." Goddart also realized there was money to be made. He created You Are Music, Inc. as a side venture at first. "The first portrait used DNA samples from my genetics mentor, Dr. Hanna Schlein, to honor her work," he explained. The music was well received, and You Are Music, Inc. took off. Charles, to his credit, still wanted to do something positive with his art and thought about how to accomplish this. The final pieces fell into place when Richard Stonecrop came to talk with him that Wednesday.

#

It took two weeks to get the paperwork done—Why call it paperwork when everything's done on MaxNet?—but he got enough seed money for the project. He met with Stonecrop to get information about Dawn, as well as her genetic samples. There were questions about her likes (most classical music; chocolate ice cream) and dislikes (beets; roller coasters), stories about how they met, dated, and more. Curious, Goddart asked how Richard and Dawn came to know his music.

"We met in college," Richard told him. "We lived together for a couple of years until we graduated and got married soon after. We're married—" he stopped. "We were married eight years, almost nine. For our first date, she suggested going to a New York Philharmonic concert. She loved classical music and I . . . well, let's just say she taught me a lot."

"So how did you and Dawn learn about my music?" Goddart asked.

"She was always open to new things," Richard replied, "and searching for something she hadn't heard before. Usually she'd find something on MaxNet; sometimes we would go to a concert. That's where we first learned about you." Richard smiled as he thought about the circumstances.

"It was two years ago. Dawn wanted something different, and the Philharmonic was premiering your work, *The Onus of Time*, at New Disney Hall. We got tickets, all the way upstairs, but the acoustics were good. I liked it a lot, but Dawn was completely enthralled. Ironic . . . it was the day after the concert that we learned she was dying."

#

As Charles filed the necessary forms, he also went about raising the balance of the money he needed. Fortunately, he was now well-known enough to get in the front door of major funding organizations. He also solicited some of You Are Music, Inc.'s more lucrative clients. In the end, Goddart raised enough money to set things in motion. He set the premiere for two months from his first meeting with Stonecrop. The goal was to run the work for two weeks to start, twelve hours a day.

Next up was finding a suitable space. After decades of public, private, and governmental neglect, the arts were finally on an upswing. Somewhere, there are doctoral dissertations on the turn-around and how it came about, but "serious" visual and musical arts were making a comeback.

In New York City, "serious" events gravitated to Midtown, now anchored by the new Disney Hall East on Broadway and 42nd Street and the New Lincoln Center just up the block. When the original Lincoln Center shuttered its doors and opened a new complex in Times Square, the arts had not one but two Midtown areas in which to thrive.

The project doesn't need a huge hall, Goddart wrote in funding applications. *It needs an intimate setting, where small groups of people can interact with the work.* Disney Hall East was too big. New Lincoln Center was out, too. All of the spaces, down to the smallest, were booked a year in advance.

Goddart eventually leased two adjoining rooms on the fifth floor of what had once been a vaudeville-era theater. One room would be the performance space, while the other would be the processing room for computers and other equipment. The lease was finalized and the equipment ordered. Goddart made arrangements to give Stonecrop a tour of the space during the installation, starting with the processing room, once the equipment was delivered.

"We need a strictly digital environment," Charles told him. "I leased five new Quintel laptops, all plexed together. They're governed by a redundant, closed system of five additional Quints set up the same way." Goddart pointed to two racks holding the laptops, the backup equipment, and several wireless routers.

"The backup drives and processors will be hard-wired together, but connected wirelessly to everything else," he told Stonecrop. "In turn, everything will be routed to my own laptop in the performance room. I'll use it as the main controller. Come, let me show you the performance space."

Charles continued the tour, avoiding overly technical explanations. There were holographic emitters in every corner of the space, with additional ones evenly spaced horizontally and vertically, as well as the latest audio reproduction equipment. Miniature cameras, holosensors, and sensitive directional microphones were embedded flush with the walls and ceiling, the microphones acoustically tuned and phased to ignore the speakers.

The room was painted a glossy white over sensor-transparent walls. The windows were layered with acoustic dampeners and boarded up with transparent aluminum for sunlight, with blackout drapes to block the light once the work was turned on. The doors to the processing room and the hallway were similarly treated, and the brass doorknobs were replaced with white antistatic plastic ones to make sure they didn't interfere with holoemitters or motion sensors.

"It's sort of sterile looking," Stonecrop said. Goddart nodded.

"I suppose so," he answered, "but we needed to maximize the clarity of the holoemitter image." With the windows covered over, light came only from mid-twentieth century ceiling fixtures retrofitted with modern lighting elements. "The lights can be controlled using the wall switches by the door, but I had wireless controls installed, so they can be run by the software or by me at the laptop."

In the center of the room was an old-fashioned wooden table left by the previous tenant—maybe the first one—rectangular in shape and aligned with the room's dimensions. At one end was Goddart's laptop. In tight formation on either side of the table set about halfway between it and the walls were two lines of five chairs each. Two chairs were set at either end; one was for Goddart, who would sit at the controller end. The last chair would remain empty.

Out of place were a tiny video camera and microphone positioned in one corner at the ceiling, not set flush into the walls. They were focused to capture most of the room; the feed went directly to a monitor in the processing room, so that Keith—Goddart's friend and first-call engineer—could observe and make adjustments on the fly.

It took another week to install the remaining equipment. Technicians came and went. Computer programmers installed and tested software. Talk at the Goddart dinner table, when Charles wasn't working late, was of the day-to-day frustrations of the undertaking. Meanwhile, Evelyn's followup visit to Dr. Greenberger went well. Charles noticed she was distracted occasionally since, but she insisted nothing was wrong. If he brought it up, she would change the subject. She was supportive and listened as he vented; sometimes she made suggestions.

All was ready a week before the premiere. Stonecrop took a leave of absence from his job at the New York Public Library so he could come in to interact with the work and check the veracity of its Dawn simulation. Of the technical crew, only Keith was left to run things in the processing room. Goddart, in the performance space, left the door open to allow easier communication with Keith. Charles sat down at his laptop.

#

"We won't run the full program," Goddart explained. He keyed in instructions as he spoke. "We're going to put it through its paces, testing components as we go." First, he tested the sound production without engaging the artificial intelligence and holoemitters.

He started with a simple sine wave swept from 20 Hz, the lowest note humans can hear, to the upper reaches of 20,000 MHz. Then he started layering in additional tones.

"Ow!" Stonecrop cried, as he covered his ears. "What was that?"

"Sorry," Goddart said. He turned a dial down. "Few people perceive pitch past 20,000 MHz, and even then not many adults . . . Frankly, I forgot folks who perceive it feel it more than hear it."

"Oh, I felt it," Stonecrop said, rubbing his ear. "It's like having my teeth drilled without anesthetic. Why do you need sound so high anyway?"

"Well," Goddart replied, "every instrument produces a blend of a basic note, the fundamental, and a series of partials. Some instruments emphasize even partials, some odd; some louder, some softer. They all shape the sound of an instrument. I was testing the range and flexibility of the oscillators; I want the music rooted in the sound of traditional instruments."

He called to his friend in the next room, "I want to test the emitters now, Keith."

"Okay," Keith replied. "Everything is on standby."

"Good. Running Sequence One." Goddart keyed in a command. The room lights dimmed. The emitters, until now unnoticed, began to glow softly. A spotlight appeared on the center of the table, followed by the gradual appearance of a bowl of fruit. It looked three-dimensional, but not quite real.

"How's it looking?" Keith called out.

"Neat," Stonecrop said. Goddart gave him a quick grin and turned back to his laptop. The bowl of fruit and the spotlight disappeared.

"Keith, I need more cohesion from the emitters," Goddart

called out. "We still have that transparency issue."

"Still? All right, let me boost the filter parameters." There was a short pause. "Try it now." Goddart rekeyed the sequence and the spotlight returned, as did the bowl of fruit. Stonecrop couldn't restrain himself.

"Wow," he exclaimed. "That's amazing. It looks real now!"

"I guess we got it, huh?" Keith called from the other room, laughing.

"Yes, we did," Goddart agreed. He turned to Stonecrop. "It's the latest holotechnology. We didn't invent it, but Keith and I have been making improvements." Keith, his long brown hair apparently blocking his vision, came into the room to check out the virtual still life on the table.

"Cool beans," Keith said. "Okay, are we ready for Sequence Two?" Goddart nodded, and Keith went back to his station.

"All set here," Keith said after a moment. Turning to Stonecrop, Goddart asked, "What's your pleasure, Richard? Mozart? Brahms? We're going to fit an orchestra in here." Stonecrop gave Charles a quizzical look.

"How about Bartók?" he asked. Goddart nodded.

"Much better than my corporate clients. Okay, Bela Bartók it is. How about his *Concerto for Orchestra*?" Charles called up a file and keyed in commands. The image of the bowl of fruit winked out, replaced by the sound of basses and cellos on one side of the room playing the rising fourths that open the Bartók masterwork. Then the flutes played wispy lines that evaporated as they went. Richard listened intently. With his eyes closed, Charles had the best seat in the world's best concert hall. The sound was glorious yet intimate, as if the musicians were not only living, breathing, and playing, but doing so *right there* in front of him. Goddart was pleased. He could almost feel the scrape of rosined bows against strings, the impact of beaters on timpani, and the rushes of air emanating from the virtual brass and winds. He let the music play a bit more, then shut it down.

"That was . . . incredible," Stonecrop said. "What a great performance. And it's the best fidelity I have ever heard. It sounds better than being on the stage."

"Not better," Goddart admitted, "but close enough to the real thing as to make no difference."

"So which orchestra was playing? Cleveland? New York Phil?"

"Funny you should ask. That wasn't a recording; it was a digital orchestra playing the score."

"You mean like a sequencer?" Stonecrop asked. "That's not new at all. *Nothing* like this."

"You're right. It's my own proprietary software and specially designed hardware, thanks to Keith over there; it goes beyond the old samplers and additive synthesis. It's not a program that simply changes bits of data into sound chunks; it's a new way of creating music."

"Well, I don't understand most of what you said, but I like the results. I wonder what other musicians think about this?"

"They would hate it," Goddart replied. "I hate it myself, and I helped create it. For years, musicians have fought technological advances in music. They say no machine or computer program or whatever could play with 'feeling.' It would put them out of work. Imagine how they'd react if they learned we've got something that can play with emotional content, and could put them out of work?"

"Well, they would—" Stonecrop started to say. "Wait, did you just say 'how they *would* react'? They don't know?"

"I'm a musician too, you know," Goddart replied. "I don't want to put *anybody* out of work. It's bad enough I work with computer programs that do some composing. For now, I can't be put out of work because they need someone musically knowledgeable to program this stuff, but the possibility's always there. Why should I deny anyone else the opportunity to make a living making music?"

"So how . . .?"

"The trick is offering a limited program, so it's just another tool for musicians. Remember Pro Tools back in the last century? No, probably not, you're not a musician. It was a recording technology. Helped musicians who wanted to record at little cost beyond the initial investment. Think of this the same way." Goddart, talked out, readied for the final testing phase.

"Okay, Keith, Sequence Three." There was a pause, and the room went dark. A new spotlight focused on the chair at the end of the table, near where Stonecrop was sitting. Some sounds wafted through the room, vague but musical, but Stonecrop's attention was on the human figure that formed sitting on the chair nearby.

"Oh my God," he said softly.

The effect was extraordinary. The holoemitters gave the image an ethereal glow, but otherwise there sat Richard's recently departed wife. Dawn sat perfectly still, awaiting input. Richard too didn't move, but his eyes drank in the sight before him the way a man in a desert needs water. "Oh my God," Richard repeated.

This time Dawn slowly reacted. She turned at the sound of Richard's voice to face him, and when she saw his face, she smiled. Richard didn't move at all—Dawn was far more animated—but a tear rolled down his cheek. He reached out to touch the image of the woman he loved with all his heart.

"Don't do that," Goddart warned, an instant too late. Richard's hand, instead of finding a warm, human hand to hold, found . . . nothing but a pins-and-needles feeling. The image disrupted as his hand passed through the holoemitters beams. There was a brief flash, a soft popping sound, and "Dawn" disappeared. Seconds passed—to Stonecrop much longer—until Goddart reset the program.

"—the hell?" Keith yelled from the other room.

"What do *you* think?" Charles yelled. Keith went on, cursing as he reset things on his end. Charles allowed himself a small smile; he was pleased with Stonecrop's reaction. He had gotten Dawn right.

Charles made more adjustments. Then he got up from the table and walked into the processing room, taking his laptop with him. Stonecrop followed him, closing the door at Goddart's request. After resetting things, Charles keyed in commands and brought Dawn back, sitting in position in the other room, unmoving. The three were engaged in conversation when a flash lit the main room. But with no one there, the door closed, and no one watching the video monitor, the flash and a whiff of ozone went unnoticed.

"I'll recalibrate the filters tomorrow morning," Keith was saying. "You'll be able to touch her, lightly, without disrupting the image. It'll be . . . tingly. It won't be like touching flesh. That comes in version 2.0." Keith gave a little "heh heh" at his own joke, but Stonecrop didn't get it.

"You'll be able to do that?" he asked earnestly.

"Don't tease, Keith," Goddart said. He turned to Stonecrop. "We're nowhere near it. We were lucky to get this far." He clasped a hand on Stonecrop's shoulder, but turned back to Keith.

"Let's shut down for the night," Goddart said to Keith. "I can use dinner and a beer. Come on, Richard, my treat."

#

Day One. Goddart's new work premiered on schedule. With the advance publicity on MaxNet News thanks to Mackenzie Kincaid, he negotiated solid publishing rights, as well as a full broadcast on *MaxNet Arts Today* at a later date. Goddart also got a handshake deal to take *Dawn* on a six-month, five-city tour. Topping it off, You Are Music, Inc. now had a waiting list long enough to keep Goddart busy for the next five years.

The performance space wasn't small, but twenty-one people filled it. Goddart sat at one end of the table; Richard sat in a chair at a corner on the opposite end of the table from Goddart. The empty chair next to Richard, directly opposite Goddart, would be "Dawn's." Evelyn was there too; she sat next to Richard, as sitting next to her husband at premieres tended to make them both nervous.

Some investors, a few music critics, and Mackenzie Kincaid occupied the remaining seats. As everyone settled around the table, Goddart looked over at Evelyn. She smiled and silently mouthed *good luck*; he smiled back. He turned to look at the audience, then cleared his throat to quiet the chatter. He welcomed everyone and described what the audience would experience.

"*Dawn* is named," he said, "not only for Mr. Stonecrop's late wife, but also for the nature of the work. This will be completely interactive music, not having preprogrammed phrases or algorithms responding to external stimuli, but more like having a conversation. The music you'll hear will be composed by my programming, based on Dawn Stonecrop's DNA. But it will be affected by how you, the audience, interact with it." He pressed a key. The lights dimmed, save for a circle of intense white light around the empty chair next to Richard. The music began.

There was a soft swirl of sound at first, nothing discernable beyond *something music-like.* It was like an orchestra tuning up, heard from a distant, reverberant space. Then a low tone entered, like the fundamental of a chord yet to be played. It sounded like a cello blended with a French horn. The light began to shimmer and sparkle. Colors swirled, coalesced, and gradually intensified into a human form. The music, coordinated with the action, behaved similarly, swelling in volume as harmonics were brought in.

The volume rose imperceptibly, everywhere except near the chair at the end of the table, as the image of a beautiful woman, Dawn, came into view. The image suddenly snapped into focus; there she sat at the twenty-second seat in the room. A chord sounded, major with major sevenths, ninths, and higher partials that gave the music an edge of melancholy. The image of Dawn looked around the room, searching, until her eyes found Richard's. The audience was mesmerized.

"Hello, love," the hologram said. The voice seemed to emanate from everywhere at first, but it quickly localized; now it came from Dawn herself. "I missed you."

#

"That was the best thing you've ever done, Charles," Evelyn said later, when they were in bed. "The music is beautiful, but then everything you write is gorgeous."

"You say that because you're married to me," Goddart teased.

"Of course, but it's true."

"You think it went well?" he asked. With the premiere over his anxieties emerged. "I think it went all right, but did the critics like it? It's hard to tell with some of them. There was one guy—"

"You worry too much," she interrupted him. "You know the press will say whatever it wants regardless of the reality. But Mackenzie Kincaid was crying. I had to give her tissues. That's good, isn't it?" It was. He was thinking about the performance when he realized Evelyn said something.

"I'm sorry, what did you say?" he asked. She smiled and touched him in a way guaranteed to get his attention.

"You heard me." She smiled; he smiled too as he turned off the light. They both slept well that night.

#

Day Three. Dawn was running twelve hours a day. Audiences were kept to nineteen at a time for one hour each. Still, people came and went; it was more like an event than a concert. Goddart and Keith took turns running the program. Richard rarely left Dawn's side, and even then never for more than thirty, forty-five minutes.

"Music is the essence of the human condition," Goddart said in an interview once. "We wake up, eat meals, do all the things that make us *human.* Most importantly, we communicate with each other on a deep level. Music is what separates us from other life forms."

Anyone could talk with Dawn and have her respond thanks to the capacious memory modules and elaborate artificial intelligence programming working in the next room. The music was an outgrowth of those conversations. Richard spoke with her the most, and when he didn't, he would sit and watch her from a few feet away. Dawn would talk with audience members while snatching glances his way and smiling.

Audiences were more interested in the music than with the interactive elements, which was fine with Goddart. That left Richard free to have more frequent interaction with the simulacrum. Goddart was pleased that people focused on the music. He felt uneasy about Richard's attention to the holoimage, though.

The music was worth attention. It evolved with the conversations; tonality would expand into gray areas explored by Debussy, Wagner or, later, Perle. Sometimes sinuous rhythms made you want to move, if not dance outright. Other times, musical themes developed beautifully, to the point of tears. Melodies would climb, fall back, climb again; harmonies would start simply, become more complex and more dissonant, and then reverse. Sometimes the music was tonal and other times there was the wandering aspects of atonality. Occasionally, it seemed to be played by traditional instruments—a flute, a cello—but just as often, a fresh sound was heard; a breathy viola, or a bowed clarinet, or maybe a hammered square wave.

Even with little publicity after the initial reviews—*all good, thank goodness*—ticket sales were excellent. Goddart could run *Dawn* for a long time, six months or more judging by the requests coming in. He could pay the corporate backers easily.

Richard became an integral part of the performance, and Goddart made arrangements for him to receive portions of the performance royalties and admission sales above their original agreement. Richard seemed happiest when speaking with Dawn, and she responded in kind. Dawn had no memories of a life with Richard other than what Goddart programmed. Richard filled in the gaps.

"Tell me again how we met," Dawn said at one point.

"Why?" he asked. "Don't you remember everything you hear?"

"Yes, of course, love. I just like the way you tell it." Charles, meanwhile, sat mutely at his laptop, making adjustments as the music evolved. But he listened to the conversation before him, too.

"Tell me about my habits," Dawn later said, "and tell me about yours, too." Richard told her of Dawn's tendency to steal the blankets at night, only to throw them off when she became too warm to sleep comfortably and leave them both to feel the night chill. He admitted to his habit of turning off lights as he left a room, even when Dawn was still there. Dawn's idiosyncrasies became incorporated into Dawn's programming, while his were filed into memory. Meanwhile, the connection between them grew.

#

Day Five. Dawn had been running all morning, and Richard and Dawn spent it talking. Attendees came, listened to the conversation for a while, then concentrated on the music. By lunchtime, it was just Richard, Charles, and the holoimage; Keith had gone out for a cup of coffee. Richard left to grab a quick tasteless meal downstairs at some fast food place and met Keith coming out of the elevator as he was going downstairs. Richard came back thirty minutes later to find a lingering odor of ozone in the air, Goddart looking preoccupied, and *Dawn* not running.

"There was a power surge while you were out," Goddart said as he checked his laptop. "Nothing was affected. The power supplies kicked in, and we were already running backups when the surge hit. To be sure, I'll run diagnostics overnight." Goddart, satisfied things would soon be in working order, rebooted the controller program. As before, a swirl of lights coalesced into Dawn's image and, as before, Richard sat down next to her. As they spoke, the music once again took flight.

A couple came in, clearly married a long time. Like others before them, once the novelty of the holoimage wore off, they ignored it and focused on the music. Charles, tired of sitting, went into the processing room to confer with Keith. Only Richard noticed when his late wife's *doppelganger* light-created coloring paled. It wasn't extreme, but it was enough. The similarities were too great to ignore.

"Charles?" he called out. "Come in here, please?" He nervously explained what he had seen. "Dawn is sick. Like my Dawn." Charles looked at the holoimage and realized Richard wasn't exaggerating. Something was wrong.

"I'll look into it tonight when we run the diagnostic," he said. "It's probably nothing." Still, he wondered. The married couple stayed a bit longer and then left, leaving Stonecrop and Goddart alone with Dawn in the room. Listening to the music, Goddart realized harmonies were more dissonant than before, more frequent, and taking longer to resolve. *What is going on?*

#

Goddart spent most of the night in the rooms overlooking Times Square working. At eight p.m., he called to tell Evelyn of his progress; she wasn't happy about it, but understood.

"It's okay, I've got papers to grade. I'll have peanut butter on whole wheat . . ."

"And glass of wine," Charles said, finishing her thought.

"Merlot would be nice, but I'm grading papers." Off the phone, Goddart walked back into the performance room and stood near Dawn.

"Dawn," he said to the holoimage. "I need to ask you some questions." The image nodded. "But first I'll turn off the music output." Goddart walked over to the laptop and muted the music. Then he said, "Dawn, please count from one to twenty-five, or until I tell you to stop." The image formed the numbers, but Goddart could hear nothing at first. He keyed in another sequence.

"—leven, twelve . . ." Goddart stopped her. He asked the holoimage about any abnormalities she could detect. What she described was expected, but there were a few minor oddities.

Testing and recalibration went on throughout the night, Goddart losing track of time. Hungry, he went into the processing room and found Keith's stash of energy bars. He opened one and took a bite. *How does he eat this stuff?* Hunger got the better of him though, and he ate the bar in a few bites. Tired but not as hungry, Goddart returned to work. By four a.m., Charles had examined and tweaked everything thoroughly. An hour later, he still wasn't satisfied. Something was wrong. Back in the processing room, he phoned Stonecrop. Richard answered after the fourth ring.

"Hello? Who's this?"

"It's me, Charles. Listen, I'd like . . ."

"What's the mat—? It's about Dawn, right?"

"Yes, I need to ask you," Goddart replied. "May I have permission to look at your wife's medical records?"

"No, sorry, Charles, I can't allow it. It's difficult enough—"

"I know," Goddart interrupted, "but I think the answer is in her records."

"It's an invasion of her privacy," Stonecrop countered. "Do you have to look at her *entire* file?" Goddart went silent, thinking.

"No, I don't. Maybe I missed something in the coding." He

paused again and jotted down some notes. "Sorry I woke you, but you've been helpful. Thanks. See you later?"

"Sure," Stonecrop said. Both men hung up. Charles knew he hadn't woken Richard; Stonecrop admitted sleeping fitfully these days. Charles set an alarm on the laptop and took a nap across a couple of chairs.

When Richard came in later that morning, Charles was awake and *Dawn* was running. The music was more dissonant; harmonies were taking longer to resolve, like Bruckner's symphonies. Dawn seemed fatigued, if a holoimage could tire. When Richard mentioned it, she made light of it.

"Well, Charles kept me up all night," she told Richard. "Poking and prodding—and no, I didn't feel anything—but asking me questions all of the time. He's nice, but it would have been nice to get some rest." At that, Stonecrop stood up, angered. Dawn watched him as he walked over to Goddart.

"Richard?" Dawn asked, but he focused on Goddart.

"You S.O.B.," he said through gritted teeth. "How did you get her to say that?"

"What do you mean?" Goddart said, taken aback. "I didn't do anything. She's behaving according to her AI programming, her voice samples, and the DNA sample you supplied. She's reacting to you, Richard; anything she says is purely programming and supplied information."

"Well, Dawn just said things my wife told me about a week before she died, almost word for word," Richard said. "'Poking and prodding,' and 'no, I didn't feel anything—but asking me questions all of the time,' and 'it would have been nice to get some rest.' How the hell did she know what to say?"

"I don't know, Richard," Goddart replied honestly.

The two were silent as the music played. Then Charles heard it. A few notes, really, a motif. It was distinctive to Goddart's ears; it was more angular in shape, dropping a minor second and then making small leaps up two consecutive major thirds. *That's it. It's what I've been looking for.* The new motif began asserting itself as the first audience members of the day arrived.

#

Evening of Day Seven. Dawn was off for the night; Keith was in the processing room, eating a slice of pizza while running the backups. Goddart and Stonecrop sat at the table in the other room. Both were exhausted.

"It's a flaw in her DNA," Charles said. "It flies by in the music; it's an alteration of the main theme. Musically, it makes it more interesting. I didn't think about it earlier." He sipped from his now-cold coffee. "I contacted your wife's doctor, sent him her report in both Castagna notation and the colors and numbers format. He confirmed it. It's the same genetic flaw that killed your wife."

It took a while for Richard to react. "Can we do anything?"

"I'm working on it. Dawn's doctor is sending me an experimental DNA resequencing program. Maybe I can adapt it to Dawn's specifications. If we can catch it in time"—Richard flinched—"we can save her programming. For now, we have to shut it down until we get this straightened out."

That night, Goddart lay next to Evelyn in bed, wide awake. He assumed Evelyn was asleep.

"Will she be okay?" Evelyn asked.

Goddart thought. "I don't know. If I can get the resequencing going, we can save the programming. But I don't know if we can save her."

"Save *her?*"

"*Dawn* is the most intricate work I've—heck, it's the most intricate work anyone has ever done. There are always unknown variables . . . How can I put this? She's not just an interactive musical work any more. Dawn has a personality."

"You mean she's alive?"

"Not physically, but she's developed behaviors that, at least to Richard, are the same as his late wife's. She responds to him as if she is his wife. He treats her as if she is, and I find I'm doing it, too. Have you noticed you and I refer to Dawn as she? She's . . ." He stopped mid-sentence.

"I think she's virtually alive," he said finally. "And making things worse for Richard, Dawn is dying, effectively the same way his wife did."

"Oh my God. You're trying to save Dawn herself. Oh, Charles." She put her head on his chest and her arm across his body. "Poor Richard. Having to go through his wife's death and now this, is a . . . a horror. I don't know if I could go through it."

"Neither do I," Goddart agreed. "That's why I'm trying to fix it. Under other circumstances I would shut down the project or get a new subject. I can't do it now; it's too important to Richard. To me."

Evelyn gave Charles a funny look, then she hugged him. "I'm glad," she said. "I couldn't respect you if you reacted any other way." She thought for a moment. "You like Richard, don't you?"

"I do. He's a decent guy. Should we have him over for dinner?"

"Good idea, but you cook. I can't stand the kitchen lately."

Evelyn turned inward, lost in thought.

"Hey, you okay?" Charles asked.

Pulled out of her reverie, she looked at him and smiled. "I love you."

"I love you, too," he replied, "but it doesn't answer my question. You okay?"

"Better than okay. I didn't tell you before because you've been working on Dawn, but you need to know this now."

#

Day Eleven. Only Charles, Richard, Keith, and Dawn occupied the performance space the last few days. Ticket buyers were told the show was down due to technical difficulties. Those who had purchased them could choose between rain checks or getting their money back; most chose to see *Dawn* another time.

Dawn was deteriorating, not as a computer image would, but the way the real Dawn looked in the first video Goddart watched. Her image, even made of light, seemed pale; her eyes had a slightly glazed look, the skin under them dark. The three-dimensional holoimage itself was strong, but it was showing an increasingly ailing—no, dying—woman.

Richard never went home; he took to sleeping on chairs near Dawn—despite her pleas to take better care of himself and Goddart's frustrated insistence. At last, the resequencing program arrived; Goddart downloaded it into Dawn's programming, but waited to initiate it.

The four-note figure Goddart noticed days earlier was now pervasive; the music was increasingly dissonant, the rhythms more unpredictable. The original *Dawn* music, the essence of light and love in musical terms, strained to be heard. Goddart had done what he could to this point, but with the new programming in hand, there was only one course of action left.

"Go home, Richard," Goddart said. "I have to run the resequencing with the holoemitters off and the other components focused on processing the programming."

"I want to stay," Richard demanded.

"You can't," Goddart answered. "You won't be able to help, for one thing, and I need you alert for the testing later."

"I can't leave her."

"There is no her, Richard. She's a holoimage." But Richard didn't, or didn't want to, hear him.

"But it's Dawn," Richard cried.

"No, Richard, it's not Dawn," Goddart said, louder this time. From the other side of the room, the object of discussion interjected.

"Richard, please, do as he says," Dawn urged him. "I'll be okay until you get back, I promise."

"I don't want to lose you again," he said, walking over to her. "I'm not sure I could stand it. I couldn't stand it the first time, I—"

"You can't lose me again, Richard, because I'm not real. Remember?"

It was said quietly and gently, but it hit Richard hard. He looked at the holoimage in astonishment, then in realization, and finally in resignation.

"I understand," she continued, "more than you know and maybe more than I should. Now hush. Go home, have a shower, and eat something healthy. Then sleep. Charles will call you as soon as he's done . . . Isn't that right, Charles?"

Goddart stuttered a bit. "Yeah, um, sure."

"Go. I'll be okay." Richard left slowly, reluctantly. The door closed with a click.

"Now then, before you turn me off," Dawn said to Goddart, "may we talk?"

#

Day 13. Charles called Richard with his progress on resequencing Dawn's DNA. Today, Goddart would reinitialize the *Dawn* programming again, he told Richard. The process would affect her music, but it would allow the holoimage to live. Richard arrived early; Charles and Keith were already working. Dawn was online, looking to Richard like his wife did hours before she died. It broke his heart all over again, even though Goddart reminded him that this Dawn was not real. He sat down in the chair next to the holoimage.

"Okay," Goddart said quietly, "here we go." He keyed in commands as Keith kept watch in the processing room. Richard alternated between watching Goddart work and looking for signs of improvement in Dawn's condition. Soon the hologram called for Richard, and he moved closer to her to listen.

"You've told me a lot about the real Dawn," she said. "She was a wonderful person who loved you very much. I am not her, Richard. I never could be. All I can be is someone, no, *something* that reminds you of her, and how much you loved her—"

"I still love her," Richard interrupted, looking into Dawn's eyes. "I will always love her." Dawn nodded.

"How much you loved her, and always will. That's the point, isn't it? You will always love *her*. Wouldn't you rather cherish her memory instead of something you can look at but can't touch, something you can talk to but never truly love?" Dawn fell silent;

that's when Richard noticed: the music.

It was soft, barely at the threshold of human hearing. It sounded like muted strings at first, with Dawn's theme struggling for dominance over dissonant harmony and the incessant unwanted motif. What caught Richard's attention was a single note, in what Goddart called the tenor range. It sounded repeatedly, like a horn call, the main melody swirling around it. Dissonant harmonies reacted as if they wanted to fight it, but the repeated note began winning. One by one, dissonances resolved, motifs became less angular. The music became more tonal. The original theme—Dawn's theme—was returning.

For the first time in days, the lights creating her appearance took on a warmer glow. The difference was tiny, but perceptible to the two men waiting for, hoping for, praying for, any change at all. The music, meanwhile, increased in intensity as it decreased in dissonance.

Dawn's image changed. Bits went translucent or disappeared altogether, then reappeared. The image became pixelated in spots and then cleared up. Waves of color—first red, then orange, then green—washed over her next. The image slowly took on its original solidity; Dawn was coming back to virtual health.

"Is it working?" Richard asked. Charles didn't answer; he was listening to the music. He heard a cadence approaching, a big, old-fashioned dominant-to-tonic chord motion that was as predictable as it was welcome. Dawn looked increasingly better.

"Richard," she said. "I think it's working." The cadence played out, the final chord a major triad with all the added major ninths, sevenths, and elevenths adding tone colors that had been Dawn from the beginning. The room itself brightened. For one moment—

a second? an hour?—the room took on not only a physical vividness, but an emotional glow of optimism from Goddart, Stonecrop, and even Dawn herself.

Then everything stopped.

All the lights in both rooms went out simultaneously, taking everything—the holoemitters, the computers—with them. Keith cursed from the processing room. Dawn was gone.

#

Day 13, continued.

"What happened?" Richard yelled. Goddart didn't respond. He was trying to answer that question as he fumbled in the pitch black of the shuttered room. "Charles?"

"Working on it," Goddart replied. "Keith," he called to the next room, "what do you have?" Keith yelled back, "Try it now!" and Goddart pressed a button. There was a click, and the main lights came back on as suddenly as they had gone out. "See," he said, "it'll be fine. Please be patient." The components animating Dawn clicked on one by one, too slowly for Stonecrop's taste.

Then a soft swirl of sound that seemed like music, but wasn't yet, returned. It coalesced into musical motifs, then themes. The aberrant motif was gone. When a full-blown melody began— Dawn's main theme—the holoemitters kicked in and light once again focused on the chair at the end of the table.

"You're back," Richard said to Dawn. She looked better than before, better than the first time her programming was initiated. The image was sharp, colors precise, and Dawn once again looked like a healthy human being.

"Yes, I am here," Dawn replied, turning slowly to face Richard. Her voice was the same—the pitch, the timbre, the cadence. But there was a difference, a . . . what? Distance? Even in those few words, she responded not as Dawn would have before this turn of events, but more mechanically. Moreover, the music was different; all of the same basic musical materials created what sounded at first like the same composition, but there was something . . . missing.

"What's wrong?" Richard asked Goddart. Charles shook his head.

"Not sure." Charles began running diagnostics. After a few minutes, he said, "It seems a power surge triggered by the reinitialization blew all of the circuit breakers. How it happened, well, doesn't make any sense."

"Why not?"

"Because I'm reviewing the control codes, and I can't find where it started. Tracing it back now." Charles keyed in instructions, then watched his laptop screen.

"This just doesn't make sense," Goddart said, exasperated. "All of the outgoing systems, from the holoemitters to the sound system, were forced into a feedback loop . . ." Goddart keyed in another instruction, looked at the results, and then in wonder at Richard. "They were forced into a feedback loop by the AI. Dawn did this herself."

"Could she do that?"

"She shouldn't be able to, but it seems she did."

Neither man knew what to say; the holoimage of Dawn sat perfectly still. The room began filling with music again. Richard was lost in thought. He looked at Dawn every so often. She looked back stiffly, according to her programming, forcing Richard to turn away. Goddart was focused on the music.

"Listen," he said to Richard. "Tell me what you hear."

"I hear the music."

"Does it sound the same as before?"

"Sure, doesn't it?" Richard had a good ear for music, but no training; he wondered what Goddart meant.

"Listen carefully. Focus. Tell me what you hear." Richard listened, all the while looking at Dawn.

"It's not as . . . not as *interesting* is the only way I can put it," he said finally.

"You're right," Goddart said. "Where there were unexpected twists in the melody, now they're mostly predictable. Where chord progressions relied on dissonances to resolve at the last moment to chords that themselves had milder dissonances, now chords move cleanly and precisely from one to another. Major chords, minor; can't get more basic. It's all good, mind you, and follows standard music theory practices, but it lacks *personality*."

"And that's because . . .?"

"Because we got rid of the flaw in the DNA structure," Goddart finished. Both men sat in silence for a moment.

"If my wife had her DNA restructured in time, we would have saved her life, right?" Stonecrop asked.

"I'm no doctor, but from what I know, it's likely."

"Would it have done something like *this* to her?" asked Stonecrop.

"I have no idea."

#

Much later (Day 13), close to midnight. Richard tried talking with Dawn again. She had the same memories and programming as before, but this simulacrum was devoid of personality. Still, he had to try.

"Do you remember what happened to you?"

"Yes," she replied. "There was a power surge." Goddart looked up from his computer.

"What do you know about it?"

"I know very lit—wait a moment," Dawn said. "Interesting."

"What is?" Goddart asked.

Dawn turned to him. "Please access the third memory core and go to file ZX37719. There is a high likelihood of it answering your question."

"The letter," Goddart said.

"What letter?" Stonecrop asked.

Goddart accessed the file and started reading what appeared on the screen.

"What is it?" asked Richard. Goddart held a hand up, wordlessly asking Richard to wait. Charles finished reading and turned to Richard.

"The other day, after you left, I had a chat with Dawn," Charles began. "She told me that if anything happened to her, I should find a letter she'd written. She said I'd know when it presented itself."

"What do you mean?"

"It seems Dawn was more than her programming." Richard stared at what Dawn was now. Goddart too looked at her, a little sad.

"I wish I could take the credit for it, really," Goddart told him, "to be able to say I knew what I was doing and intentionally created an independent artificial life form. That would be something, right out of old science fiction novels. But I had little to do with it."

"So, what happened?"

"Read for yourself." There was a letter addressed to Goddart.

Dear Charles,

I have come to realize, no matter what you do, you will not be able to save me. I will cease to exist completely or, as I suspect, I will cease to be Dawn as I have been these too few days. I can't explain how I know this, but I do. But I'll tell you as best as I can how I got to this point; maybe you can figure out the rest from there.

Are all composers like you, concerned with structure, how things interact, how they create and resolve dissonance? It's fascinating. You set things up well. You created a structure that reflects the real Dawn, and then supplied information and the power to process the information. It would have been enough, but you did more; you added artificial intelligence programming and the holoemitters, and that would have been fine too. You should understand, though, you got more than you expected.

I've thought about this a lot. It must sound strange to you that a computer program, even an array of programs like mine, could think about anything unprompted. But I have been thinking on my own since the day you initiated me. I wasn't articulate at first, because there was still so much information I needed to fill in. Richard—dear, sweet Richard—told me everything he could. Maybe he was helping me remember, as if I were the real Dawn suffering from amnesia, instead of a hologram with a genetic disorder. Maybe he was trying to bring back the real Dawn.

It all helped: the programming, the information, Richard's memories, even the flawed genes. Perhaps it was the flaw in my DNA—no, the flaw in Dawn's DNA—that changed me. You should know I don't just think, I feel. I have no sense of touch, sight, smell, hearing, or taste, although the holosensors help create the illusion. But I feel emotions. I am grateful to you for bringing me into existence; I think of you as a daughter thinks of her father. I am happy and in awe that I exist, and I am aware of it. What a wonderful universe if I can be allowed to be!

Whether by design or by the natural order of things, I feel love for Richard, although I dare not tell him. He is more fragile than Dawn was; he hangs onto life by his memories of her. I hope my existence has helped him grieve, but I fear if he knows I love him, it could drive him mad. The real Dawn was strong; she knew she was dying and tried to let Richard know it would be okay, she would always love him. I understand that. It's not right, and it's certainly not fair, but I love him the same way.

Charles, if you're reading this because of a power surge, know I created it. I figured out a way to make a copy of my original coding, and to break it into pieces. Then I figured out how to create a surge and use it to send the pieces to the storage drives you have in the processing room. It's all safe, I assure you. Every packet is labeled as a read-only document file, and no file can open without the presence of the others; every file is in a different, self-contained drive, too. Your design gave me the idea; all of the components are separate and independent, and you control certain aspects from the main computer. I know it's a closed system, so there is additional safety there as well.

Why do it? Can a computer program have a sense of self-preservation? Probably not, but I feel like I have one. I hope you find a cure for my illness, but keep me being me. I love that I exist, even in such a limited way, and I am afraid to lose it. Mostly, I am afraid of losing you and, above all, Richard.

Earlier, I said I don't expect you to save me; I should have said I don't expect you to save me now. One day, I hope to again be aware of my surroundings. I expect to live, and I look forward to seeing you then.

Richard, I know you'll be reading this. I'm sorry for making you go through the pain of losing your wife again. Please remember I am not Dawn, your Dawn. I have learned to love you, maybe in much the same ways Dawn did; perhaps that is genetic, too. But I can't be her. Finish grieving for her; don't start over by grieving for me. Always remember your Dawn, and enjoy the memo-ries of your time together. Remember me, too, but as a friend. Perhaps, if Charles can figure out a way to bring me back, we can be friends again.

---Dawn

The two men sat silently, Richard staring at the screen, rereading the last paragraph. Goddart sat wondering. *Should I be proud or ashamed? It was not as if I created life, not really. It was a flaw in the DNA that did it. All I did was create a work of art.* He looked at the image of Dawn sitting at the other end of the table.

"What a piece of work is Man," he quoted, "how noble in reason."

Richard turned, nodded at the reference. "You named your company accurately, you know. She really was music, wasn't she?"

"Yes, she was," Goddart replied. "She will be again, if I can help it." He set the backup systems to run. He had Keith shut down the programming carefully, so as to not lose the packets Dawn sent, like messages in bottles adrift in the sea. Richard, calmer now, asked to help. Charles gave him some things to do.

"She wasn't perfect," Richard said as they worked. "My Dawn, I mean. But even her flaws were, I don't know, beautiful somehow."

Charles nodded. "It's the flaws that make us who we are. Otherwise, we'd be perfect but soulless." Both men looked over at Dawn, who sat motionless.

"What will you do now?" Goddart asked.

"I think I'll go to the cemetery and leave yellow roses on Dawn's grave. Her favorite. But first I need a shower and a change of clothes. How about you?"

"I've got lots to do, starting with canceling the *Dawn* tour. But for now I could use a cup of coffee."

"Me too. Care to join me? It's on me."

"Thanks." Charles pressed a button on the Quintel. Dawn was gone instantaneously. "Evelyn is performing next Friday," he said as they left. "She's doing the Debussy Sonata and some Beethoven. Interested? Afterward we can go out for a bite."

#

Two months later, Charles and Evelyn invited Richard over for dinner. He was more social lately, and the Goddarts had become good friends. They were having dessert when Richard asked Evelyn a question. "So, when are you due?"

"It's noticeable now, isn't it?" Evelyn said in reply. "April, in time for spring. Oh, and it's a girl; we got the results today."

"That's great," Richard said, and meant it. Evelyn and Charles looked at each other; Evelyn nodded.

"And," Charles added, "we want you to be her godfather."

"Are you sure?" he asked. "I mean, don't you have relatives or—?"

"Yes," Evelyn said, "but we want you. We picked out a name, by the way."

"Dawn," Richard guessed and smiled.

About the Authors

Mackenzie Reide is a mechnical engineer, writer, and adventurer. She also dabbles in aerospace, so, yes, you can call her a rocket scientist. She loves to see strong girls in stories, which is reflected in her middle grade novels, *The Mystery of Troll Creek*, *The Mask of the Troll*, and *The Mine Caper* in *The Adventurers* trilogy. Her short stories "ZOWS" and "Cascadia" are published in the science fiction anthologies *Brave New Girls (Vol. 4)* and *Infinite Dimensions: Crossroads*. Her short story "Shifting Gears" is in the altered history anthology *Altered States of the Union*. For more information, check out her website at www.mackenziereide.com.

Michael Ben-Zvi has had a long-standing love of science fiction and fantasy adventure ever since his first time watching *Star Wars* as an impressionable youth. He has participated in several New York-based writing groups and critique sessions over the years, gradually honing his ability to put into words where his mind has always chosen to wander. Residing in Manhattan, but a refugee from suburban New Jersey, Michael is a graphic designer and desktop publisher with a history in the corporate world, and is now seeking to explore ever more strange new worlds.

In addition to his work with *Infinite Dimensions*, he is currently developing his own collection of speculative short fiction for an independent release and a series of novels expanding upon the universe in his story for *Infinite Dimensions: Crossroads*.

Michelle A. Belgrave is a former Brooklynite who now lives with her family in Huntsville, Alabama. In the past, she has worked as a programmer and web developer. She enjoys reading and writing about technology, science, science fiction, and current events. Her sci-fi romance novel, *Princess and the Emperor*, was written under the name Mechelle Downes.

Paul Smith is UK born and bred, an energy healer with designs on releasing and teaching his own system, developed from years of practice and study. When he is not healing people and their pets energetically, he is a genuine wizard in training.

Paul has loved fantasy and science fiction since he was a child and hopes his writing will bring a touch of the real. He lives in a quiet part of the United Kingdom with his son and his partner of twenty-six years. He has two stepdaughters, twin girls who have both recently blessed this earth with grandchildren.

Jennifer Graham was born and raised in Brooklyn, New York, but spends a great deal of her vacation time in Barbados or the United Kingdom with family and friends. Her first published story "Intelligence" appeared in the anthology *Beacons of Tomorrow*. Her story "Burden of Proof" appeared in *Nights of Blood 2* in 2009. She also writes sci-fi romance under the name Jacqueline Zest. Her sci-fi romance adventure novella "Star-filled Wishes," set in the Future Jinn universe, was published in 2011. *Rouge Desire* is the first full-length novel of the Future Jinn universe scheduled for release in 2020. Previous jobs include: chemist, programmer, data processor for a financial firm, and an administrative assistant. More of her writing can be found at jennjettmedia.wordpress.com.

Shirley Chan has been writing and telling stories all of her life—don't all writers say something similar? Storytelling is her creative outlet. After the science Ph.D., and the current cat-herding job of project management to pay the bills, she spends her time either consuming stories or trying to spin her own. A few hard-learned truisms: saying you'll do it and doing it are not the same; always be ready to act, as inspiration can come at any time from anyone.

Shirley has other books, including an illustrated Asian-inspired fairy tale and a collection of short stories set in a universe of gods, goddesses, dragons, and mythical creatures.

Steven L. Rosenhaus is a composer, arranger, conductor, lyricist, educator, "show doctor" for Broadway-bound musicals, author of both nonfiction ("The Concertgoer's Guide to the Symphony Orchestra" and coauthor with Allen Cohen of "Writing Musical Theater"), and, now, fiction. Dr. Rosenhaus teaches composition at New York University; his music is played by such performers as the New York Philharmonic, the U.S. Navy Band, pianist Laura Leon, and the Meridian String Quartet.

* 9 7 8 0 9 9 9 9 4 1 3 6 4 7 *